BLOOD & SAPPHIRE

© 2026 Lexi Caron. All rights reserved.

No part of this publication may be reproduced, distributed, or transmitted in any form or by any means, including photocopying, recording, or other electronic or mechanical methods, without the prior written permission of the publisher, except as permitted by U.S. copyright law.

NO AI TRAINING: Without in any way limiting the author's exclusive rights under copyright, any use of this publication to "train" generative artificial intelligence (AI) technologies to generate text is expressly prohibited. The author reserves all rights to license uses of this work for generative AI training and development of machine learning language models.

For permission requests, contact the author at: lexicaron@yahoo.com

This is a work of fiction. Unless otherwise indicated, all names, characters, businesses, places, events and incidents in this book are either the product of the author's imagination or used in a fictitious manner. Any resemblance to actual persons, living or dead, or actual events is purely coincidental.

Editing by Black Dahlia
Cover art by Rii Finley:
   iStock Photo 1317397885 Licensed.
   iStock Photo 2020619579 Licensed.
Internal illustrations by Rii Finley:
   iStock Photo 514729950 Licensed

ISBN:
978-1-970774-03-0 (Paperback)
978-1-970774-04-7 (E-Book)
   Prose Ink LLC. North Carolina
   Proseink.com

   1st edition 2026

To the people who said I'd never be good enough.
Fuck you.

Chapter One

Sapphire

I gripped the steering wheel of my 1969 Mustang so hard that my knuckles turned white. The red foreclosure letter mocked me from the passenger seat. After looking for a job for months, this was my last resort. I took a slow breath, staring at the gray building ahead. The online ad for this bartending position had said 'Not for the faint of heart'. The lone bar nestled against the forest edge, with its sterile parking lot devoid of cars or trash, reinforced that notion.

I checked my makeup in the visor. *Presentable.* The dark hair and hazel eyes staring back at me were so unlike my Mom and Dad's. The memory of their blue eyes was a gift to me now, just like the Mustang. If I lost the house, the Mustang was all that I'd have left of them.

As I crossed the lot, a swift breeze wrapped around my legs, raising goosebumps on my arm.

Why did I decide to wear a pencil skirt?

Silently cursing my wardrobe choice, I reached the black-vinyl-covered doors. My gaze shifted to the sign by the road that read: *Vampart Bar*. Before I finished knocking, the door swung open and a tall man wearing a black vest, filled the doorway. The way he towered over me did nothing for my sweaty palms.

This is Joshua?

"Who are you?" he asked gruffly.

"Sapphire." I said, my voice shaking, "We spoke on the phone yesterday, I believe."

He moved aside, and I swallowed as I stepped into the building, thankful for the warmth. Brown, high-top tables were scattered throughout the room with a handful of pool tables in the back corner. A strange smell of smoke and something metallic drifted through the air and tickled my nose. But it was the karaoke platform in the back corner that caught my eye. Overall, it looked like all the other bars I'd seen, yet the air had a thickness to it that I couldn't quite put my finger on.

Once we sat down, Joshua began reviewing my résumé. I bit my lip, crossing my legs. Gingerly, I opened myself up to the world around me, trying to feel his feelings, but no emotions came from him.

My stomach dropped.

As an empath I'd always been able to feel people, a gift I kept secret from everyone, except my mother. On her deathbed, she warned me not to tell a soul, or else the wrong kind of people would find me. A gift and a curse.

Yet now, the silence echoed.

"I see here you've had many jobs, but never stayed long." Joshua tilted his head. "Is there a reason?"

My hands shook in my lap for a brief moment.

"Oh, that." I let out a wry laugh. "I used to get migraines. Missed a lot of work because of it in the past. It won't be a problem now."

I couldn't tell him the cause of those migraines came from my *ability*. I've since learned to control it, but it still hovered over me like a shadow.

"Hmmm. As long as it doesn't cause any issues." He went back to reading. "Have you ever worked with other demons before?"

Other demons?

"I'm sorry, could you repeat that?"

"Have you ever worked with other demons before?" He repeated, nonchalantly. "Actually, what type of demon are you?"

My already sweaty palms shook. *Get a grip, Saph, it's probably a themed bar.*

"Oh, I'm not really into cosplay. Do I need to be to work here?" I asked, hoping only I could hear the shaking in my voice.

Joshua burst into laughter, his eyes lighting up. I looked around the room, half-expecting to find hidden cameras.

"You're a riot! The vampire demons will love you! I usually only hire other vampires, but..." He shrugged, "desperate times."

This had to be a full immersion bar. I needed to stop letting my anxiety get the better of me.

"I'm a," I paused, wondering what demon from D&D suited me best. "A witch." My thumbs slid against each other as I fidgeted.

"A witch?" He rubbed his chin and eyed me. "You'll be a favorite here, I can tell. We only serve blood and alcohol, so you don't need to know how to mix drinks. Pay is twenty an hour, plus tips. Would you be okay starting tomorrow?" He stood and extended his hand to me.

As I rose, my legs failed and wobbled beneath me. After hundreds of no-calls and failed interviews, I couldn't pass up that kind of money. Not even if it felt... off.

"The sooner, the better." I shook his hand, ignoring the sinking feeling in my stomach.

"Perfect. Please follow me, and I'll show you around!" He slapped the bar and stood up.

I followed him.

As we walked into the kitchen, my mouth gaped open at the sight before me. All the appliances looked untouched, and the metal on the stoves and fryers gleamed. The white tile floors shone like no one had ever walked in there. The only thing that looked used were the two industrial-sized fridges by the door. I traced a finger on the edge of the counter: no dust.

"Do you not serve food here?" I asked, staring at my surroundings.

"Nope! Vampires don't eat much. This was all here when I bought the place. It would be more expensive to get rid of it. That pretty much sums up the tour. Do you have any questions?" He asked as we walked back to the middle of the bar.

"What about house specials?" I pointed out. My eyes shifted back to the bar counter.

"Tomorrow's shift starts at 7 pm. Kathy will be here to explain anything you may need." He extended his hand to me, and I shook it once more. "I think you'll make an excellent addition to the team, especially with your humor!" Though he beamed, his shoulders looked stiff.

While walking to the car, a shiver slithered through me, but there was no wind in sight.

That evening, I arrived at the restaurant my friends chose for dinner. As I stepped inside, I scanned the room for them. A welcoming atmosphere greeted me. Small brown booths and slated partitions filled the space.

An influx of other people's emotions burst through me. Exhaustion hit the hardest as a yawn escaped my throat. The anxiety from the couple behind me made my hands tremble. I closed my eyes and took a few deep breaths, shutting the world out.

I spotted my friends and slid into the booth seat across from them.

"How did it go, Saph?" Emily asked, twirling a strand of her indigo hair over her shoulder.

"Honestly, it was odd," I said.

That got their attention as they stared at me. Isabelle waved a hand, her dark purple hair swaying while she waited

"He asked what kind of demon I was, and said they usually only hire other vampires." Even as the words left my mouth, I felt silly.

"Demons?" Isabelle asked, taking a sip of her water.

"Well, no, more like cosplayers, I think. I know it sounds strange, but I need the money." I sighed and rested my chin on my hand. My eyes drifted over the menu, and my stomach let out a low growl.

"I'm buying," Emily said without missing a beat. "That's weird, though. Hopefully, it pays well. When I was a waitress, some days I didn't even get 20 dollars in tips." There was a slight annoyance in her voice.

"Ow! Rude." She laughed as Isabelle gave her an elbow to the ribs.

"I don't think you're helping, Em." Isabelle rolled her eyes, and we laughed.

"Oh, I do hope you find a hot guy, too. You've been single *forever*!" Emily exaggerated.

"I don't know if I'm ready for anything," I admitted.

The girls exchanged looks, then turned back to me.

"Saph, you're thirty-two now." Isabelle reached for my hand, placing hers over it. "Don't let some ex-boyfriend ruin you forever."

"He crashed my car, among other things." I pressed my lips together. "Guys, I really don't want to talk about this."

"We know life's been hard for you, Saph, but finding happiness is okay," Emily said gently.

"She is right, Saph; if it weren't for you guys, I never would have made it out of my depression." Isabelle motioned her hand between Emily and me. "It's okay to take a chance. You might find something great, like what I have."

"Can't I be happy with just this?" My lips curved up in the corner.

"I think you forget we're your best friends and know your darkest secrets," Emily teased. "You need adventure and a big man to help you forget the hard times!"

Isabelle nodded in agreement.

Emily was right. Over the last five years, we found each other at the lowest points of our lives and managed to get through everything together. Isabelle lost her husband to cancer, I lost my parents, and Emily had just been diagnosed with Bipolar Disorder. We were a group of misfits, but we fit together like pieces of a puzzle.

I hadn't sought out anything serious in years. It never crossed my mind. The idea of finding a guy at a cosplay bar didn't sound riveting either. I was never the nerdy type. I preferred the dark and mysterious.

"Alright, alright, I surrender. Maybe I will *look* for an adventurer." I rolled my eyes, and we let out a soft chortle.

"How did you find the ad anyway? I looked after you told us about it, but nothing came up," Emily asked, raising her voice over Isabelle's obnoxious slurping sounds.

"Oh, I was at the free Wi-Fi café, and a guy and I were talking about the birthmark on my neck when he pulled up the ad." I shrugged.

Isabelle smiled. "As long as it pays well, that's all that matters."

I raised my hands in mock surrender and laughed. "Can we eat now?"

Chapter Two
Sapphire

When I arrived the next night, the parking lot was filled with cars, banishing the haunting emptiness of yesterday. I shut the door of my yellow Mustang and walked toward the building, my heart beating erratically as my breath caught in my chest.

Above me, constellations clashed against the beautiful dark sky. Music flowed from inside. Metallica's "Enter Sandman" rang in my ears. There were no speakers in the kitchen, but it was still loud.

"Hey, new blood." A soft voice echoed from a woman standing by the bar as I stepped inside. She ran a hand through her messy pixie cut and looked me up and down with a smirk. "You're smaller than I expected, but Joshua didn't tell me how attractive you'd be." She said with a wink.

I blushed, heat flooding my cheeks. "Sapphire." I extended a hand.

She shook it. "Kathy. And don't worry, only new vampires bite." She and handed me an apron.

"Where's everything?" I ignored her comment about vampires and tied the apron around my waist.

"Blood's in the fridge and alcohol's on tap. That's all the vampires need unless a confused human walks in. That's rare though, since only demons can see the bar." She said with a shrug, but her tone was oddly serious.

Unless a human walks in? Is everyone here really that into roleplaying? "Wait, what do you mean? I see the bar, and *I'm* human." I pointed out.

Kathy stopped in her tracks and turned back to me. Her eyes drifted to the bar door, as if someone invisible stood there.

"Ha! Joshua said you were funny," she mused, then gave herself a little shake and let out a quick laugh. "Anyways! Let's get to work, shall we?" She locked our arms and dragged me toward the bar.

Kathy danced around the entire building, pointing out where things were. "If you want good tips, leave them be unless they ask for something. Most demons want to be left alone. I guess you could offer them blood right from the tap." She gave me a teasing wink.

I stood like a deer in headlights, trying to process her directions. The words left her mouth, but I couldn't hear anything but a ringing in my ears.

God, how am I going to do this?

"Okay, new blood. First customer of the night will be yours. I'll be floating around if you need me." With a shimmy of her shoulders, Kathy walked off.

I leaned over the counter, revealing a bit of cleavage. The scraping noise of a bar stool drew my attention to two men coming in. One with brown, Ivy League hair and a rose tattoo on his shoulder. He sank onto the barstool, grinning at me. The other stood behind him with his arms crossed over his chest, layered blonde hair and soft stubble shadowing a strong jawline. He wore a leather jacket and ripped jeans that showed his form well. But it was their eyes that held me.

Both had entirely black eyes. Contacts maybe?

Why can't I feel anything from them? As I stretched my senses towards them, I got only emptiness in return. Unnerving.

"Hey Dollface," said the Ivy League. "You must be the new bartender Joshua hired." His deep, rumbling voice lured me in as he rested an arm across the bar.

I shifted my eyes around the room, looking for Kathy, and tapped a finger on the counter. She was nowhere in sight.

"That'd be me." I quipped with a smile. "I'm Sapphire. What can I get for you guys?" I straightened as I spoke and put my shaking hands behind my back.

Breathe.

"I am Ezra, that's Kyler." Ivy League said, jabbing his thumb over his shoulder at the blonde in the leather jacket. Kyler, I guess. "You will see us a lot, so remember our faces. I would like two bags of A-negative, please."

I turned toward the glass shelves behind me and looked at them, then gritted my teeth as I realized the liquor bottles were all empty. Laughter erupted behind me.

"Forgive her, she's learning." Kathy placed a hand on my shoulder and I jumped.

Where did she come from?

"Bah!" Ivy League Ezra chortled. "Joshua should pay me for all the times I have had to explain how to serve drinks.

Kyler, go check on the kingdom, will you?" he waved his companion off, eyes never leaving mine. My gaze dropped to the floor, avoiding the smirk curling on his lips that sent an uneasy shiver down my spine.

Wait...kingdom? These guys took DnD *way* too seriously.

"The blood he wants is on the top shelf of the fridge," Kathy whispered into my ear.

I swallowed and nodded. "Let me get that drink for you." I could feel Ezra's eyes following me as I walked into the kitchen.

I entered the strange, too-clean kitchen. My phone vibrated in my pocket.

Emily:
> How's the hunt for tall, dark, and adventurous?

Me:
> Em, I've been on the clock for all of ten minutes. LOL.

I chuckled and slipped the phone back into my jeans. I crossed to the fridge and yanked it open. A cloud of cool mist buffeted my face and I quickly batted it away, then gaped at the bags of blood hanging in neat little rows. They looked perfectly authentic and were arranged by type. I grabbed a bag labeled A-negative. Curiosity took over, and I popped off the IV block, sniffing the contents. My nose crinkled at the metallic smell that filled my nostrils and color drained from my face.

It's real!

The kitchen's back door called to me louder than anything ever had before. Every alarm bell I had rang as I darted to it. My pulse throbbed in my veins. My hand gripped the knob, but the nagging voice in my head echoed one thought.

If you walk away now, you'll be living in your car. Everything your parents built for you, gone.

I hesitated and let go.

A hand grabbed my shoulder hard and flicked me around with brutal force, bringing me face to face with Ezra. He slammed me into the door, pinning his body against mine and glared at me with piercing eyes. Nausea tinged in my stomach. The door handle dug painfully into my back, but I didn't dare move. I shuddered, realizing no one was in the kitchen but us.

No way out.

He pressed himself against me like a rock, hands gripping my hips.

"How did it smell?" Ezra purred, his beady black eyes met mine.

I blinked "I'm s-sorry?" My heart beat faster as a wicked grin crossed his face. I pressed my hands flat against the door, shaking.

"How. Did. It. Smell?" He rested an arm above my head with his warm breath caressing my neck.

"M-metallic," I whispered. "How'd you know I smelled it?"

I shifted my body, trying to escape his grasp, to no avail.

"Call it an educated guess." His fingers moved to my neck, sweeping the hair away from the spot I knew all too well.

Small tingles slid through me as he traced my unusual birthmark.

"How long have you had this?" A low growl filled the air. He continued to inspect the spot, tracing it.

He should have scared me. My heart pounding loudly in my ears told me my body was scared, at least. Yet, I stood in place watching him, studying him almost analytically.

"My entire l-life," I managed to squeak out, my body betraying me.

"How are you hiding your demon form?" He gripped my hair and pulled my face up to meet his watchful eyes.

"I-I don't know what you're talking about."

Ezra punched the door beside my head. I yelped, throwing my hands up. An unusual warmth trailed down my arm, and fire appeared on top of my index finger. My brain went into overdrive as I shook my hand. The tiny flame flickered away, but my body quaked with fear.

Yet still...I was more intrigued than scared. Like I was watching my body be afraid, but the fear didn't touch me.

Fire?

"There is only one demon who could have this mark. It is written in all the old texts. Nothing would be able to hide your power."

I was frozen in place. It didn't seem like he noticed the flame.

No, my mind played a trick on me, nothing more.

A memory of my mom's dying words sprang to mind. '*You are a demon. An angel will guide you when the time is right.*' I'd always believed those were ramblings from the drugs keeping her comfortable at the end.

Where is my angel now?

"I'm just a human girl trying to keep her house." My lips quivered as tears filled my eyes. The words sounded like lies, even to me.

"Do you believe demons exist yet?"

Yet?

Ezra stepped away from me and bared his teeth. Fangs formed where canines were. I stumbled away from him, trying to steady myself, and knocked over a mop. Its clatter echoed on the pristine walls. I kept my eyes on him.

"Do not worry, Dollface, you will accept the truth soon." He bowed his head to me and vanished in a blink. I stared at the spot for a moment, fearing I was having a stroke. Then remembered... the fire!

I held out my hand, looking for any sign that a flame had been there. No burn marks, no heat, nothing.

I panted, trying to catch my breath, but my hammering heart made it impossible.

What the fuck is happening!?

This time, there was no hesitation. I ripped my apron off and threw it on the ground, darting out the door.

I didn't bother looking back.

Chapter Three

Sapphire

I drove home as fast as I safely could, but even that didn't feel quick enough. Road signs passed in a blur, and horns honked while I weaved through traffic. Before I knew it, I was home.

The tires skidded as I whipped into the driveway. I bolted for the front door, slamming it shut behind me, and pressed my back to it. I placed a hand on my heaving chest. The quiet made my thoughts echo louder.

Am I going crazy? There's no way fire *came from my hand! And the way Ezra just* vanished...

Slowly, my breathing returned to something resembling normal. I tried to move further into the house, but fear rooted me in place. It consumed me. I pried myself away from the door and drifted into the living room where shadows danced in the familiar darkness, tricking my mind into believing I wasn't alone. I shivered, goosebumps trailing down my arms.

I flicked on the lights. The emptiness reminded me of the truth.

I'm the only one here.

Needing a distraction, I dragged myself to the kitchen. Every movement felt slow and heavy like wading through deep water. Even making a simple sandwich drained me.

By the time I lifted it to my mouth, nausea churned inside of me. The smell of the tuna no longer appealed to me. I jammed the sandwich into a baggie and tossed it in the fridge, hoping I'd be hungry later.

Anxiety lingered no matter how much I tried to ignore it. There was no logical explanation for the flame on my finger. Ezra believed I was a demon. Mom had called me one on her deathbed.

No. No. No.

This is all wrong. I need sleep.

With each step up the stairs came a mocking creak. Vampires or demons, whatever the hell they were, couldn't be real. They were stories in books. *Myths.*

Concrete filled my bones as I collapsed onto my bed. The scent of clean sheets and the hum of the fan gave me a sense of peace. I was home, safe.

Yet, sleep never came.

I tossed and turned for hours, sweat dripping down my forehead, my nightgown clinging to my skin. Moonlight danced between the trees outside my window. I rolled onto my back and stared at the ceiling. Thoughts ran rampant in my mind.

Looking toward the clock, the red numbers glared brighter than normal.

Three in the morning.

Ezra's fangs. The fire on my finger. The metallic scent of blood. It all kept flashing in my mind. He had me pinned, scared enough to run. But now? Curiosity had taken over. Something drew me into the world he belonged to.

I ditched the covers, breathing in tight, short breaths. The old floors groaned under my bare feet as I went into the office.

My eyes drifted to the neat stack of boxes in the corner of the room. The impending foreclosure meant I started packing. I paused, slumping my shoulders, thinking about all of the things I'd have to sell to make this month's payment. Blankets Mom made, games we played together as a family, and even college books would have to go. The idea of those memories slipping through my fingers brought tears.

Thirty-two years of life were held within these walls. This was where I grew up. Where Mom found her love of wedding dresses. Where Dad taught me to read and do calculus. Mom taught me how to fix the car here. If the house got taken away, how long would it be until the memories fizzled away, too?

I sighed and opened my laptop. My foot tapped rapidly on the wood. The blank screen soon turned into a frenzy of websites about vampires and fan discussions. I scrolled through the pages of results.

Demons burn in Hell!
Click.
Vampires make good sugar daddies.
Click.
Lucifer will rise again.

Click.

None of the results had any helpful information. I gave up by the fourth page. The internet didn't have the answers I needed.

Perhaps no one did.

Looking down at my hands, I hoped for a magical answer.

I shut the laptop and paced the length of the office. The more I moved, the more I questioned, the more heat filled my body. I scratched the base of my neck for relief. More of my mother's words drifted into my head.

You are destined for a world beyond a simple mortal life.

Were her ramblings more than hallucinations? Did she know about demons? I needed answers.

Darting around the house, I searched for anything Mom could have left behind. Closets, boxes, and even totes in the basement came up empty.

I ran a hand through my hair and groaned. "This is fucking pointless."

I was looking for evidence that shouldn't exist. Of course, I didn't find anything.

A family picture on the wall caught my attention. My parents and I stood next to a giant snowman we built when I was fourteen. Those were happier days, at least until Mom died. Until Dad drowned his sorrows in a bottle and died three years later.

A warm tear slid down my cheek, and I wiped it with the back of my hand.

No matter the truth, if demons were real or not, I couldn't lose my home.

"Are you going to guide me now?" I asked the ghosts of my past.

The answer never came.

I needed air. I couldn't breathe being in the house, suffocated by memories. I threw on my hoodie and shoes before stepped outside. Crickets chirped into the night as cool autumn air wrapped around me. I breathed it in, my mind stayed focused on what tomorrow might bring.

Assuming I still had a job.

The air in my lungs became tight as I gripped my neck. Then, as quickly as the feeling came on, it disappeared, stopping me in my tracks.

"I heard my brother scared you earlier. Are you alright?" A deep voice asked.

Kyler leaned against the large tree. His leather jacket and wind-blown hair stuck out to me. My heart beat faster at the sight.

Don't run. I told myself.

"Why would you care if I'm okay?" I asked with fleeting confidence.

Kyler rolled his eyes and pushed off the tree.

"Despite pop culture, demons aren't all assholes, Sapphire."

"Your brother sure is," I murmured.

He let out a deep laugh that drowned out the noises of the night. The nip from the cold air tingled on my skin. We stood in the yard, the only light coming from the moon.

"Name's Kyler, in case you forgot. Feel free to wear me, I mean my name, out anytime."

I caught a glimpse of the amused smile that crossed his face. My shoulders relaxed.

"I'm going to level with you. Ezra sent me to check on you. I don't want you scared, not of me, and not of demons. So, any questions you have, ask away."

I turned towards the Mustang; it shone in the moonlight. I ran a hand over my arm, debating running away. Perhaps this was too soon, and I wasn't ready for the reality. For the truth.

"What are you? How does being a demon work? Where do you come from? Do you burn-"

Kyler threw his hands up in the air.

"Whoa, whoa. Slow down. Why don't we start with the basics, and then over time, I can explain the rest? Deal?"

I nodded.

"Do you want to go inside? You look cold." He pointed to the goosebumps on my arm.

I glanced at the front door and swallowed. Although I was cold, I didn't want him in the only place I felt safe.

"N-no. Let's sit on the steps." I gestured toward the stairs leading to the front door.

"At least take this."

As we sat down, he wrapped his jacket around my shoulders. I stare at him, wide-eyed. Kyler couldn't be more different than Ezra.

"Thank you." I wrapped the jacket tighter around my shoulders.

"Alright! Demons and Magic 101 starts now!" Kyler laughed. "What's eating you the most?"

I looked down at my hand, thinking back to the warmth and the flame.

"Magic. Do you have powers?"

"Damn, asking the big questions right out of the gate. Yes, demons have elemental powers. Fire, lightning, things like that." He folded his hands in his lap.

"How's it work?"

"You have to focus on the magic you want to use. The effort you put in is what you get out. I have fire, so my arms get warm. It's also how I phase." He looked toward the sky. Blues and oranges lie on the horizon.

"Phase?" I asked.

"It's how we get around. Think of a place or person, and boom! You're there." Kyler laughed to himself.

"That's how you knew I was here?"

He nodded.

I covered my face with my hands. Only one question lingered in my mind. Only one question I wanted to ask. But the truth scared me more than anything.

"How do you know if you're a demon?"

He gave me a sideways glance and took a deep breath.

"Hell-born demons have black eyes that can change to mortal colors. They can summon magic. Some long-extinct demons had abilities like feeling others' emotions, or moving things with their mind."

I turned to him and bit my lip. I opened myself up, and I couldn't feel Kyler.

I can't tell how demons are feeling.

The thought brought me a piece of solace. At least one spot in my life would be quiet.

"I've got to get going. The sun isn't good for my skin. We will talk more soon. I promise. I hope you come back to the bar." He popped up and stretched his arms above his head.

"Here." I passed him his jacket. "Thank you."

"Anytime, beautiful."

He took a step back and looked all around. After a minute, he was surrounded by fire and disappeared.

My mouth fell open. No heat or burn marks were on the deck.

Demons are real.

I stared at the empty yard, heart racing.

How did I move on from fear to acceptance so quickly?

Everything Kyler told me should be impossible. Just stories told to scare kids.

But Kyler isn't a story.

And I'm not a kid anymore.

Chapter Four
Sapphire

That night, I took a deep breath, standing in front of the back door to the bar. I looked at my hand and thought about what Kyler said. I focused all my energy on making the fire to come to my hands again. Nothing happened. I laughed to myself.

I wasn't a demon.

What a ridiculous idea.

Even though I decided to go back to work, my nerves stayed on edge. Inside, the noise from the customers sounded like a dull roar. I put on my apron and headed toward the bar, where Kathy loomed with a mop in hand. She looked up and beamed.

"Sapphire! You came back!" Throwing the mop down, she half-sprinted to me, pulling me into a hug.

"Bills won't pay themselves," I muttered, awkwardly patting her on the back.

"Joshua said it can slide this time, since Ezra talked to him, but I wouldn't make it a habit of skipping out like that."

"I won't," I said, trying to convince myself more than her.

"Since you're here, can you clean those tables over there? I could use a smoke break." She pulled out her vape and waved it around, then pointed to a group of tables by the bathrooms.

"Yeah, I've got it."

I noticed a tray and a cleaning rag already on one of the tables. I stepped over and gathered the dirty glasses scattered around. Since the bar had been open for hours, a slight whiff of blood filled the air, killing what little appetite I had.

"Did you hear? The prince believes he has found the lost princess! He said something about her ability to feel others' emotions! Isn't that wild?" The blonde demon to my right asked, leaning close to her male companion.

Lost princess?

"Are you drinking contaminated blood or something? The lost princess is exactly that. *Lost.*" He scoffed and waved her off.

"Oh yeah? Then how come he's spending more time in the mortal realm?" The blonde fluttered her arms around wildly.

I continued to clean with leisure around them. Leaning over the table for a better earshot, I stacked a few glasses.

"Because our prince is up to no good, like always." The man chugged his drink.

With nothing left to clean, I strode back to the bar. Pouring leftover blood into the sink made the aroma even stronger. I gagged internally. The sound of shuffling made me look up.

"You are back. Does this mean my brother explained everything to you?" Ezra asked.

I glanced up at him and tugged the corner of my lip into my mouth. My shoulders tensed, but I attempted to shrug it off. He sat on a barstool in front of me, resting his chin on his knuckles.

"Not really."

"I'm assuming you have more questions then?" he asked with a grumble.

"Who are you, really?" I took a rag and cleaned off the counter where he sat—anything to keep my shaking hands busy.

"I am Ezra, Prince to the Vampires in Hell." He leaned back in his chair.

A darkness flickered in his already black eyes. I blinked at him, and my mouth fell open.

He sneered. "Do not worry, I'm a gentle prince. Kyler is my second in command, a duke essentially. The politics of Hell beyond that would not make any sense to you. Do you plan on staying here?" Ezra asked and licked his lips.

"I-I think so." I idly cleaned mugs in the sink.

Ezra glanced toward a few vampires sitting in a corner before he spoke again.

"I will be back in a few minutes, Dollface." He pulled out a cell phone and walked out the front door.

I slumped my shoulders and got back to work. Following Kathy's movements, I went around the bar, grabbed leftover mugs, and brought them to the sink. The hot water slid over my hands as I began to wash them. They continued to tremble as my mind wandered.

A few customers sat around the bar. I moved about the room, taking orders and clearing off the high tops. I kept thinking about Ezra. How could he be a prince? My feet dragged as I returned to the bar counter.

"Are you a vampire?" I asked Kathy when she returned to the bar.

She gave me a tooth-filled smile as two fangs came out where her canines should be.

"I had assumed you were a demon, too, since you can see the bar."

"Nope, I'm a mortal." I shrugged. "What kind of powers do vampires have?"

"Well, for starters, we have the power to hear really well." A woman laughed as she took her place on the bar stool. She had her long purple hair in a braid on top of her head. Her partner sat beside her and tipped his hat at me.

"Steffan and Alexus. They come in often." She smiled at them.

"Hey, Kath." Steffan smiled back, then turned his gaze to me. "We also have elemental powers. Although it's usually fire, it's very rare for a vampire to be able to use anything else."

"I'll get their blood since you have questions." Kathy went to the kitchen. I watched as the door swung open with a swoosh before turning my attention back to my customers.

"Why not ask Ezra all these questions? I'd like to think he'd explain who we are more." Steffan removed his hat and placed it on the counter, revealing his black hair.

"Oh, please, husband. That man only cares about himself." Alexus huffed and leaned against her elbow.

"That *man* is still our Prince, wife. I'd keep my voice down if I were you." He urged her.

"I think he's just been too busy to answer her questions." Kathy waltzed over with two bags of blood and poured them into mugs. She did have a point. Ezra had not been around recently. I had not seen him in a while.

"In other news, I have a second job as a secretary, on top of my dietitian job." Alexus grinned before taking a sip of her blood.

"A vampire as a dietitian?" I laughed.

"Ironic, isn't it?" Alexus smiled, revealing her fangs.

"It also sounds chaotic to have two jobs. When do you sleep?"

"Can't hold this one down if you tried." Steffan placed a hand on his partner's shoulder.

"I love chaos. What can I say?" Alexus shrugged and patted Steffan's hand. Kathy walked off and did her usual dance around the bar tables, taking care of people and cleaning up.

"I've been building a new Jeep. Keeps me busy so I don't have to miss my wife." Steffan said with a slight grumble.

Vampires or demons just did everyday things. Granted, I have yet to meet the ones in Hell or one that would be considered bad. They had to be out there somewhere.

"We should get going. Work starts soon." Alexus said more to Steffan than to me.

"Don't remind me. Thank you for your ever-wonderful service, dear." Steffan tipped his hat once more and slid me two hundred dollars. I opened my mouth to thank them, but they were already gone. I held the bill momentarily and slid it into my pocket.

My gaze drifted to the karaoke bar. A smaller demon sang some country song. Others threw darts. I couldn't deny their existence any more, but they seemed normal.

"Waiting for me to arrive, beautiful?" I looked up to see Kyler's face looking back at me.

"I wouldn't say waiting." I murmured.

"I'm glad to see you came back. Hopefully our talk helped." Kyler's warm smile gave me hope.

"It did," I admitted.

"Why'd you take this job anyway?" He asked, watching me.

"See, we mere mortals have this thing called bills. Do they even have those where you're from?" I curled my lips up sarcastically.

"Hey! I may not be a 'mere mortal', but in my 350 years of life, I've paid many, *many* bills. And I come from Hell."

I blinked at him. He was proud of himself.

"Could you... Could you repeat that?" The words stumbled out of me.

"357, technically, but after 230 they're all the same." He took a swig of the blood. "As I was asking, what kind of bills are you trying to pay?"

"That's an awfully personal question coming from someone who is three centuries late getting to the retirement home," I shot back.

"My heart!" He grabbed at his chest. "I think I'm having a heart attack."

"Have to have a heart for that to happen." Ignoring his melodrama, I returned to cleaning dishes in the sink.

"Sapphire! I'm shocked! Shocked, I say."

Kyler and I both started laughing.

"Bartender, can I get a beer?" A male demon leaned over near the end of the counter.

Kyler's face pulled back into something serious.

Kathy darted over, but I shook my head. "I've got it."

After a quick nod of acknowledgment, she went back to waiting on others.

"Fang leader," the demon spat in Kyler's direction.

"Baku," Kyler responded in short.

"The prince finally let you off your leash?" Baku asked.

"I'm not a dog." Kyler gritted his teeth.

Dog? Is Kyler the one Ezra left in charge? I need to learn more about these two. About everything.

Even though I couldn't feel the demon's emotions, the tension rattled my nerves. Stepping away to pour the beer gave me a reprieve, if only for a moment. Baku threw me a twenty-dollar bill and stomped away.

"What was that about?" I asked, walking back over to Kyler.

"Nothing, he's being a pig-headed jack-"

Before my eyes, a ring of lightning appeared. There had been no crack of thunder or sound of static, simply blue bolts and a low buzz. Ezra stood in the middle, nodding his head towards Kyler, who bowed. I looked between them and then back out to the bar. I didn't know if I could get used to this, but I would try my hardest.

"I am back, Dollface." Ezra's voice filled the room.

He touched my hand, and his eyes met mine. His ever-alluring facade pulled me back to reality. I couldn't place what drew me in yet, but I would find out.

Deep inside, a small voice told me I belonged here.

I needed to find out why.

And fast.

Chapter Five
Sapphire

"Take a break, Dollface. Someone has to put this crowd out of its misery." Ezra jerked his chin toward the demon butchering a Miley Cyrus song over the microphone.

I threw the wet rag over my shoulder. "I'm still on the clock, Ezra."

"What Joshua doesn't know will not hurt him. Who is going to argue with the Prince? It is fun when you are with me, come on." He motioned towards the platform.

I glanced at the karaoke machine and two microphones. The demon continued to belt whatever song while the crowd booed. The words on the flat screen scrolled quicker than he could sing them.

Ezra might have been right.

"Go ahead, Saph. I can handle the bar." Kathy winked over her shoulder at me and bowed her head toward Ezra.

"Fine. You get one song." I put up my index finger for emphasis. "One."

He gave me a wicked grin and took my hand.

Singing used to be a strong passion of mine. My first choir concert I won first place, and Mom and Dad took me for ice cream after. Did I still have vocal control like I did when winning all those choir contests as a child?

Ezra stepped onto the platform, and the room went quiet. "Beat it."

The demon who sang bowed and quickly retreated from the stage.

The prince handed me a microphone and went through the list of songs. The demons in the bar watched us with curious eyes while he settled on something. I bounced on my heels, waiting.

Once "Broken" by Seether started playing, I knew exactly what he wanted. Ezra began to sing, and the crowd stared in awe. His voice matched the tone of the song almost perfectly.

My voice soon joined in the melody, and a roar of cheers erupted in the bar. The lyrics slid off my tongue like I wrote them myself. Vibration in my vocal cords came as naturally as it did in my youth. I looked out to see Kyler beaming at me. My joy matched his. For the first time in a long time, my head was clear, with no noise or pain. No emotions flooding my body. Even my worries of being a demon drifted away.

I was free.

The thrill of the moment ended when the song did. Putting the microphone back, I went to step off the stage.

Ezra caught my wrist.

"Stay, I will pay you for the entire night," Ezra insisted as I turned to him.

"I'm not leaving Kathy alone. Besides, I need the tips."

"It's fine! You can cover my vacation days next week, since you bailed on me twice now." Kathy said.

I looked around, trying to figure out where she came from.

"I hate to interrupt, my prince, but something in Hell needs your attention," a stern looking, curly haired demon said.

Where did everyone keep coming from?

"What now, Orpheus?" Ezra asked.

They walked over toward the bar. Orpheus bent forward, whispering. Ezra's eyes bulged, and his nostrils flared. He balled his hands into fists and let out a sharp growl.

Kyler grabbed my hand. "Let's play another song while Ezra proves he has the biggest ego in Hell."

After choosing "Bring Me to Life" by Evanescence, Kyler opened his arms. A red guitar materialized in his hands.

"How the hell did you do that?" My voice rose an octave higher than I anticipated.

"I'll explain later when I have you all to myself." He waggled his eyebrows. "Ready to show off again?"

"I told you to have this dealt with!" Ezra boomed from by the bar.

"Let's sing," Kyler and I said simultaneously and laughed.

He strummed the cords of his guitar like his life depended on it, never missing a note. During the chorus, he sang in such wonderful harmony that it echoed mine. Who knew demons made good musicians?

"Looks like I am going to Hell, Dollface. I will see you soon." Ezra furrowed his brow as he walked towards me.

He didn't say another word before disappearing. I curled my lips in the corner of my mouth, letting out a breath of relief.

"I wouldn't read too much into it. He's a control freak." Kyler followed me as I stepped off the stage.

"Is he angry often?" I wrapped my apron back around my waist and stood behind the counter.

"*Often* isn't the word I would use." He scratched his cheek.

"Well, thanks for keeping me company while he... did that. I should get back to work."

Ezra made me nervous. I didn't feel as comfortable around him. Seeing how angry he could be put me on edge.

"Oh, good, I could use a drink." Kyler slid onto a stool.

Before grabbing more blood, I looked around. Demons were laughing, drinking, and having a great time. Nothing I ever would expect from Hell's creatures.

"Here you go." I smiled at Kyler and slid him a mug.

"You know, you sing like an angel." He mused, taking a swig of blood.

"Thanks, I had a few lessons." I shrugged, angled on an elbow.

"Great throat control."

My cheeks burned. I shouldn't have felt at ease the way I did with him.

"I could get used to this view. I'm glad you stayed." He licked blood from his lip and smiled.

"Yeah, I am too. I still have a lot of questions, though."

"Does that mean you're sticking around?" Kyler tipped his head back, drinking the last drops, then pushed the mug back to me.

"That's the plan, anyway."

"I'd better get back, but like I said, wear me out anytime, beautiful. See you around." Kyler gave me a nod.

Fire swirled around him, and then he was gone. I stared at the empty space, wondering what the hell I was doing with my life.

After my shift ended, I trudged into the kitchen to remove my apron and count tips. The coins clattered onto the counter that I pulled from my pocket. I realized I had forgotten the tip jar. Voices could be heard on the other side of the door. I paused. My palm lay flat against it, but I decided not to push it open when a voice spoke.

I perked up and leaned closer to the door.

"He is convinced she's the one. If he keeps spending all his time here, Lucifer is going to have his head," Orpheus said.

"He keeps abandoning the throne to watch her." Kyler responded.

"Yes and the other princes already have problems with him letting our other vampires run free." Orpheus said, huffing.

"Look at how happy she was today, Orpheus. I won't let him ruin her like all the others." Kyler's voice rang out.

"You know she could be listening. We will discuss this later," Orpheus responded.

The bar fell silent, leaving me with more questions than answers.

How long until Ezra realized I wasn't a demon?

Chapter Six
Sapphire

I rolled out of bed, deciding to call Emily and Isabelle and tell them about the bar. Of course, I had to leave out the demonic parts. I had to keep the vampires secret. I didn't know if my friends would be safe.

"So you're saying there are two hot guys?" Emily's overjoyed voice echoed over the phone.

"Em, she said they have black contacts, and pretend to be vampires. Doesn't sound much like her type." Isabelle retorted with an audible grunt.

"Yeah, you're right, she needs an adventurous bad boy. No nerds."

"Maybe a little nerdy, she does play those video games."

"Uh, guys, I'm still here. Besides, I've only known them for a few days. Let's reassess next week when we go to the mall." I laughed and stretched before heading downstairs.

"Deal! Lunch break's over. Later ladies, love ya." With a click, Emily hung up.

"We just want you to be happy. Love you." Isabelle sighed before hanging up.

They meant well, and I knew that. The pressure to find someone to be with annoyed me. I didn't need a man to help me navigate life or make me happy.

I grabbed a yogurt from the fridge. Standing against the counter, the empty living room stirred up ghosts of the past. I could see Mom with a dress over her lap and a needle sticking out from her between her teeth. Dad would waltz in and call us his favorite girls. Every day, it was our little routine. The vision filled my chest with a familiar warmth.

Throwing the spoon in the sink with a clank, I closed my eyes and tipped my head back.

What am I doing mom?

The peace was interrupted by my buzzing phone, bringing me back to the present.

Stupid spam messages.

I grabbed my laptop and my bills, then sprawled them out on the coffee table. After crunching the numbers, my shoulders relaxed. Between tips and my check on Friday, I'd be able to give the bank enough to keep the house. The ringing doorbell drew my attention.

My eyes widened as I opened the door. Kyler stood, peering at the Mustang, with the wind blowing his hair around. He turned to me when I cleared my throat.

"Did you read every vampire novel with stalker vibes, then think *Yes! I'm gonna impress Sapphire with this*?" I crossed my arms and tapped my foot, frustrated. "Showing up here is not actually romantic in any way. It's creepy. The first time was fine, but what's your excuse now?"

"You weren't at the bar, and I got worried," Kyler stumbled over the words.

"You're not helping yourself right now. I work nights, and in case you didn't notice, the sun's up." I pointed at the sky. "Good to know you don't burst into flames though. I wouldn't want to explain that to the neighbors."

"You need to stop reading those books, too." He shook his head. "Besides, you don't seem scared that I'm here."

"As you said, I read those books." I shrugged.

I should have been scared, but my body didn't tremble or quake. My heart wasn't even beating erratically. This was the second time he'd shown up unexpectedly, but if he'd help me navigate the demon world, I wouldn't push him away.

"You're safe, that's all I needed to know. I'll leave now." He turned away, and I unfolded my arms.

"Why did you assume I wasn't safe?"

"You work with demons now. Sure, we're mostly okay, but there are still some who... could harm you." He turned back to me with a softness to his features. His black eyes somehow looked lighter.

"You're not my keeper, Kyler."

"But you're a keeper." He winked.

I rolled my eyes, "Any excuse to flirt, huh? Do I have to invite you in, or is that a myth too?"

"I don't need an invitation, but I won't come in unless you want me around." His voice had a somberness to it.

Respectful vampire, check.

"Don't make me regret this." Narrowing my eyes, I stepped to open the door wider.

With his ever-annoying smirk, Kyler loped into the house. He looked all around until his focus landed on the bills. In a blink, he grabbed one and flopped down onto the couch. I glared at him.

"So much for those manners." I snapped, scooping up all the other notes and yanking the one from his hand.

"Do you want a drink?" I pushed my bills into a drawer and headed into the kitchen.

"Are you offering me your blood?"

Even with my back turned, I could hear the grin in his tone. I huffed. Ignoring his question, I grabbed a soda. With a can in hand, I sat next to him on the couch.

"Were you worried about me, or my blood?" I teased, popping open the can.

"Bit of both." He stretched his arms above his head with a groan.

I enjoyed the comfortable silence. Not being able to feel the demon's emotions kept my emotions buzzing to a low hum. My eyes closed as I let the world around me fade into the background. Kyler's warm presence brought me peace I'd never known.

A safe quiet.

"Kyler, can I ask you a question or seven about your world?"

"Ask away, beautiful."

"At the bar, you said you can summon things?"

"Yeah. I can summon blush to your cheeks with a look, watch!" He gazed at me and parted his lips slightly. I watched as he bit the inside of his mouth ever so gently.

"Ugh! That is not what I meant, and you know it!"

"But it worked, didn't it?" He nudged my shoulder.

"I regret letting you in." I put my arms over my chest, but couldn't help my laughter.

"Fine. Fine. Yes, demons can put anything into their own little pocket dimension, which we call the outer world. It depletes a big part of our magic energy, though." He held out his hand. "Our elemental magic is unlimited, luckily."

I watched in awe as fire twirled around his fingers. The flicker of orange glow danced across his face.

"Whoa." I reached close to the fire, heat prickling along my skin.

"Please don't burn yourself. I'd *hate* having to nurse you back to health."

"I'm sure it would be absolute *torture*." I teased, slouching back into the couch.

"There are things already in the outer world, but we don't know exactly what the Gods put there for us." He closed his fist, and the flames vanished.

"The gods?" I fidgeted with the pull tab on my soda. "All my life, I've been told there's one god. I can't imagine anything else. Not that I've ever been religious."

"Think of it this way, every religion has an idea of God or Gods. The Greeks had twelve! We have... eight."

"What about angels? Lucifer?"

"Lucifer is very real, and a fallen angel in Hell. Not like you are thinking, though. There is a god of angels, and he created Lucifer to watch over us demons." Kyler lay his head back and closed his eyes.

I sat in silence reflecting on everything he told me over the past two days. My world changed rapidly, and I could barely keep up.

"I'm sorry, I know that was a bit of an information dump. Are you okay?" Kyler asked after I stayed quiet for a while.

"There is so much I don't know." I sighed and ran my hand through my hair.

Kyler laid a hand on my thigh, "Don't worry, I'm an excellent teacher."

The doorbell ringing interrupted our laughter. We exchanged looks before I pushed myself off the couch to open the door.

"Do I have a sign that says 'Vampires Welcome' somewhere?" I pressed my tongue to my cheek, annoyed when I saw Ezra standing there.

"I am here to collect my brother and ask you on a date." Ezra glanced over my shoulder.

I froze. My breath caught in my lungs.

Date?

"Way to ruin the night," Kyler grumbled, stepping next to me. "My prince."

"Saph? You, me, the bar, two weeks? I will be busy in Hell until then." Ezra took a step closer.

"Why do you want to go on a date with me?" I raised a brow.

"You are the first mortal to work at my bar. I want to know you better. Maybe we will end up liking each other, is that so bad?" Ezra asked.

I stared at him for a minute, then turned to Kyler. My heart thumped in my ears.

Perhaps a date would help me feel better about all of this.

"It's a date." I managed to fumble out. "But if either of you shows up unannounced again, I'll surround the house with garlic!"

Judging from their laughter, it wasn't much of a threat.

Chapter Seven

Sapphire

My friends and I sat at a table in the mall's food court. The noise from people's emotions buzzed inside me. One by one, I tuned them out. I hated going anywhere busy; it always took a lot out of me. Emily and Isabelle sat across from me, idly chatting.

Emily wore a pink corset that exposed too much cleavage, and Isabelle wore a pantsuit. They were opposites, but you'd never know from the way they leaned together, scrolling through thirst traps on the internet.

It had only been a week and a half since I started working at the bar. I had not seen Ezra or Kyler for a few days and found myself thinking about them.

Or at least, Kyler's sarcasm.

"Right, Saph?" Isabelle asked, drawing me away from my thoughts.

"What?" I blinked.

"Ugh! See! I told you. She's probably daydreaming about her two nerds." Emily waved her arms around.

"They sing and have muscles for days. I can't say I blame her." Isabelle shrugged and put her phone down.

I rolled my eyes at Isabelle. "I'm sorry. What'd you ask?"

"I didn't ask anything. I-" Emily stopped mid-sentence, her mouth gaped open. I turned around to see what, or in this case, *who*, caught her attention.

Ezra stood behind me.

"Sapphire, your friends are beautiful. I should have tried getting to know them sooner." Ezra gave a wolfish grin.

He pulled out a chair beside us and leaned back. His baby blue eyes sparkled. The normal black color was nowhere to be seen.

The air around me chilled. There he was, showing up out of nowhere again. I looked towards my friends.

Emily angled herself on an elbow closer to him. Isabelle rolled her eyes but also shifted closer in her seat.

"Tall, dark, and adventurous indeed." Emily batted her eyelashes.

"You shouldn't be here." I hissed at him.

"Did you not miss me much, *Princess*?"

The way he said the word princess soured in my mouth. Did he still believe I was some demon? What happened while he was away?

"Are you going to treat our friend right? She's been through enough bullshit," Isabelle said, narrowing her eyes.

"Yeah, you're handsome, but don't think for a second we won't protect her from douche canoes," Emily added with a nod.

"I will treat her like royalty." Ezra's eyes stayed locked on me.

"I like him, Saph," Emily said, puffing out her bottom lip.

I crossed and uncrossed my legs. A heavy uneasiness lingered inside of me.

Something darker wrapped around Ezra. He scanned the mall before returning to me. "I have to get back to... work. But I had to check on you, Dollface. I'll see you next week for our date. Another time, ladies." He stood, bowing his head.

"Give us one second, guys," I said to the girls and pulled Ezra over to an empty table. "What things, precisely?"

"You really want to know?" He shoved his hands into his jeans' pockets and looked down at me.

I gulped. "Yes. Tell me something, please. Anything. If we're going on a date, shouldn't I know *something*?"

Ezra looked around the mall, rubbing his chin. Once his eyes met mine again, he groaned.

"This is a one-time deal. I hate talking politics. That's all I do. I've been working on making a treaty with the witches. It's better for my future plans if all the other princes in Hell are on my side."

"There are other princes in Hell?" I asked him.

"Yes. Three others." He nodded.

"What plans do you have?" I asked.

I tapped my foot on the ground. My skin felt like bugs were crawling down my arms.

Ezra leaned down and whispered in my ear, "Sorry, Sapphire, that is not something I am going to concern you with."

When he said my name, a sliver of tingles ran down my arms. The dominance in the way he said it made me question him, like he was hiding something. I rubbed my forehead.

"Why not?"

"Because you do not belong in Hell, yet. When the time is right, I will explain things to you. You should get back to your friends." He angled his chin towards the girls waiting for me. "I will see you soon."

As he walked off, I took a few deep breaths. My heart always sped up in his presence. My mom's voice kept repeating three words: *trust your instincts.*

Every time I thought of her, a different kind of pain tugged at my heart. Why would she say those things? It couldn't be a coincidence that Ezra acted as though I were a demon.

Plus, the fire on my finger had no real explanation.

"Everything okay, Saph?" Isabelle asked from her seat.

"Yeah, we were solidifying details of our date." I shrugged and sat back down, slinking into my chair.

"He's hot. I'd go on a date with him too." Isabelle nodded.

"It's just at the bar, nothing fancy. Anyways, let's go shopping." I sat up straighter and looked back where Ezra had been. A small wave of comfort crawled over me, knowing he left.

"Emily, don't you have a date tomorrow?" Isabelle asked.

"Yeah, I do! Do you want to see what he looks like?" Emily had been going online to find dates. She was not one to ever settle; she was having too much fun.

There were weeks she would go on a date with a different guy every day. Other times she would find someone she really liked and see him for a few months. They always broke up in the end though, as Emily would find some silly reason to end it. The last guy: his shoelaces had to be bright blue. I always assumed it was because she got bored. It made it all the more intriguing that she wanted me to settle.

"Duh," Isabelle said.

Emily pulled out her phone and scrolled. She held up her phone. We both leaned in and admired the picture. The guy had dark hair and three different piercings on his nose.

"His name is Rick. He rides a Harley and likes the same music I do." Emily mused. "What's up with you, Isabelle?"

"Nothing too exciting. I have too much going on at work, but it keeps my mind busy. I do need an outfit for a formal dinner I'm having with the CEO's next week, though." Isabelle took another bite of her food.

After five years of friendship, she didn't tell us much, but we respected that, knowing what she had been through. She let us into her world when she was ready. The three of us were three peas from very different pods, but we loved each other all the same.

"Okay! So, I thought we could go to a few shoe stores, maybe HotTopic, wherever you guys want to go." Emily smiled as she shoved the last bite of noodles into her mouth. Her words turned the conversation for Isabelle's benefit.

"I'm ready when you guys are." Isabelle stood up and walked off to throw away her trash.

Isabelle led the charge on this adventure. I hated the escalators as we went. I felt like I would fall backward at any moment. My hand gripped the rail till my knuckles were white as I tried not to become a weeble wobble in the middle of the mall.

The store was small, but there were racks of dresses in various styles and colors. We moved to the back and found a rack of peach colored dresses. That was Isabelle's favorite color, and it always looked amazing on her. Emily found a slip dress and ushered Isabelle to the dressing room. She begrudgingly abided. When Isabelle came out, she looked beautiful beyond words. The dress sat perfectly on her curved frame and brought out the color of her eyes. Emily and I exchanged a look before nodding in agreement.

"That one." We chimed in unison.

"This is why I only go shopping with you guys," Isabelle laughed. She had never been good with style, but Emily was both of our go-to's for this sort of thing. If we needed help with numbers or anything related to science, that was where Isabelle excelled. My natural talent was telling them useless facts about things unrelated to anything.

"Saphy?"

I stopped in my tracks, blood draining from my face. The noise of the mall muffled around me, and the reminder of years of pain stung deep inside. I'd know that voice anywhere.

Isabelle wrapped her hand around mine, squeezing.

Could this day get any worse? I'm a magnet for bad luck, even with humans.

"Hello, *Bret*," I said through gritted teeth.

"Fuck off, douche. She doesn't need your bullshit," Emily hissed.

"I simply wanted to say hi," A coy smile tugged on his lips.

"I don't have much to say to you," I groaned.

"I miss you, Saphy." A tinge of sadness dripped from his voice.

The hundreds of people in the mall made it impossible to tell what he honestly felt.

"I doubt that. Considering you left her for the bimbo." Emily picked at her nail.

Then, the second worst thing that could happen, *happened*. His blonde-haired beauty bounced over and laid a hand on Bret's shoulder. Her light giggle made me roll my eyes so far back I gave myself a headache.

"This is her?" The woman laughed, eyeing me. I took a deep breath and tried my best to calm myself.

Another reminder that I didn't belong here. I had Emily and Isabelle, but *people*? I could never find a place where I fit. Eventually, my ability pushed people away.

The blonde whispered something in Bret's ear, and I felt ten inches tall. My eyes burned.

Don't cry, not now.

"C'mon, Saph, we don't need to deal with this." Emily said.

The air in my lungs was trapped and the pull I felt floored me. Turning, he towered beside me, and I could breathe again. A relief washed over me. I shook my head. Relief washed over me. Why? Who knows?

"Babe, seriously, you know you can't leave me alone in the shoe store. I thought I lost you!"

Before I could respond, Kyler pulled me against him.

His lips met mine.

The scent of a log fire radiated from him. Warmth filled every crevice of my soul, and abruptly disappeared when he pulled away.

I wrapped my hand around the base of my neck. I'd never felt that kind of spark before.

Emily and Isabelle looked at us with raised brows and wide eyes.

"Enjoy it while it lasts, man. Look at how much she let herself go! Look at those bags under her eyes." Bret chuckled.

The blonde whispered in his ear, and their laughter continued.

I lowered my eyes to the floor and sniffled. Kyler shifted beside me.

"Once you're comfortable, her true colors come out, and you discover what a worthless lay she is." Bret laughed and began to walk away.

Kyler moved.

He tapped Bret on the shoulder, and when he turned around...

Kyler's fist cracked against Bret's mouth.

Passersby stopped and stared, unable to look away. I was no better, watching the scene unfold. Blood dripped from Bret's nose, and I slapped my hand over my mouth.

"If you ever talk about my girl like that again, it'll be the last time you speak."

Bret's Adam's apple bobbed. He took off as fast as he could. The blonde chased after him, yelling his name. My hand hid my gigantic smile. People went back to their business, and the four of us burst into laughter.

Kyler had chased Bret off and defended me. Almost like something out of a comic, but he existed. *And that kiss.* I touched my lips.

"That was chivalrous," Isabelle said, eyeing Kyler.

"Are you ok, beautiful?" He turned all of his attention onto me.

"Yeah. . . Yeah. I'm okay, thank you." I breathed out.

"I'll let you ladies get back to it." Kyler leaned down, his breath brushing my ear, "Don't worry, I'll always save you."

He shoved his hands in his pockets and walked away.

The longer I had a foot in his world, the more connected I felt. The more I wanted to be around him.

The more I ached for something more.

"Saph, Kyler just kissed you." Isabelle looked at me. "Are you okay?"

"It was a nice kiss." I touched my lips. "I'm okay."

"Oh damn. She like's him. Like *a lot*." Emily laughed.

I rolled my eyes. "Let's finish shopping."

Chapter Eight
Sapphire

Sitting at one of the high-top tables in the bar, I bounced my leg. I wore my uniform since my shift would start right after.

What does someone even talk about on a date with a vampire prince?

He didn't like to talk about Hell or himself. Ezra had a mystery wrapped around him. A riddle I felt compelled to solve.

Kyler, on the other hand, made everything simple. I never had to wonder with him. Pulling at the seam of my shorts, my mind wandered to his delightful sarcasm. The way he made me feel seen in such a short time gave me flutters.

And that kiss.

Kathy cruised over from the bar and bent against my table. She slipped out her vape and took a quick puff.

"You're a bit early for your shift, Sapphire," she said, tilting her head.

"Yeah, I'm waiting for Ezra. We have a date." I sighed.

She leaned in closer and whispered, "The prince can be a bit ostentatious, but don't take it to heart."

"Is there anything else I should know?"

"There's discourse in Hell. No one actually likes him. He kisses Lucifer's ass, and everyone is worried he's going to start another war. I'm not saying don't date him, but I am saying be careful."

I gaped at her. Nothing she said sat right. Why would he want to start a war?

"Thank you for telling me. I appreciate it." I gave her a small smile, which she returned.

"Us gals gotta stick together." She winked.

The air around us got thicker. A static slid across my skin before silent lightning formed the prince. Kathy straightened and darted off without a word. My mouth went dry watching Ezra sit across from me.

"Sorry to keep you waiting. I had a.... meeting in Hell." He looked around the bar, then back to me.

I gave him a once as a speck of blood slid down his mouth to his chin. A shiver shot through me as he wiped it away, without even looking at me.

"What kind of *meeting*?"

"The boring kind where some demon cries about a loved one dying. We live for hundreds of years, the pain will go away." Ezra waved a dismissive hand.

I folded my hands in my lap, trying to ignore how heartless he sounded.

"What's Hell like? Is it fire and brimstone? Are lava monsters walking around everywhere?"

"You watch too much television." Ezra held his chest as he let out a thunderous laugh. "Hell is beautiful, warm like the

Arizona desert in the late spring. And just as dusty. We have villages and castles where the princess and Lucifer stay. Do not worry, you will see soon enough."

I shifted in my seat, moving away from Ezra.

"I'd like to see Hell, one day," I murmured. "Not any time soon, though."

"Once I make it a safe place for you, we will go." He angled closer.

"When it's safe?"

"Stop talking about Hell, Sapphire." He rubbed his temple with two fingers. "It is not important. Not yet," he snapped.

"You brought it up," I whispered, shrinking into my seat.

His tone lightened. "Would you like some food, Doll-face?"

"We don't serve food here."

An irritated sigh came from him. "I did not ask if you served food, I asked if you wanted any."

"Cheese pizza?"

"Alright, be right back."

He phased away, and I peered over at the clock. Kathy wandered around in her usual fashion. I was awed by the way she took care of the bar by herself. I could barely serve demons without her help.

"Here you go." Ezra phased in, static filling the air.

He placed a Chicago pizza box down and opened it.

"Did you just go to Chicago... for me?"

"Do not act so surprised. I can do some nice things." He picked up a slice of pizza and took a bite. "What do you want to talk about?"

"I don't know much about you," I pointed out with a shrug.

"What would you like to know?"

"Everything." The words muffled by a mouthful of pizza..

"I am a prince, not much more to say there." Ezra shrugged, eyeing the bar again. The demons around us avoided his gaze.

"I'm sure you had a childhood, even if it was hundreds of years ago." I laughed awkwardly.

"I did, but I assure you, it was boring. My dad had a firm hand; he was strict. Mom, well, she had been an angel before she died." He clenched his jaw. "I got taught to rule."

"Did you always want to be a prince?"

I ate more pizza, and Ezra summoned another.

"Want? Oh dear Sapphire, as the son of a prince, I had no choice. It was always where I would end up. My father's throne." Ezra stared off into the distance.

"Did you like your father? Was he around during the war?"

"Who told you about that?" His hand flexed on the table.

"Is that important?"

"I suppose not." He grit his teeth. "My dad was dead long before the war. And no, I am not talking about it." He leaned back in his chair and crossed his arms over his chest.

"But I want to know, Ezra."

If this was my world now, I wanted to understand it better. If he really did plan to take me to Hell one day, I wanted to know what I was in for.

"Gods, Sapphire! Stop fucking asking! The last thing I want to do is answer another demon's questions! Especially when she asks about shit she has no business knowing!"

I froze, stomach dropping. The word *demon* echoed. Demons glanced our way.

I wondered if I could shoot fire at him now. Nothing happened to my dismay.

"Jerk." I pushed the pizza away from me.

"That's not how I meant it. Stop looking so sad." His regret didn't reach his eyes.

"Ezra, my prince, you are needed in Hell." Kyler's voice hit my ears as his fire formed him.

He bowed and Ezra rose to his feet. The black metal armor Kyler wore showed off his hidden muscles. A long silver sword stretched across his back. I bit my lip, gawking. He noticed me staring, and a smirk crossed his lips.

"I will see you soon, Dollface," Ezra said.

Before I could respond, he pressed his lips firmly against mine. My shoulders locked. His kiss did nothing for me. My skin crawled with bugs.

Only when he phased away did the tension in my bones ease. I stared at the spot he left empty and sighed.

He got upset over a simple question. Just like always Bret did.

Kyler reached out and touched my hand. "Are you okay?"

A spark flew through my body, and noise filled my head. Dizziness consumed me.

Anger.

Pain.

Sadness.

Happiness.

Joy.

It wasn't just noise, but emotions pinning me to my seat. The all too familiar tightness in my chest tugged hard. Kyler pulled his hand back, staring at me in shock. The emotions flickered away.

What the hell was that?

"I'm okay. I think." I placed a hand over my wildly beating heart and took a deep breath.

"Do you want to talk about something else?" He asked.

I nodded, not wanting to focus on whatever the hell that was.

"How do you like working here? Now that you've had time to adjust?" Kyler asked, sitting on the stool his brother left.

"It's not bad for the money. I've been expecting someone to be an asshole, but demons are so chill, it's almost annoying. Where's the fireballs being thrown and mortals getting eaten?" I responded, thankful for the distraction.

"You want us to be assholes? Don't think I've heard that one before." Kyler rubbed his chin.

"No, I don't want you to be! I'm saying it's strange." I shrugged. My eyes glided around the bar at the demons relaxing.

"I'm telling you, you read too many books. Only rogues eat humans. Why do you think we have blood bars? Besides being able to hit on hot bartenders?"

I rolled my eyes. "You can't help yourself, can you?"

"With you around? No. Let me take you on a date."

"What?"

"You know, I take you to dinner, and you realize you want to spend your life with me. We live happily ever after!" Kyler mused, resting his chin on his knuckles.

"A date? Wouldn't Ezra be mad?" I stood and wiped crumbs off my pant leg.

"Does he have to know?" Kyler shrugged.

I scrunched my face. "You always appear when I feel like I need rescuing."

"I am a man of my word. So what do you say? I will take you anywhere in the world you want to go. Sky's the limit."

"Okay, Kyler, you have a deal. Pick me up at 8 tomorrow night."

"Hell yeah! I'll see you tomorrow, beautiful."

And just like that, he was gone.

I rose, staring at the bar. The cascade of emotions still had my stomach in knots. Opening and closing my sweaty palms, I went to grab my apron for work.

Chapter Nine

Sapphire

I admired myself in front of the mirror. The long black dress sat snug on my curves with my hair was braided in a bun. The dark eyeshadow brought out my hazel eyes. After slipping on my black heels, I sent a picture to the girls. *Instant notification flood.*

Emily:
> *This is for a date?*

Isabelle:
> *Who are you, and what have you done to Sapphire?*

Emily:
> *OMG! She really likes him. My evil plan worked!*

Isabelle:
> *But which him?*

Emily:
> *Good question.*

Emily:

> *How was your date with Ezra, anyway?*

I rolled my eyes.

Me:

> I'll tell you guys about both later. This one is with Kyler.

I looked myself over one more time in the mirror. My eyes shifted to black, and my heart began to race. Every muscle in my body locked up. I blinked repeatedly and shook my head.

No. No. No. Please.

The doorbell rang, startling me. My eyes shifted back to hazel, and I let out a deep breath. Wiping the tears from my eyes, I hovered by the door. This couldn't be happening.

Why did my mind keep messing with me? I imagined the color shift.

The doorbell rang again.

Kyler would be waiting on the other side, but I couldn't bring myself to open it. My stomach clenched. I glanced back over, and my eyes stayed hazel.

"Saph, I can tell you're in there, you okay?" Kyler called from outside.

Taking a deep breath, I found the will to open the door. My jaw hit the floor.

Kyler stood in a full-blown black suede suit, with his copper blonde hair combed down. "Try not to drool like that all night." He swiped at his shoulders and smirked. "Are you okay?"

"Shut up. Why are you dressed up? And yeah, I'm okay. Had to finish getting ready." I looked down, avoiding his gaze.

He waltzed into the house. "I told a beautiful woman I'd take her anywhere in the world. I expected you to want something off the wall and fancy. If you wanted fast food, then I'd still go like this if it meant you'd smile." He took me in before adding, "You do look absolutely gorgeous, by the way."

"I wanted to go to Italy, but it's two am." I hoped he didn't notice the heat in my cheeks.

"I do know a place in Venice that's open."

"Why am I not surprised?" I shook my head.

"I can phase us there. It might feel a little... weird the first time."

"I think I can manage, for Italy."

He pulled me against his body. Flames surrounded us in warmth. Swaying in Kyler's arms, I rubbed my eyes. I reached toward the flame. The heat wasn't overbearing; I didn't even sweat.

When the flames died out, we stood outside a cafe along the canal. The moon glistened, and gondolas floated in the water. The smell of sea salt whisked through the air on a light breeze. Old Venetian Gothic-style buildings arched alongside the canal.

My lips parted.

We were actually in Italy.

Kyler's mouth curled up.

"What?"

"Nothing, just enjoying the view." He shrugged and took my hand.

We veered over to a table in the back corner. As I looked around at all the people sitting near us, no emotions tingled within me.

"A demon cafe?" I tilted my head.

"Did you know when you try to feel our emotions, there's this pull to our magic? It's this reverberation in my chest. Feels funny." Kyler rubbed at his chest.

"I'm sorry. I don't want to make you uncomfortable."

"I didn't say you made me uncomfortable," he said without hesitation.

I crossed my legs and looked back out toward the water. "Why did you ask to take me out?"

"Ezra set a low bar." He shrugged, and I raised a brow at him. "Okay, Okay. My brother is not what he appears to be. All the other princes of Hell detest him. I just don't want him to ruin your smile."

I gave Kyler a nod. The moon reflected over the water.

I thought back to Dad and who he became once Mom died. Perhaps Ezra changed for a reason, too.

"Are you okay, Fire?"

"What did you just call me?"

"Fire," he said.

"Why?"

"Because you light a fire deep within me that I didn't know was there."

My cheeks burned. "If you keep flirting with me, I'm going to assume you're in love with me."

"Fuck, you caught me." He laughed with his chest.

A waitress came to our table, speaking fluent Italian. I blinked at her, but Kyler took over and conversed with her like it was second nature. I leaned on my elbow and stared at him in amazement.

"Now, who's in love with who?"

"You're ridiculous." I rolled my eyes.

"I'm *not* hearing a no." He raised a brow.

"Why do you always appear with Ezra?" I asked, purposely avoiding his retort. "Or after him? Like at the mall?"

"I'm Ezra's second in command, his fang leader. Which is a fancy way of saying, I have to follow him everywhere."

"What does a second in command do?" I tilted my head.

"I'm in charge of his realm when he's gone. I'm also in charge of his legion and do his bidding." His voice cracked. "It also means if he dies, I become prince." He ran a hand over the back of his neck.

"Do you want to be a prince?"

"No." He shook his head. "There was a war 130 years ago. Ezra sat on his throne while I watched good people, *friends*, die." Kyler balled his hand into a fist on the table. "I vowed to stay with the people. No throne is worth the death that follows."

"I'm sorry. I can't imagine that pain, but I do know loss." I placed my hand over his fist.

He slowly lowered his shoulders.

"How do you feel about Ezra?" I asked.

Kyler grunted. "I'll never be anything to him. I'm only his second because mom begged. I think if he finds someone as capable, he'd get rid of me."

"As in?"

"Who knows when it comes to him." Kyler rubbed the back of his neck.

"He's convinced I'm a demon."

"I know." Kyler nodded.

"My mom told me on her deathbed that I have an angel watching over me," I whispered. "Her death sits in the front of my mind always. It's why I stayed at the bar."

"And your dad?"

"Dad died the same day Mom did. Not in a physical sense, but he drank his grief away for the next three years. I was 16 and had to grow up overnight."

Kyler ignored the plates of bolognese placed down in front of us. Instead, he stared at me for a long time.

My heart beat fast, and my palms sweated. *Why is he looking at me like that?*

"Why do you suddenly look so nervous?" he asked.

"No reason. I-I'm fine." I breathed out. "Why are you starting at me?"

"I was thinking about something." He tapped his finger on the table.

"About what?" I arched a brow.

"I will pay off your house."

"What?" I jerked my head. "No. I can't ask you to do that."

"You're not asking. I'm telling you. If that house holds happy memories for you, then I will make sure you get what I still don't have: a place to call home."

"Kyler I-"

Orpheus appeared next to our table, speaking fast. "Ezra is looking for you."

"What does he want now?" Kyler groaned.

"I don't know, but I will take Sapphire home."

Why did Ezra always pull Kyler away?

I chewed on the inside of my cheek and sighed.

"Told you he ruins everything," Kyler huffed. "I will see you soon, Fire. I promise."

We stood, and Kyler pulled me into an embrace. His warmth surrounded me. I inhaled the smell of a log fire.

"Come, Sapphire. I won't be able to hold Ezra off if he finds us here." Orpheus extended his hand.

I reluctantly took it, and Orpheus phased us back to my house in a blink. I wobbled a little as I stepped away from him.

"Thank you for taking me home, Orpheus. You have no reason to be kind." I slunk into the couch.

"Kyler is a good friend," he said "If you are important to him, you are important to me. I'd be remiss if I didn't warn you about the path you're headed down, though. There is far more beyond the veil that you have not been allowed to see. Dangerous things."

"What do you mean?"

"I can't say more. If they find out I even told you this, I will be sent away. I must get back now."

After he left, I paced my bedroom floor.
What am I going to do?

Chapter Ten
Kyler

Ezra had his head buried in paperwork when I phased in. Not sure what he spent so much time on it for. All he ever did consisted of sitting on his shiny throne and ordering everyone around. Never lifted a fucking finger.

The clutter on his desk made the messiest people look clean. Books opened to random pages, and pens scattered about. His finger slid along a page in rapid movements.

Asshole.

"You wanted to see me, sire?" I crossed my arms.

He didn't bother looking up from whatever project sat situated before him. "I need you to get the treaty papers from Alfonso."

This prick called me from my date, for this?

I took one deep breath, trying not to make a decision I'd regret later. "Brother, any one of our lesser legionnaires could deal with this," I spoke through gritted teeth. "Can I send Orpheus, or Amdis?"

"I am your prince *first* and brother *second*. You *will* address me as such. I do not trust anyone else to run this for me." He paused and looked up at me with a wicked grin. "Unless you were in the middle of something… important?"

I balled my fists at my sides. "No, sire. Nothing important at all."

"You are in a suit. Are you sure?" He gave a knowing grin.

I gulped. "I am going to go now, sire." I phased away before my mouth said what I was thinking.

Alfonso's gate guards gave me a nod before lifting it. I strolled through the courtyard.

Why castles? The whole of Hell got modernized, but princes had to feel important.

Shades of red with black clouds blissfully floating covered Hell's sky. But inside, the pungent smell of wet dog reignited my anger as I walked into the library. I was so sick of everyone calling me *dog* when this asshole was one.

Alfonso studied a map, towering against a shelf. He ran a hand through his dark hair, pushing it out of his face. I cleared my throat and waited to be noticed like a peasant running a fool's errand.

Hearing my explanation, he groaned. Then sent me back to the main entrance of the castle to wait for him there. The silence in the halls echoed eerily. Many of Alfonso's pack stayed in the mortal world.

Being sent to this side of the realm, I decided to visit my friend once this charade ended. Zariah would undoubtedly love to be graced by my presence. And I wanted some company.

Alfonso came into view with a rolled-up paper in hand. Dust covered his fingers. He must have gotten that from the long-lost archives. Why did Ezra need it? If he planned on changing territory lines it could start a war. We just got out of one, I sure as shit wasn't ready for another. Neither were my men. I knew it didn't matter though. If he wanted war, he'd make war.

Shithead.

"Tell your brother hello for me. I want this back after he's done." Alfonso handed the roll to me, narrowing his eyes.

"Sire." I bowed my head in thanks and left. I had no reason to stick around longer.

The sky above me darkened in the little time I with Alfonso. Sapphire would undoubtedly be sleeping by now. I grumbled while I walked, kicking up dirt. Phasing back to Ezra would have made more sense, but what's a pit stop when you've been reduced to a glorified paperboy?

"Kyler! Brother! What brings you to my neck of the woods?" Zariah greeted me as he pulled me inside.

His small living room and the smell of meatloaf welcomed me. I glanced towards the kitchen, where I could hear Sylvie, Zariah's mate, humming to herself.

"Oh, you know, being Ezra's bitch." I flopped onto his couch and scratched my head.

He sat down across from me. His dark hair tousled around his ears. I towered over him by a good foot since he was one of the shorter wolves from the pack. The yellows of his eyes looked darker than normal, more tired.

"Kyler! Language!" Sylvie called from the kitchen.

"Sorry, Syl!" I yelled back. "He called me to Hell to get this stupid roll of paper. Anyone could have gone," I grumbled, tossing the roll to the ground. Hiding my face in my hands, I let out a low moan.

"You're feistier than normal. What gives?"

"Nothing. Ezra is being extra douchey lately. He's asked me to up the level of guards on duty. I've had to deal with three times more prisoners the last few days, and he keeps going on and on about Lucifer not knowing what's coming. Plus, he's sending me on bitch-ass errands like getting this treaty! He's fucking lost his mind." I stopped hiding my face.

"Are you sure we can't help you get away from him? It's been 300 years, man. He can't keep abusing you." Zariah furrowed his brows.

Sylvie stepped out from the kitchen and placed a hand on his shoulder. Her long crimson hair was such a contrast to his dark locks.. I admired how well they fit together.

"No, you guys do enough for me. Who knows, maybe things will turn around for the better soon?" I scrunched my face.

By the looks on their faces, they weren't buying it. Hell, I wasn't buying it. Nothing had changed in hundreds of years; why would it get better now?

"At least stay for dinner." Syl smiled my way.

"I'd love to, Syl, no one cooks meatloaf like you, but I've got to get back. I really needed to see a friendly face. Murdering your brother isn't a good look." I gave a half laugh.

They exchanged a quick look.

"She won't take no for an answer, man. You know this." Zariah laughed up at his old lady.

An ache sat in my chest. I longed for this. For a mate and a cozy home with no responsibility. It was a dream that seemed worlds away. An impossible dream that couldn't happen. Ezra would never allow me to have this. Never allow me to find happiness.

"Alright, alright." I threw my hands up in mock surrender.

"Good, because it's already done. Go sit at the table." Sylvie shooed us away.

We laughed and sat down at their small round table. Zariah folded his hands and rested his chin on them. He took a gander at me.

"While Syl is distracted, be real here, man. What is eating you? Because if it's truly Ezra, we can make a plan. I've watched you deal with so much bullshit." Zariah flung a hand out in anger.

I knew exactly what bullshit he meant. Years of abuse, and blood on my hands, all for my ungrateful brother to sit on his throne unharmed by war. Untouched by famine. He didn't have to watch people he loved die. He stayed safe from the real evils that belonged in our world.

Fucking asshole.

"What could we really do? He is practically untouchable. Alfonso loves him. The other princes are not his biggest fans, but they'd never go against him. Not without someone stronger at their backs. He has everyone so fucking afraid. Lucifer could give two shits as long as he's left alone." I leaned back in the chair and stretched a leg out. Frustration curled around my mind.

"You've thought about this for a long time, haven't you?"

"Only two hundred years or so."

"Kyler."

"Yes, I have thought about it a lot. Zariah, I've killed so many innocent people for him. There is blood that can never be washed away, no matter how many times I clean my hands. No matter how much good I do, the darkness lingers."

A heavy quietness drifted into the room. Sylvie brought in a pan of meatloaf, and her eyes shifted between us. She pushed her tongue to her cheek and huffed.

"That is it. Kyler, you need to get away from that godforsaken place. I don't care what it takes, but you *will* get out." She stomped her foot.

"Sylvie-" Zariah started to speak, but she put her hand up.

"No, Kyler is family. We take care of family."

"Yes, ma'am," Zariah and I said in unison.

"Good, now I will hear no more of this. Let's eat."

We dug into dinner. Laughter stocked the air as we chatted about life, and my problems drifted away. This was my family, not by blood, but by choice.

After hugs and saying a quick goodbye, I phased back to Ezra. He still had his head in his desk as I firmly placed the treaty down. I didn't bother saying a word to him and turned to walk out.

"Oh, brother," his sing-song voice sent a chill through me, "Can you also go make sure our spot is secure for the demons' ceremony next week? I'd hate for Dante to have one less chair."

I took a deep breath, ignoring the shaking in my core.

"I doubt the prince would leave out a chair for a fellow prince." I knew if I turned around, my face would give my anger away. That is, if my feigned civility didn't first.

"Go check. Or you will be in charge of torture for the next hundred years. Do I make myself clear?" Ezra said sharply.

"Yes, sire."

"Oh, and Kyler? Next time you visit your friend, before doing as I ask, you will spend a week in the dungeons. You reek of dog." He held his nose.

"I went to Alfonso's castle. Of course, I smell of dog." I rebutted.

"And meatloaf?" He quipped.

"May I go now, sire?"

He waved his hand and shoved his face back into his work, unrolling the treaty. With a sigh, I phased away. There were no more niceties to be had with him. Not when he wanted to prove he held the power. As if anyone could forget.

Instead of going to Dante, I stood in front of my mother's tombstone. The demon graveyard chimed with a silence fitting only for Hell. Not even a breeze disturbed the dead. The heat had a heaviness to it, as if to keep the buried in the ground. I touched her pillar and lowered my head. My chest rose and fell with each slow breath.

"It was always easier when you were around," I whispered.

I felt utterly alone in this world. Ezra would continue to abuse his power over me and anyone who got in his way. There had to be a change soon, or I would burn it all down. The pressure in my chest tightened with every breath. My high rank and status in Hell meant nothing as long as my brother remained alive.

As long as he had control.

Clouds drifted above my head when I looked up. Taking a deep breath, I centered myself. Holding resentment did do me any good. The world continued to go on.

There happened to be one person I wanted to see. After the errands were done, I'd get back to Sapphire.

After all, I needed to ask her about the Mustang.

Chapter Eleven
Sapphire

I sat on the floor surrounded by boxes stacked in the office. Ezra knew me now; I couldn't run away. He'd always find me as he did at the mall. Knowing I would be stuck in a life of demons, that left only one thing to do: unpack. The house would be paid off with no more foreclosure hanging over my head. I might as well get comfortable.

Kyler mentioned magic a few times. Perhaps I could find a way to protect myself from the demons. Or at least stay off their radar. I didn't know enough about their world, but I did trust Kyler.

Only Kyler.

I pulled memorabilia from the box closest to me. Trophies from childhood and pictures of a happy youth were sprawled out around me. A smile lined my face when I found the last family photo we ever took.

Mom was lying in her hospital bed. Dad had one arm around me and one on Mom's shoulder. My hands tingled at the memory. In the quiet, I heard their laughter. Even within hours of death, Mom had been smiling.

"Wow. I didn't know you could smile that wide," Kyler said, leaning on the door frame.

I jumped in my skin, dropped the picture, and grabbed at my chest. "Fuck, Kyler! You're going to give me a heart attack coming in like that!"

"Sorry, you looked so happy, and you know I love seeing that. I didn't want to interrupt." He sat down cross-legged beside me.

I picked up the picture and handed it to him. "It was a few hours before she died," I whispered, leaning against his arm.

He looked over the photo, and a light smile crossed his lips.

"You had a beautiful family, Fire," he said, placing a hand on my thigh.

He lingered on the picture, his thumb tracing a corner back and forth. He blinked, and his black eyes turned blue; red lines spread across the whites of his orbs. The silence in the room spoke louder than any words could.

Kyler handed the picture back to me. I put it down in my favorites pile and went back to rummaging through boxes. He sat beside me for a while, passing me things.

"Ah-ha! I knew you had professional lessons!" Kyler blurted as he pulled out an award from choir.

I took it from him and laughed. "Was it that obvious?"

"It was. Oh, I forgot! I brought you something."

He pulled out a small keychain from his jacket pocket and handed it to me.

"What's this for?" I looked at the tiny red guitar in my palm.

"So you can remember how good I am with my fingers." He smirked.

"You're ridiculous." I laughed.

"Only for you." Kyler nudged me with his shoulder. "What's the deal behind that Mustang anyway?"

"My mom gave it to me for my sixteenth birthday."

"She's a beauty. What's the specs on it?"

For a moment, I thought back to the day Dad taught me how to replace the carburetor. Taking care of the Mustang became a ritual when he was home.

"It's a Mach 1 with a 428 supra cobra jet engine. It has stronger connecting rods. There's close to 400 horsepower along with 330 foot-pounds of torque. Is that enough, or should I go down to the smallest detail, like the hood pins?" I smirked at him and spun the keychain around my finger.

His mouth dropped open, and his eyes bulged. "Good Gods, I am so hard right now." Kyler shimmied his shoulders and laughed.

"I take good care of Stella, thank you very much." I huffed at him, failing to hold back my own laughter.

I put the keychain on the desk beside me and spotted a small lavender-colored box underneath. I definitely did not see that when I rummaged through the house before.

I lifted the lid, and small particles of dust flew out, causing me to fan them away. A spiral journal sat on top. After wiping more dust off, I noticed my name scribbled in Mom's writing.

"What's this?" Pulling it out of the box, the worn pages somehow felt heavier. Opening the notebook, I froze at the handwritten words.

My darling Sapphire,

If you're reading this, then you have probably discovered the truth- demons and angels exist. Before Lilith brought you to me, your guardian angel came to visit. He told me you are the only demon of your kind. That Lilith and Apollyon sent you forward in time to keep you safe. They ruled over Hell after the original Lucifer. That's all I know. The gods can only intervene so much. Magic protects you for now, but one day your powers will fully awaken, and the demon you are will be free. Remember that you are strong and to always rely on your instincts. Your father and I loved you with everything we had. No matter what happens next, don't forget that. I'll write more when I can.

-Love you, always

Mom

By the end of the first page, my vision blurred. I stood with my hands trembling. The journal fell from my grasp, and I kicked it across the room. My head shook fervently. Mouth went dry. Tightness gripped my chest. Kyler shot up with pursed lips and a furrowed brow.

"No! No! No!" I wailed, pulling at my hair with both hands. The world began to spin.

"Fire? What's wrong?" He placed a hand on my shoulder.

"I'm not a demon! It's a lie!" I yelled, shoving him off me.

Warmth filled my arm and slid down my hand. A burst of fire wrapped around my fingers. There was no scent of burning flesh, but of burnt dust. Gasping, I shook my hand violently until the flames vanished.

It's true.

It's all true.

The fire from my finger, my eyes turning black.

Demon.

Tears streamed down my face as I bolted to the bathroom. All the contents of my stomach came hurling out. My world came crashing down around me. Everything I had ever known changed in the blink of an eye.

"Fire?" Kyler came over to me with the journal in his hand.

The words my mother said on her deathbed weren't drug-induced hysteria, and now they pounded louder in my mind.

You are a demon, and destined for a world beyond our own.

"I'm.. the demon...princess." I tried to talk through my agony, but all that came out were wails of pain.

Another twirl in my stomach, and I heaved into the toilet again. Tears poured from my eyes. I rested my head against the cool porcelain and wept.

Wept for the life I lived.

Wept for the life I no longer knew.

Wept for the death of who I thought I was.

Kyler dropped down to his knees, pulling me against him. My entire body shook fiercely as my tears fell. Air barely escaped my lungs.

"What I'm about to say is going to sound impossible, but I am begging you to trust me," he whispered into my hair. "Go to your shift at work tonight, pretend everything is normal."

What does normal even look like now?

I was a demon the entire time. Everything I had ever known was a lie. My family, my friends, even my home, all lies.

I belong in Hell. I'm a monster.

A demon.

My heart ached as I gripped at my chest.

"I'll get Vealla to help us. She is the princess of the witches. If there's magic keeping you hidden, we'll find out. You're not alone in this, but I can't protect you if we don't play this smart. I swore to always rescue you, and with the Gods as my witness, I always will."

I nodded at him, still unable to form words. I couldn't tell if it was the tears or the reality of my world turning upside down. Ezra knew who I was all along. I'd never be safe.

"What's going to happen? Who- who are you protecting me from?" My voice broke.

"Everyone."

Chapter Twelve
Sapphire

It appeared quieter than usual as I stood behind the counter at work. Tilting an elbow on the sink. I tried to dry mugs, willing my hands to stop shaking.

All I could see were memories of my life. I thought back to every moment that never made sense. My hand not burning on the stove when I was eight. My empathic ability. The fire from my fingers. It had all been the demon inside me.

Kyler's words echoed, but I didn't even know what normal looked like anymore.

I belong in Hell. I was never meant to be here.

Tears threatened to swell again. I dug my nails into my hand, sending the pain anywhere but my mind. Why didn't Kyler appear like all the other times? He promised to rescue me.

He promised.

I didn't know if a witch could truly help me, but I needed to hope for something. Even if it meant releasing what lingered inside me. At least it would give me an answer. Any answer.

Why me?

A cold hand grabbed my shoulder. A demon spun me around and extended his fangs out. Fear gripped deep within me. The world moved in slow motion as his teeth came to my neck. I wanted to scream in pain, but no sound left me. I watched the bar blur as my vision clouded.

The feeling of warm liquid slid down my collar.

"Kyler," I whispered to the spinning room.

"Get off of her, you spineless dog!" Ezra's thunderous voice shook the room.

Static slid down my entire body. The world darted into darkness. In my head, I heard my mother's words again.

You are a demon.

"Sapphire! Sapphire! Can you hear me?" Ezra's voice sounded a million miles away.

I blinked, vision still blurry. The light from the ceiling had me dazed. I held my forehead in my palm. My head ached as the world around me came back into focus.

Ezra's face hovered close enough that his warm breath hit my cheeks. Kyler looked fuzzy, standing at my side. I pinched the bridge of my nose, sitting up. When I could see, I lingered on Kyler. He had a white knuckle grip on his sword.

Loud noise rang in my head, but no one spoke. It took me a minute to realize emotions hit me like bricks. Anger, fear, rage, everything blended together. My hands twitched, and my head pounded. I scrunched my face at the strong metallic smell now wafting in. Demons surrounded us, gawking.

I ran my hand over my neck. Expecting to feel blood, yet nothing.

Despite feeling completely out of control, my heart beat steadily in my chest. My breath caught in my throat. The world around me overflowed with vivid colors. And I could feel *them*.

I could feel the demons.

The demon inside of me rose to the surface.

"Are you okay? I could not get to you in time." Ezra sounded sad, but a hint of darkness settled in the air.

Kyler shot Ezra a dark look, then extended a hand to help me up. I took it and rose to my feet. I couldn't understand the glare through the fog. Emotions bounced around, making it impossible to focus.

My legs wobbled, forcing me to grip the counter for balance. I leaned on my elbows and covered my ears, but the noise raged on. I tried to curl into myself, wishing everyone would go away.

I took the silence for granted. Now, I couldn't turn it off no matter how hard I tried.

"Leave us," Ezra demanded.

"Sire, we can not ignore what happened. Are you going to tell her?" Kyler asked, looking at me, frowning.

What the hell happened?

"I will do what must be done. Now find that rogue and deal with him swiftly," Ezra hissed the order.

"My prince." Kyler bowed, but his eyes never left me.

"I'm okay." My weak legs and quaking hands told a different story.

Only a dull roar drummed with the other demons gone. Ezra inspected me closely, but I ignored his leering. He took a step closer, invading my space. A spike of anger flashed inside of me.

"I have something to tell you."

Ezra reached for me, but I jerked away.

"You knew I was a demon the entire time, and yet you did nothing to help me. You didn't even explain Hell to me. Not the rules, not what to do, nothing!" I growled, surprising both of us.

"I failed you, and I am sorry." He sighed, but his eyes drifted past me.

Anger burned through me. I curled my fists at my sides. Two fireballs shot out from my hands, and the smell of charred wood filled the air.

Ezra laughed manically as he poured water on the floor.

"Dollface." Ezra stepped closer and pushed a hair behind my ear.

A lump formed in my throat at his touch.

"I think it is best if you come be with me in Hell," he said "You cannot control your powers. There are... *others* who would use that to their advantage. You belong next to me on the throne. You belong *to me*." Something wicked flashed in his smile as he reached for me again.

"I don't trust you." I stepped away from him as the fire from my hands burnt out.

Click.

The sound of a shotgun loading went off in the distance. It sounded so far away yet so close. Ezra snapped his head towards the door and then back at me. The sound coming closer made my legs weak all over again.

"Get down, Sapphire. That is a hunter." Ezra's voice was low.

"A hunter?" My breath became shallow as I backed into the wall.

"I told you, you are a demon. Hunters go after us when there is a surge of power. Now get the fuck down," Ezra growled, pointing his finger at the ground.

I hid behind the bar counter. The steps outside got closer. The cold tiles sent a shiver through my body, or was it anxiety? With all my senses heightened, I couldn't tell. I shut my eyes. First, my demon came alive inside of me, and now this.

Will it ever end?

"We should really stop meeting like this," Ezra snapped as the steps entered the bar. I didn't venture a look to see who was on the other side.

"Where is everyone? I was hoping for a party," another male voice said.

I prayed Ezra had this under control.

My breaths quickened. The footsteps came within feet of where I was. I put a hand over my mouth to hide my whimpers.

"Just sent everyone home. Sorry, but I am sure I can still give you a party favor." I could feel the wicked smile in Ezra's voice.

Someone landed a punch. Heavy anger filled the room. Glass broke above me, almost in slow motion, as the shards fell. Instinctively, my arms raised above my head.

A shard pierced my elbow. Pulling the piece of glass out, a small amount of blood poured out. The wound healed in an instant, no mark to be seen.

Woah.

My skin had never done that before.

Brown boots stood in front of my face.

"Don't worry, darlin'. That demon isn't going to hurt you anymore. I'm sorry for what I'm about to do, though."

Something hit my head hard. The world spun, and that blissful darkness took over once again.

Chapter Thirteen
Sapphire

How does a demon pass out anyways?

The glass at the bar didn't do anything to me, yet I managed to black out twice now.

Taking in my new environment, animal heads lined all four deep brown walls. The bed's satin sheets wrapped around my body in a cozy cocoon. The quaint charm of the room gave a false sense of hope with a smell of wood burning hit my nose.

I took a deep breath and tried to calm the shaking in my bones. My eyes scanned the room again, stopping at the antler mirror. My irises were hazel.

How is that possible? Shouldn't they be black?

I hugged my shoulders, bringing my legs to my chest. Anger rose to the surface.

Fuck. Ezra.

He should have protected me. Should have told me more about demons, about who I was. He could have phased us away! Instead, he left me to my own devices, unsure of anything. How could I handle this? I needed to calm down.

Shooting an accidental fireball in a hunter's cabin wouldn't be the best idea.

I pulled out my phone and raised it.

No signal.

Fuck.

How the hell am I getting out of here?

A shotgun unloaded. My eyes shot to the door.. The smell of gun cleaner became suffocating. Heavy footsteps headed my way, the smell stronger.

"You're safe now, darlin'." The hunter's voice rolled through the room. A scent of pine trees clung to his shirt as he sat next to me on the bed. He extended his hand to me. "I'm Sam."

I kept my hands in my lap, not knowing if I'd shoot my power out again. I fidgeted with my fingers, avoiding his gaze.

Watching from the corner of my eye, he smiled. It had been enchanting in a way, as it lit his entire face.

"I don't know who I am." I bit my quivering lip.

The truth.

The undeniable truth.

Whatever identity I had before, gone. I turned into a demon with nowhere to go.

"There are clothes in the bathroom if you want to change. Belonged to my wife." Sam pointed to a brown door. "Then we can figure things out."

I gave him a nod, swallowing.

The clothes hung over the edge of the tub. He had expected me to want to change. I began to hyperventilate and squeezed my eyes shut.

Fuck Ezra.

Fuck this.

I slowly slid off my clothes until nothing but my underwear was left. I wanted to cry; my eyes burned. Yet, no more tears came.

Looking in the mirror, I touched my face. My eyes flashed to black.

Shit. Shit. Shit. Shit.

I blinked frantically, willing them to change back. After a tense moment, they returned to their normal hazel color.

It had happened the night of my date with Kyler, and I shoved it off. Now I couldn't deny the hard reality.

"You okay in there?' Sam called out.

"Yes, just a second!" I quickly threw on jeans and a T-shirt.

I put my hair in a messy bun, took a deep breath, and patted myself down. Content with my eyes staying their color, I walked out. Sam sat waiting for me on the bed.

"Thanks... For the clothes, I mean."

"How did you end up in that bar? I'm assumin' you didn't know it was a vampire den." He cleaned his shotgun with a rag, still watching me.

"I thought it was some cosplay-type thing." I shrugged and sat back down on the bed.

"You didn't even bat an eye. I just told you vampires were real." He raised an eyebrow.

Where is Kyler? I need to escape.

"I always felt magical things were real." I hoped my shaking voice didn't give way to the fear clutching me.

"They're very real. I hunt and kill them. I'll take you home, but you need to know things. I wouldn't want you to end up in this position again." Sam rested his hand on my thigh, and I shifted away.

"Like what? Don't I just look for whoever doesn't appear in the mirror?" I laughed a little.

"You're so beautiful, you remind me of my wife." Sam moved a stray strand of hair behind my ear. A chill slivered its way down my spine. "Vampires are actually a subset of demons. All the myths you've read are not true. Demons are evil, and they all deserve death."

I turned away from him as my chin wobbled.

Do I deserve death? Am I evil?

"Every demon has a crest. The most powerful have two symbols, while lesser demons have one. That's how Lucifer divided them." Sam looked toward the door. His gaze drifted beyond whatever was there.

"Are you okay?"

"Yes. I'm fine. Demons are scum; they only care about themselves and will kill anyone to get what they want." Sam grunted and placed his gun over his lap.

"They c-can't be all bad." I whimpered.

"Listen, demons come from Hell. Perhaps not biblical Hell, but a place where vermin belong. They fight wars over succession and kill for petty reasons. Stay far away from them if you want to survive."

I couldn't say anything. He believed demons were vermin. How could I blame the hunter? He knew more than I did of their world.

My world.

"Come with me." He shot up and guided me into the living room.

A bear skin carpet with creepy eyes lay in the middle of the floor. The fireplace raged on as the flames cracked and popped. Sam handed me a frame. In it stood him and a woman in a white dress.

I turned my head to the window. The air around me became thicker, and panic slid into me. A shadow darted across an opening in the trees.

Something lurked out there.

I squinted, aiming to get a better look, to no avail. My heart thumped in my ears.

"The vampire prince killed my wife, Jasmine, in front of me." He didn't notice the figure outside, but his voice sharpened.

A flicker of anger and guilt surfaced.

Sam walked over to a cabinet and pulled out a silver dagger. Anger rose deep within him, and a red aura covered his body. It went away in an instant. I rubbed my eyes, wondering if it had been there at all.

Auras were only something I experienced twice. Once when Mom died, and again when I met Emily. Neither time made any sense, but this time, anger accompanied it.

"I'll use this blade to kill Ezra. Slice right into his chest and take his heart out like he took mine." He spun the blade between his fingers. "Now, where do you live?"

"I d-don't remember," I murmured. The last thing I needed was a hunter showing up at my home.

If I even went back to it.

"Let's go to the local hospital, then. Maybe they can figure it out."

How do I get out of this? Can I do the vampire compel thing? Is that a demon's power?

As we walked towards his truck, I scanned the forest. Whoever lurked here seemed long gone.

I stared at Sam as he drove, waiting for him to notice my gaze. He turned to me and curled his lips up in the corner.

"You good? You look like you have to go to the bathroom somethin' fierce."

I sank into the seat and leaned my head against the window. Tears that I didn't know I had left fell silently.

My world changed, and I had no way out. Isabelle and Emily clouded my mind. Would I ever see them again? Or was I too much of a monster now?

Sam walked me into the emergency room, and we waited in line. The mixture of emotions caused tremors in my body. Listening to an older gentleman cough repeatedly pushed my senses over the edge. The clock ticking on the wall echoed in my mind.

Tick. Tick. Tick. Tick.

I covered my ears again, with little luck. I became dizzy and off balance. I wanted to run, but the fear of accidentally causing harm to someone kept me in place. I had to wait, like a lamb to the slaughter. My eyes darted around for an exit, and I found one.

The bathroom.

A wide grin crossed my lips. My chest felt lighter. Soon, I could get away. It didn't matter where, as long as it was far away from the hunter.

Far away from people.

Once it was our turn, I slid away. Sam didn't notice as he was distracted by the nurse.

The bathroom smelled like ammonia and puke. I slammed the stall door shut. The metal door was cool against my forehead. My breath was trapped in my nose, and I didn't dare try to inhale the horrible scent. Closing my eyes, my thoughts shifted to the bar. The smell of cigarettes and blood replaced the puke. Opening my eyes, I stood in the middle of the bar.

Glass and blood remained splattered on the floor. Reaching down, I grabbed a shard of a broken mug. I slit my palm open and gasped. My hand healed itself on its own, and there had been no pain. I could heal, but to what extent?

The bar being quiet felt eerie, but everyone was still here.

"Fire! You're alive!" Kyler darted to me, holding me against his chest. His fingers wrapped in my hair, pulling me closer. "Are you okay? What happened?"

"Ezra is fucking useless." I looked up at him. "He didn't save me!" Static slid down my arm and through my fingers until a blast of lightning cracked across the room. My chest rose and fell hard. Kyler watched me carefully.

"You don't know how to control your powers. I can see how angry and hurt you are. Look, after the demon attacked you, I came to rescue you. Once I had you in my arms, you absorbed a piece of my soul essence. There is a piece of me tied to you now. We are destined in a way so few are. You feel it too, that pull to me."

"What're you saying, Kyler?"

"You're the only one of your kind. The lost princess. Let me protect you."

I collapsed to my knees. "Ezra said I belong to him." I covered my face with my hands.

"He won't protect you, Fire. He is never around, you got attacked, and a hunter took you. I can't claim you, to take you from him. It would be a death sentence. The rules of Hell don't work as they do in the mortal world, no matter how much I burn for you. But, I can protect you and keep you safe."

"Why can't you claim me? I don't understand."

"If a prince claims you, no one else can, except Lucifer. It means you are his, and his alone. If I claimed you..." He paused and looked down at his hands. "If I took you from him, I'd be considered a traitor to the crown."

"What do I do, Kyler? I don't want to live like this. I hate this! I hate it!"

"We will figure it out, Fire. I swear to you."

Kyler held me again, ignoring the tears wetting his shirt. The walls closed in around me. The air in my lungs couldn't escape. My entire world crumbled around me. I leaned away from Kyler and stood up, wiping away my tears.

"I need time," I whispered.

I closed my eyes again, attempting to phase away. At first, I didn't move, and groaned. When I tired again, I managed to phase slowly.

Chapter Fourteen
Sapphire

A cool breeze wrapped around my body. Waves crashed against my feet with the tide. The water calmed the storm that raged inside of me. Kyler couldn't claim me. I would be stuck with Ezra forever. A thought that made me want to die. Made me want to scream and beg whatever god or gods there were to take back my demon. All I wanted was my mortal life back.

The moon reflected off the water, reminding me of the night Mom died.

Oh, Mom, what do I do? I asked the universe, as if it would answer. As if it cared.

Her face ran through my mind. The loss of her warm embrace hit me as the waves swished. Mom loved me even knowing I was this... this *thing*. Dad would have too, in time, I think. Or did he know? Neither of them ever judged me or expected more out of me than what I was capable of. If only she could be here to tell me what to do now.

It felt like being stuck in a dream, but no matter how hard I tried, I wasn't waking up. The image distorted and became a waking nightmare.

Some angel I have. I huffed and kicked the sand.

The quiet calm of the beach did nothing to soothe the pain. I still had so many questions. I felt where the bite on my neck had been. Not even a scar lingered on the skin.

I took a deep breath and listened to the sound of the water. The ocean air smelled of sea salt, reminding me of my date with Kyler.

Every time his presence was felt, I could breathe. Things came easily with him near. With Ezra, I never knew what version of him I'd get. I clenched my fist tight at my sides.

"Are you happy now?" I screamed out, not sure who I had asked.

I didn't know what would come next, but nothing would ever be the same.

My friends could never know what became of me. All that I had in this world was my childhood home, but if they went looking for me, that is the first place they'd look. Where could I go?

I'm so lost.

"Of all the places I thought I would find you, this was not it." Ezra's deep voice came from behind me.

I didn't want to see him, not now. Nothing he said would make me forgive him. And nothing could make this right.

"I have questions." My voice came across harsher than I anticipated.

"If you want answers, then fight me."

"Excuse me?"

"You have no control over yourself. If you want to know what you can do, fight me. Figure it the fuck out." His voice boomed as he rolled up his sleeves.

"Fine." My nostrils flared.

I didn't know anything about fighting, except the things I had seen on TV. My powers were useless; even if I felt stronger, I had no control.

Biting my lip, I swung my foot. Ezra grabbed my ankle, pushing me into the ground. A low growl escaped my lips as I popped back up. Rage filled his eyes when my fist met his face. He lunged at me, slicing my face with one of his talons. Blood dripped down my cheek for a second before my face healed.

God damnit, Ezra!

He cracked his knuckles but didn't move. The way he watched my every move angered me more. He knew I had no chance against him, but he wanted to see it in this twisted game we played.

A violent scream escaped my throat. I was a game to him. Another way to prove he had the power.

In a burst of speed, I ran at him. Ezra slid to the side, causing me to miss him. Static erupted in my arms, and lightning wrapped around my fingers. For once, my emotions causing my powers to be unpredictable, worked in my favor.

Our eyes met, and I threw the bolts at him. He dodged, moving in a blur every time I aimed for him. The wicked laugh that came from his lips sent a feeling of dread through me. Tired of the games, I decided to see if I could push a different limit.

"You'll fucking answer my questions." A surge of power sat inside of me. "I know what happened between you and that hunter!"

"Do you think you know the truth?" Ezra's tone came out angrier than I had ever heard before. The emotions inside him surprised me. Fear slammed into me. His eyes bulged.

"NO! I don't know anything!" I shouted. "I don't even know what the fuck I am!"

"The truth is that you are *mine* now. It does not matter what you are."

I screamed and turned my back away from him. The wind whipped my hair around. The sound of crashing waves held me in place. Heat from my tears filled my eyes.

How did I have more to cry? I felt so weak and so naive.

"You will never be worthy of me if you can foolishly listen to a hunter."

Worthy of him?

"At least he told me more about you than you ever did," I said calmly.

"Stay away from him. Or else."

"Or what?" I spat.

"Or you will end up in the dog house, too," he said matter-of-factly.

"Fuck. You." I gritted my teeth.

He was the second male in my life to become something different than what I knew. I shook my head, ignoring the flashbacks in my mind. They surfaced anyway.

Dad tripped over his own feet, stumbling into the kitchen. The house smelling of stale food and vomit. He would shout about how I killed Mom. After the crashing of a beer bottle against the wall, I ran to my room and cried. The feeling of emptiness grew in the pit of my stomach that day.

"Saph," Ezra's voice lured me back to reality. He touched my shoulder. "I am sorry. I honestly tried to see if he could tell you were no longer human. I pretended to be unconscious, and I did not realize you were gone. I tried to find you, but the hunter must have his cabin warded. I could not tell where you were inside, so I left."

The world stopped moving, the weight of his words blaring in my ears. My hands shook. My chest heaved with anger.

He used me as bait.

He let me get taken.

He had been the shadow in the woods. He could have saved me, but left me alone.

I stepped closer to him and placed a finger on his chest.

"You left me!" Hunger shot through me, and a light blue glow swirled down my arm.

Ezra's eyes went wide, and he shoved me off as hard as he could. I fell back into the sand. He looked down at me with his beady eyes.

"You need to be careful! You could kill someone if you touch them without controlling yourself! This is why you *are* coming to Hell." His said.

I looked down at the sand, away from him. Lifting one hand up, I scanned my palm.

I can kill someone with a touch? God, I am a monster.

"What am I?" My voice cracked.

"A soul-eater. Now stop acting like this." Ezra gritted his teeth.

"We'll see who is worthy of who," I whispered.

I got up and went to phase away, but Ezra gripped my arm. The force sent a ripple of pain through me.

"I will give you forty-eight hours to get whatever affairs in order, then you will come to me." He pulled me closer and growled in my ear. "Or I will find you and drag you to Hell myself. After killing your pretty little friends. I promise I will. Ask Kyler how many of his friends I killed while he watched."

Ezra phased away. The color drained from my face as I collapsed onto my knees. There was only one errand I needed to run, then I'd go to Hell. No matter who I was now, my friends would be safe.

Safe from me.

Safe from my new life.

I wouldn't lose another family.

Not again.

Chapter Fifteen
Sapphire

Orange and blues spread across the sky as the sun rose. My parents had a beautiful plot in a cemetery in Rhode Island. Small stone grave markers surrounded theirs. Nearby also had three or four burial vaults for urns, all made of beautiful marble. My parents' stone read: *Here lies husband and wife, Anna and Owen Labella,* along with their birth and death dates.

I kneeled and touched the stone, enjoying the peace. I loved the quiet, and now, with my senses elevated, it was all I longed for.

"Oh, Mom, is this the life you imagined for me? A demon who feels so lost. I wish I knew what greatness you had in mind for me because I do not feel like this is it. How could being a monster equate to greatness? Maybe I deserve to be in Hell. Why didn't you tell me the truth? Why did you leave me alone!" My eyes burned but there were no tears to cry; the ducts were empty.

"You left me a notebook, a fucking notebook! Why didn't you tell me when you were alive? How could you keep this from me?"

"She did as she was told to to keep you safe."

A deep voice echoed in my head. I turned and looked everywhere, but the cemetery had been empty.

"Who's there?" I asked, shaking.

"You are on the correct path, Sapphire."

"Who said that? Show yourself!"

I rose and spun, searching. No one came into view. The wind blew around me, yet everything sat still. The voice disappeared, leaving me by myself.

I stayed for a few hours in the brisk air. Praying seemed obsolete. What gods did I even have now? Instead, I closed my eyes and waited until my heart beat calmed and the storm inside subsided. Before leaving, I slid my phone out to send a message to Emily and Isabelle.

Me:

> Hi guys, I'll be going away for a while. You may not hear from me, but I promise I'm fine. Things are changing for me, and I need to go somewhere where my thoughts won't get someone hurt. I love you both with all that I am. Thank you for being my family.

I sent the message. If this world was dangerous, if *I* was dangerous, I couldn't be around them. I had to let them go.

I needed to let everything go.

Hell would be my new home. Nothing on this plane mattered. My friends would remain safe; they'd move on.

Standing up, I kissed the gravestone one last time before leaving.

Thinking of Kyler, I phased into an unfamiliar place. White stone walls clashed against wood floors. A red carpet lay in front of a four-poster bed. The chandeliers all lit the room. I felt like I stepped into the 1600's. Sitting on the edge of the bed, I ran my hand over the smooth comforter. The atmosphere smelled like old dust, musty, but comfortable.

Kyler came out of the bathroom in nothing but black boxers. His head tilted down, drying his hair with a towel. He didn't see me as he entered the closet and threw the wet towel on the ground. I heard fabric shuffle, and when he returned, he tightened the black buckle on his jeans.

Our eyes met.

"Oh, please, Fire, make yourself right at home." He bowed and extended both arms out.

I peered at his crest on his lower abdomen: a dove. The symbol of hope. He tilted his head at me.

"Like what you see?"

"This is a nice room you have." I slipped off the bed, walking over to him. I ran my fingers over his crest, and he straightened. His rippled chest twitched under my touch.

"Is that why you're here? To compliment my room?" He raised an eyebrow at me, pushing some hair from my face.

I looked up at him, closing the distance between us. His hands found my hips. I tried to ignore that call from within myself to be close to him, but continued to fail.

"Ezra threatened me, threatened my friends. Plus, my senses are heightened. I needed somewhere quiet to be." I held back tears.

I could have sworn I heard a growl from Kyler as he pulled me against his body.

"The jackass made me fight him. Told me to figure it out on my own. He told me... He told me he's killed your friends before." My voice broke.

Everything I learnt about Ezra made him worse and worse.. I hated it.

Kyler let out a low murmur, "It's true, but we don't need to talk about that now. The noise will quiet down soon, I promise." He pressed his forehead against mine.

"Can I ask you something?"

"Anything, Fire." He picked me up and sat on the bed, pulling me down on his lap. His hands never left my hips as I turned to see his face. A comfortable warmth sat between our bodies.

"What happens now?" My finger traced circles over his soft sheets.

"Honestly, I don't have an answer for that." Kyler looked down at my finger movement.

"What happened when I blacked out? The *first* time." I locked eyes with him. My blood boiled every time our gaze met.

"When you were attacked, and I grabbed you, some of my essence escaped me, almost like you were calling to it." He wrapped his arms tighter around my waist.

"Did I... change you?"

"Nah, you couldn't take away this sass even if you tried." Kyler popped an invisible collar with a shoulder shrug.

I rolled my eyes, and he chuckled.

"If I have an angel, it'd be nice if it would appear." I sighed. The voice from the cemetery came back to the forefront of my mind.

"An angel would definitely be helpful." He looked out his window into the darkness. My eyes followed his to see a sky full of red shades.

"Kyler, are we in Hell?" I asked as he turned his gaze back to me.

"Yes. We are."

I stepped closer to the window and looked out. A red sky with black clouds was the backdrop to a village below. Demons of all sorts wandered stone walkways.

"I'll probably never see my friends again. Or see my home." I peered down at my new world. I was so sick of crying.

"Hey, now. We'll get you to a point where you can control your powers and be able to see them." Kyler lifted my chin with his finger.

"I don't even know what powers I have. What powers other demons have. It's not like it matters. Ezra would never let me leave his side."

"Demons have one elemental power, except purebreds, who have two. I'd assume the same goes for you. Let's not worry about that, okay? One day at a time, one thing at a time." His thumb brushed along my cheek. I gave him a nod.

"Are you not from the same family as Ezra? Your crest is different from his." I asked. His hands moved up and down on my hips. The gentle motion made it hard for me to focus on the conversation. My cheeks were going to be permanently red.

"Same father, different mother. Ezra's mother died, and then our father married my mother a year later. I came three years after that." Kyler ran a gentle hand down my back. I leaned into him enjoying the closeness. It felt right; I had no reason to fight it anymore.

"What was your childhood like?"

"My dad was a dick. He tortured any vampire he considered lesser. He felt he was above most demons. My mom was beautiful, and she loved me no matter what I had done until she died at the hands of a hunter. I have exactly one best friend, and he is a werewolf." Kyler looked distant.

I knew the feelings that came with the loss of one's mother to circumstances out of your control all too well.

"I'm sorry, Kyler. No one should have to feel that kind of pain." As I ran a hand over his arm, I tried my best not to picture my own mother's death.

"When you've been alive as long as I have, you learn to accept it." He gave me a soft smile from the corner of his mouth. "Any more questions, Fire?" He wanted to change the subject, and I would respect that.

"What about me having a part of your essence? How does that work? You said we're a part of each other now."

He locked eyes with me, and his lips lifted into a smile.

"You and I are bound. You call me without even realizing it. You make me feel stronger, braver." He ran his hand over my hair, and the heat of his eyes surprised me.

"I do feel it." I yawned and lay my head against his bare chest. "But I felt it before I took your essence. How can that be?"

"Could it have been my emotions?"

"Why would it have been that? It took my breath away." I tilted my head.

"You do take my breath away." His sharp tone made me chew on my lip.

Kyler gave a low chuckle before scooping me into his arms and laying my head on his pillow. He kept his body against mine, and I snuggled into him.

What did being a demon mean for me? How powerful did being a soul-eater make me? What could I do? All of this information had my head spinning. I got thrown into a world I didn't know.

I calmed my thoughts and relaxed my shoulders against Kyler.

Even in the darkness of the room, a pulsing in my veins reminded me that who I was and who I became were no longer the same.

Chapter Sixteen

Sapphire

When I opened my eyes the next day, sprawled out on the couch in front of the bed, Kyler snored. Light from the sky shone through a gap in the curtains. A groan escaped my throat as my muscles stretched. The sheet's warmth made it hard for me to want to move.

A pounding in my head reminded me of all the tears I had shed over the past few days. I got up and walked over to the window, observing the clouds in the sky. Hell had a quaint beauty to it. Reds and oranges clashed together with dark clouds. A knock at the door made me turn my head. Kyler shot up, and his eyes met mine.

"Go hide in the bathroom. Don't make a sound," he whispered.

I did as he asked. Trying to make as little noise as possible, I closed the door most of the way. The cool air made me regret not taking the sheets with me.

"Kyler, I know you are in there." Ezra's voice came from the hallway.

I tried to see through the crack in the bathroom door. Ezra waltzed into the room. The black crown on his head was a memento of the power he possessed.

Power I had yet to see.

"Sorry, I had to make myself decent. Unless you prefer my junk hanging out while we talk... *Sire*," Kyler bowed unceremoniously.

Ezra mumbled something under his breath, then came into the room to sit on the couch. An unimpressed look crossed his face before he spoke, picking at his nails. He didn't bother looking towards Kyler, and it angered me.

"Sapphire is strong. She is definitely not a mortal, nor has she ever been. Once she adjusts to being here, I think we can train her. Make her a weapon, and finally destroy my enemies. Not until she learns her place and bows to me, of course. We cannot let her make a fool out of me."

I had to tell myself not to go barreling through the door, even though I really wanted to punch him in the face. I clenched my fists, nails digging into my palms. How dare he?

Make me a weapon, my ass.

"Things are going to change around here. She will have to learn to behave. She cannot go frolicking through the mortal realm either."

"Sire, if I may, not letting her go home would be a mistake. I do not think you should use her. She could end up killing you instead." Kyler leaned against the bathroom door, which ended up shutting it. I gasped silently and scrunched my face.

"*Hmmm.* It is not like she knows how to control herself enough to harm me. She could barely throw lightning. When she accidentally tried taking my soul, she did not pull anything. It is rather pathetic, honestly. Anyway, I am calling a meeting in twenty. Be there," Ezra said.

I looked at myself in the bathroom mirror. My eyes were bloodshot. Tired lines stretched across my upper cheeks. Sadness enveloped me. Ezra believed me to be weak and pathetic.

I would show him he's wrong. Someway, somehow. He'd learn.

How could I do anything when I had been a demon all of twenty-four hours? I shook my head and cursed silently at the universe.

After the footsteps were long gone, Kyler opened the bathroom door. I stepped back into his room, running a hand over my face.

"I'm sorry about all that has happened. I should have protected you. If I came to the bar when I was supposed to, maybe none of this would be happening." His voice shook as he looked down at me.

"Please don't blame yourself for something out of our control." I touched his face.

"Even so, I'm especially sorry for the Prince dick bag."

"Eh, my life's been full of dick bags." I shrugged.

"How many have hurt you?" Kyler made a fist, his nostrils flared.

"Enough," I said in a breath. I didn't want to open that can of worms—not now. "None of that matters because you can keep me safe." I looked up at him and smiled.

"This could get us killed if anyone finds out," Kyler said frantically. "Ezra can never know—not what I told you, not that we spent the night together, and not that I will choose you over him." He kissed me then, an urgent kiss as if he needed to ensure I knew the truth behind his words. My body surged to life as our lips and bodies connected, and whatever power moved inside of me yearned to escape.

"So, don't get us caught." I winked at him, breathlessly. "Why didn't he know I was in the bathroom? Or why not phase in here?" I raised a brow.

"No one can sense you, well, except me. Ezra bitched about it when that hunter took you. He said he tried to find you but couldn't, so he left."

That mother fucker. Is he so arrogant that he assumed I'd find him? The vein in my forehead twitched.

"As for phasing into my room, I have it heavily warded. No one can phase in here except for me, and now you, due to my essence." He gave me a cocky grin.

"No one can sense me? I don't understand."

Does my so-called angel keep me safe?

"I assume Lilith's spell keeps you hidden. Ezra could sense an area you were in, and nothing more." Kyler shrugged as he walked into the closet and grabbed a shirt.

"Would it still keep me hidden? I mean, I am a demon now. Or I always was." I chewed the inside of my cheek.

"Ezra said he couldn't find you yesterday, so I assume her magic is strong."

"He keeps trying to keep me under lock and key." I spoke low, looking at my feet. I closed my fist as flames blanketed my hands. Kyler pulled me against him so quickly it made me dizzy. The fire burned out as I lay my palms against his chest, forming the only gap between our bodies.

"I will always rescue you," he murmured into the air. "I tried to find you when he returned from the cabin, but you already made it to the bar." I looked up at Kyler.

"You came for me," I whispered.

"I could never leave you behind."

"I should go to Ezra. I have a feeling whatever fight we had was only the beginning." Pulling away from Kyler's arms, I gave him a soft smile. "For now, all we can do is play along. Please stay close." My soft words brushed against his chest.

"I wouldn't dream of leaving your side, Fire." His lips met mine once more as he caressed my back. "We will find a way out of this."

"Thank you, for everything." I moved away from him. "Don't miss me too much," I smirked, phasing to Ezra.

Chapter Seventeen

Sapphire

I emerged in a long, open hall with marble floors and six giant columns lining it. The two black doors that led to the outside were propped open. Warm air swept into the room with a faint muggy smell. A red carpet led from the massive opening all the way up to the thrones themselves. Two of the same size, black, with blood red cushions. I started seeing a color theme. *Red made sense for vampires.*

Ezra sat on the throne on the left. He looked towards me, ankle casually crossed over one knee. A tightness gripped my chest. I didn't want to be anywhere near him.

"You came back." He said, standing up.

"As if I had a choice." Anger sat low in my throat, but I swallowed it down.

"Come sit on the throne. You are not Princess until we have a formal coronation, but no one will question me—not if they want to live." He smiled, watching my face, waiting for an answer.

I nodded my head. Words wouldn't escape me.

Not that it mattered.

Ezra led me by hand to the throne. He sat me down on the right side, and I crossed my legs. The room appeared to be still. Only two guards stood by the door. Something weighed me down inside. Pride of being on the throne? Fear of being stuck here forever?

"You will not take off like that *ever* again." Ezra's harsh voice reverberated against my ear. His hand gripped mine hard, sending slivers of pain into my fingers, "Do you understand?" He growled low.

"Yes." I bit my wobbling lip and turned away from him.

The pain didn't matter as long as my friends stayed safe. They were family. I didn't get to protect myself; the same wouldn't be said about Emily and Isabelle.

"I have to call a council meeting, and then we will have to lay out some ground rules." He released my hand and snapped his fingers. I looked down and rubbed my hand. The muscles in my body tensed.

Demons began to appear before my very eyes. All the ones to my right looked to be the brawn of the operation. They had weapons and fierce-looking eyes. The ones on the left were smaller, more timid, yet somehow still fierce.

Orpheus stood to the left as well. He looked over at me, and a sweet smile crossed his face. I gave him a quick nod.

Emotions began to overwhelm me again. Everything from fear to hate to lust. I closed my eyes and covered my ears, trying to tune out the world. Panting and heart beating fast, the noise slowly drifted away. I opened my eyes to find demons watching me. Observing me like an animal in a cage.

Flames appeared in front of me. Kyler bowed to his brother, and our eyes met. He wore his dark black metal armor. His longsword poked out from behind his shoulder. I eyed him from head to toe, and heat filled my cheeks.

"Sorry I am late, Highness; I had to..." He paused for a brief moment, looking at the floor, "get something important done. Royal matters and all."

Fuck Kyler, are you trying to get caught?

He felt a little on edge, anxiety below his uncaring façade.

If only he knew I'd always choose him. There wasn't really a choice. Ezra would use me for whatever he damn well pleased, and Kyler, he saw me as someone more.

"As my second, I expect you to be on time, especially when I tell you there is a meeting," Ezra's lips pulled into a grimace. "Back to the matter at hand. I am sure you have all noticed that the throne next to me is no longer empty. This is Sapphire, and she will be your new Princess. I suggest you treat her as such." Ezra's voice dominated the room.

All eyes were on me. Kyler shifted slightly towards the thrones, but held his place in front of his brother.

"I could never accept her as my Princess or anything for that matter. We don't even know who or what she is!" A taller vamp with gray hair spoke. "She's better off dead."

Tension pierced the room. A low growl came from the vampire as he ran towards at me. I covered my face with my hands, and that familiar feeling of my firepower appeared. The sound of metal slicing through bone rolled through me. I stopped covering my face, the flames disappearing.

The vampire's head slid across the floor, his body collapsing to the ground. Kyler stood with the bloody sword in his hand. I peered over at the wall behind where the vampire had been standing, now marked with black the surrounding tapestries singed.

Kyler killed the demon for me.

Ezra's jaw clenched as he tapped his foot on the ground. No words escaped his lips in support of me. Tears swelled in my eyes. He only wanted me as a weapon and nothing more: a pawn in his game of chess.

"Does anyone else want to question me as your Princess?" I growled at the crowd of demons. They all bowed then. "Good choice."

I didn't know where the rage came from, or if it was even mine. I surprised even myself.

I took a moment to look at Kyler, who, even bowing, kept his eyes drifted to me—*cocky bastard*.

I will fight until I belong in this world. I will fight until I can be free.

The body on the floor kept calling to me. I wanted something from it. A soul? I looked back out at the crowd of demons. They all intently listened to their Prince. Once in a while, they shot a glance at me until I met it, and then they would shy away.

"Something more important than the safety of our kingdom?" Ezra asked, noticing Kyler's eyes fixated on me.

"Perhaps that of your distressed Princess." Kyler and his smart-ass tone. He gave me another exaggerated bow.

"Leave us," Ezra boomed.

The demons all phased out one by one, except for Kyler. The fewer emotions coursing through me, the better.

"Highness, I can take care of her if you have business to conclude," Kyler said in a straightforward tone.

"It is fine; she is going to be my Princess, thank you, Kyler. However, you will be her guard when I can not be around. You will protect her with your life, or it will be your head. Do you understand?" Ezra growled as the words came out.

I rolled my eyes. His constant threats were getting old.

"Yes, sire," Kyler bowed.

"Get her something to eat. I will be in the room I made up for her." Ezra took my hand and stood up.

He walked me to the door to the right of the thrones. Once we walked through the opening, I couldn't believe my eyes. The walls gray stone, and the floors dark red wood, showcasing a marvelous open room. In front of us, a marble staircase with the same red carpet lining it led upstairs.

Ezra guided me up to an open space with doors on either side. We, however, took a door to the right.

The room wasn't extravagant by any means. The bed looked big enough for one person. The walls had all sorts of swords, some metal, some golden, hanging in varying ways. A shield above the bed had his crest. I sat down on the velvet sheets. Everything smelt of old dust.

Ezra crossed his arms over his chest and eyed me. He didn't speak a word. I debated saying something to him, but feared what his reaction might be. I looked out the window toward the darkening sky.

After a few minutes, Kyler brought a person in rags and chains. Their red hair stood out to me. Could this be a prisoner?

Hunger pangs twisted in my stomach. I stood too quickly, and a dizziness took over.. I hated not knowing how to control myself. I hated the idea of what taking a soul truly meant.

"You can go, Kyler. I will call on you later." Ezra waved a dismissive hand.

Kyler bowed and backed out of the bedroom door before straightening again. Ezra shut the door and turned his hard gaze to me.

"Sapphire eat. Now." Ezra demanded.

I looked over at him, then the red head. They didn't speak or move. I watched their chest rise and fall.

"You want me to...murder this person?" I asked, shaking my head.

"It is a demon. You need your strength. Now do what I say." Ezra's forehead creased. He curved his lips up on one side, revealing a fang.

I shook my head again. I refused to become a murderer.

Ezra darted to me, his fingers wrapping tightly around my neck. He lowered his lips against my ear and spoke so low I almost couldn't hear him.

"You will do what I say, or I will make good on my promise to kill your friends. Emily would be so easy to trap. She is so desperate for attention. The way she makes sure everyone knows she is the prettiest girl in the room, I bet she tastes delicious."

The blood drained from my face while he backed away. Tears threatened to swell again, but I wouldn't give him the satisfaction. I closed my fist and sniffled.

I blinked and looked at the demon in chains, trying to figure out how to do it, how to pull the soul to me. I placed a hand on their chest, hoping something would happen. I waited, but nothing happened. Ezra watched me, unblinking.

How did I make the blue glow happen before? I needed to do this, to keep my friends safe.

Am I really going to take a life?

Ezra ran his tongue over his fangs. Pain ached in my chest. I tried again, calling the soul to me in my head. I placed my hand back on the demon, and that blue glow lit up. It flowed through my arm and into me. My body relaxed. Heat and static slid through my arms.

Ezra stepped back, a wicked grin crossing his face. My instincts took over, and every last drop of the soul came to me until nothing was left but a lifeless body.

Ezra stared at me without saying a word. I felt a surge of life flow through me like pure ecstasy. I strode past him and went into the bathroom. I put my hands on the sink and looked in the mirror. My eyes turned black. The demon deep within me woke up fully.

I woke up.

I noticed the birthmark on my neck was now black, like Kyler and Ezra's crests. I ran my finger over it. Ezra leaned against the bathroom opening, watching me with beady eyes.

I needed to get away from him.

Taking a life caused a fire to burn in my soul. Raging and screaming inside, but I remained blank on the outside.

"You are a demon, you will fucking act like it and take souls when you need to." The anger in his voice sent my anxiety over the edge.

Where is my angel now?

My legs gave way where I stood. Catching myself on the sink, I sniffled.

"I have something to show you." Ezra extended a hand to me.

I hesitated. My body could heal, but the pain from his grip stayed in my mind. There would be no time to wallow in what I had done.

My suffering had to be done in silence.

Chapter Eighteen

Sapphire

We phased into a room with no doors or windows. The walls were covere in messy handwritten notes. In front of us on the table, a map took up space. Ezra summoned a brighter light, making it easier to see.

"This is my war room. No one can enter or leave except me, and it's heavily guarded by spells. You won't be able to tell a soul about it."

"Ezra, why are you showing me this?" I stepped closer and eyed the hills on the map.

He placed his hands on the edge of the table, peering over his miniature army.

"It is *Highness*." He barked. "I'm showing you so you don't make a fool out of me." He said through his teeth.

"*Highness*." I lowered my voice and dropped my eyes.

I hate playing this game.

I hate him.

"There are three levels of Hell. The Cursed level consists mostly of werewolves and vampires." He pointed to a castle, our castle. My jaw dropped at the details, down to the small battlements.

"Then there is the Realm of the Damned. That's mostly witches and pureblood demons."

My finger glided along a river in the realm. A castle tucked into a mountain caught my attention.

"The last realm you should never go to unless you want to meet your makers. It is the Realm of Death. Lucifer's favorites, his top officials, the Knights of Death, and Lucifer himself, reside there."

I wanted to meet Lucifer. Everyone seemed to fear him. Perhaps I should, too, but the idea of him drew me in.

"Every realm has a few Princes or Princesses and their second in command. Here we have Alfonso, the alpha werewolf, and me. In the Realm of the Cursed, you have Princess Vealla and Dante. The four of us are equals in terms of power. Lucifer is the one true king. No one dares to go to his realm without an invitation." Ezra paced around the room.

"What about this smaller castle and posts here?" I pointed to the top of the realm of death.

"That is where the demon warriors stay. They do not have a prince, but Blade is the group's leader. He is also one of Lucifer's most trusted." He circled the table, studying his map and rubbing his chin.

"Is Lucifer the devil?" My finger traced along the map of his realm. He had the biggest castle on the map, and I snorted a quiet laugh.

"Not in a biblical sense, if that is what you're asking. Lucifer is still an angel, but he is not the original. His soul gets passed to whoever kills him. The Lucifer we have now is the 27th." Ezra walked over to the wall on our left. He touched one of his messy notes with a grubby finger. "This Lucifer is too passive." He murmured, tapping his foot against the stone floor.

"Hell's not what I imagined. No souls are being tortured or lava monsters walking around."

An amused smile crossed Ezra's face, and I caught a glimpse of the guy he was before, but only for a split second. He leaned against the wall and resumed his brooding manner, becoming again a shell of that man I had met weeks ago. I sighed at the distant memory.

"No, the Goddess of souls deals with that. Hell is solely home to Lucifer and demons. I will show you our realm tomorrow. There are some things I need to do tonight." Ezra stepped back over to me and took my hand.

We returned to my room, giving me no ability to process. My head spun.

I needed to learn how to use and control my powers, and fast. The war room put a bad taste in my mouth. Ezra said I couldn't tell anyone, amplifying my fears. Kathy's warning came barreling into the forefront of my mind.

Ezra summoned Kyler and told him to guard me while he went to some meeting. Kyler gave him a bow. We said nothing while listening to Ezra's footsteps fade. Kyler immediately came to me once silence filled the hall. His warmth ignited me all over.

"How are you feeling?" he asked, running his hand through my hair.

I didn't know what would happen if we got caught, but I imagined it wouldn't be good. I took a deep breath and focused on my senses.

"I don't know," I admitted. "Kyler, he... he forced me to kill someone for a soul. Is that what I am? A murder?" I looked down at my open palms, shaking. "I'm so weak. All I do is cry now. What kind of life is this? What kind of monster am I?"

Kyler took my hands into his.

"No, no! You are brightness and Fire. *My* Fire. I can swear to you, from now on, I'll only bring you someone who deserves to die. I swear on my life. Please, don't let him ruin all that you are." Kyler's voice filled with such sorrow, and I couldn't tell if the pain in my chest was his or mine.

"You promise? I won't kill someone who doesn't deserve it. Demon or not." I shook my head. "I can't live with any more blood on my hands."

"I promise." Kyler nodded, but his face twisted into something else. Pain.

Did he hurt as much as me over the loss of life?

"Every breath I take feels suffocating." Tears slid down my cheeks again. Pain aching in every crevice of my soul. I looked at my hands, expecting to see blood.

Kyler held me against his chest. I couldn't stop the wails of anger and pain that escaped me.

"You should rest. It's been a long day." Kyler kissed my forehead when my tears subsided.

I nodded, but knew I couldn't rest.

"I'll be right outside this door if you need anything." Kyler put his hands on my hips and placed a kiss on my lips.

"Thank you, Kyler." My words were barely audible.

Kyler walked out of the bedroom, and I sighed.

I wanted him to stay, but knew he couldn't. I slid into the bed and wrapped myself up in the sheets. My tears came again with full force. The vision of the person in rags facing me and Ezra's harsh words took the breath from me. I curled my knees into my chest and wept.

No matter what happened next, I took a life.

I became the monster.

Chapter Nineteen

Sapphire

Vibrant reds glistened in the night sky. It didn't seem to matter if it was day or night; a sliver of color tinted it. I lifted the covers from me and slid out of bed, pausing a second to glance out the window.

The realities of my new life weighed heavily on me. The vision of the demon I killed continued to flash in my mind, no matter how badly I wanted it to stop.

Walking to the bedroom door, I attempted not to make a sound. Before pushing the doors open, I took another deep breath.

Kyler didn't stand outside as I had hoped.

I walked to the throne room, taking small steps, admiring the castle's surroundings. Every light was dimmed as I descended the stairs. Paintings lined the walls to the throne. Many depicted battles and warriors.

The room looked a fraction brighter, and I took the opportunity to peek outside. The warmth danced on my skin. To my surprise, Hell smelled like a campfire. The air didn't feel too thick or heavy.

After a few minutes of watching the sky, I went to the throne. With my legs crossed, I sat down. It felt right to sit there.

The power coursing through me overwhelmed my senses. It needed to be used. It caused this lasting feeling like I could kill at any moment.

And I hated it.

I *did* kill. I took a life. Ezra knew exactly how to trap me like an animal. My skin crawled at the idea of him going after Emily. His threat scared me because it had been true. Emily would have gone to him so easily. I shook my head, pushing the thought away.

A ripple of flames and a ring of lightning appeared before me. There they were, the Prince and *my knight*. Ezra's lips were pressed in a fine line. Kyler, however, eyed me up and down slowly with a giant smirk.

"Hmph, she just wanted to enjoy the throne alone," Kyler mused as he exaggerated his bow towards me. I rolled my eyes. Ezra came up to me and kneeled at my feet. Then, Kyler did his own eye roll.

"Sapphire, you cannot take off like that," Ezra said with an unshakable firmness.

"Am I trapped here and not allowed to wander the castle? Wander Hell?" My tone sharpened.

"You cannot control your powers. I told you not to take off anymore." He spits.

I sighed, and both of their eyes shot to mine.

I should try to keep Ezra at bay for now.

"It is late. You should go back to bed. When I show you our kingdom in the morning, I have a crown for you." Ezra stood up and reached for my hand. My lips tugged into a slight frown.

Where is my autonomy? Where is my power?

"*Highness*, I'm not tired. Kyler can protect me, I just..." My words fell from my mouth. It seemed futile to try and argue with him.

"I think she needs air, Highness. She is still adjusting." Kyler said, taking a knee at my feet.

"Very well. Kyler, you may not leave her side, especially now. It is obvious she is too rebellious to be left alone. I expect you to keep her very close. If she gets away, you will be reprimanded. Got it?" Ezras' menacing tone sent a chill through me.

"I would never dream of getting on your bad side, sire." Kyler said evenly as he rose. Ezra nodded, and his ring of lightning took him away.

Static lingered in the air. A stark reminder that even when he's gone, his presence, his dominance, was always there.

Kyler stared at me, his eyes on my crossed leg. His look filled with a softness that melted my heart as he took my hands.

"What would you like to do, my Princess?" His wide eyes stayed locked on mine, and my cheeks flushed.

"Can you. . . Can you help me figure out my powers?" I said as low as possible in case the walls had ears.

He studied my face for a moment and nodded. Standing up, he pulled me from the chair and against his chest as his fire consumed us both.

I took in my surroundings and pulled away from him.. Our hands stayed interlocked, and his grip tightened when I went to move. My gaze turned to him, his smile reflected on my face.

We stood on sand that formed a giant oval, outside. I couldn't tell which realm we were in. I walked to the left and ran a finger over the weapons racks. My eyes caught a glimpse of a handful of white tents in the back. There had been some blood on the ground. This was a training area of some sort. Bending down, I ran my hand over the pebbles. The feeling of sticky grain slid through my fingers. A scent of metal and rust lingered in the air.

"What is this place?" I asked, admiring the metalwork of the swords.

He gestured to the area around us. "This is where we send lower demons to train, or those who are to become our warriors but need more than the usual training."

Racks of axes and swords lined one side. Some looked scary, depending on their emblem. The last rack caught my attention. The bows, both recurve and long, lined it.

Picking up a beautiful red longbow, I grabbed an arrow and pulled the string back. Kyler watched and waved his hand, summoning a target across the field. Aiming my bow and relaxing my breath, an arrow flew across the field at the string release. It made a swoosh noise as it landed in the sand, and Kyler burst into laughter. I looked at him with a clenched jaw and grabbed another arrow.

The bow called to me. I had never been big on archery before, but this one pulsed in my hand. I drew the string back once more, arrow flying, and *smack*! Not a bullseye, but still something. I took more arrows out and continued to shoot them. The muscles in my arms began to ache, not used to so much work. As I placed the bow back in the rack, my fingers lingered.

"It's interesting that you picked that bow," Kyler said, grabbing a sword and handing it to me.

He stood in the middle of the arena and beckoned me with a single finger. Swinging the sword left and right, I sauntered over to him. Kyler put one foot in front of the other, sword at an angle above his head. The way he moved with such ease... I was in awe.

"Just follow my motions. For now, we just need you to get used to the weight. I don't expect you to go fight any wars tomorrow."

We began to spar, left, right, right, left. I followed his patterns, smacking the sword against his. Clashes echoed with fury. My muscles ached with a fire I never imagined before. Every movement tugged with pain, but I kept going. I'd never break free of Ezra if I couldn't take him on. Muscle aches would be the least of my problems.

"Why's it interesting that I picked the bow up?" I asked between breaths.

"That bow belonged to my mother. She was an avid archer, and it was one of the things she made sure I could do.

Of course, I prefer my double-edged sword these days, but it was fun to learn with her." He threw the sword up, spinning it before catching it..

Show off.

Our swords continued to clash as we danced around each other. Kyler managed to stay focused while my mind wandered. Flashes of the demon's soul coming to me gripped my mind, and the sword slid from my hand.

"Everything okay?" Kyler stuck his sword in the sand and tilted his head.

"N-no. I can't get the visions of that demon out of my mind." I looked down at my feet.

"I won't lie and say those visions go away. My own demons still haunt me, but... it gets easier." He whispered.

I looked up at him, but his eyes were distant. He ran a hand over his neck, then turned his eyes back to me.

"Do you want to stop?"

"No. I need to train, I just needed a second."

Kyler nodded, and we picked up our swords. Again, I matched his movements, and the clanking continued on.

"Is there a training ring in every realm?" I thought back to Ezra's map.

"There is this one and the one in the Realm of the Damned. Lucifer has a battle arena, but it's not used for training." Kyler swung his sword at me, but I noticed the color drain from his face.

"I don't like the sound of that," I admitted.

"You handle the sword pretty well for a fake mortal," Kyler teased me, changing the subject.

"Tell that to my aching muscles." I said, my lips curling in a smirk.

Kyler shook his head and laughed, "Once you're used to this, it won't hurt. You need to build up your demon strength."

"Am I the only soul eater?" I asked.

We were panting as I put the sword tip in the sand, fingers wrapped around the hilt.

"You're the only purebloodied soul eater. Once created, soul eaters cannot have children. It's why their species of demon went extinct a century ago." He reached for the sword as I unwrapped my fingers.

"How can I be a pureblood, then? I have baby pictures; I had to be born this way. Mom said I was a demon. Maybe I should read more of her journal?" Kyler followed me to the middle of the arena. I peered down at my hands.

Suddenly, blood poured from my hand and dripped into the sand. Then just as quickly as the sight appeared, it was gone.

I'm a demon. I'm a killer.

"Honestly, Fire, I don't know. The names your mother referred to are the second Lucifer and his wife. If those are your parents, I don't know how you exist," He studied my face.

My birth parents?

"Wouldn't that also make me a Lucifer already?" I raised a brow.

"No, the soul stays with whoever killed the predecessor."

"I hate not knowing who I really am. I hate that I need to kill people to live, that every fucking time I close my eyes I see blood. I hate not knowing who I really am...hate that my mom kept this from me. I'm sure she had her reasons but damn it!" Anger rushed through me, and a lightning bolt shot from my hand, blasting the sand into fulgurites.

"Fire," Kyler placed a hand on my shoulder, "I told you before, and I'll tell you until I am blue in the face. We will figure this out. Let's start with your powers here. It's something we *can* do. I'll even let you kick my ass, but don't tell anyone." Kyler smirked, and I laughed.

"Okay, you're right. When I phase, can you tell me what it looks like? I can't exactly see myself."

"Yeah, let's see what you've got." He gestured for me to go ahead.

I phased out and back in. His mouth gaped open, eyes the size of saucers. He pressed his fingers to his lips and then, seemingly happy with what he saw, gave a sly half-smile.

"Fire, you phase surrounded by black butterflies. That was the coolest thing I've ever seen. Which is saying a lot, considering I have been alive for over 350 years. How have you not noticed that?" Kyler's voice rose an octave.

I put my arm in front of me and went to phase again. I watched as black butterflies lifted from my skin and swarmed around me.

Woah.

"I've been so caught up in my head, I didn't notice." I sighed.

"I'd like you to be caught up on my head." Kyler wiggled his eyebrows, but I waved him off.

"So hopeless."

Deciding to work on my power, I summoned another lightning bolt. Static tingled in my arm as I shot at the target. A thunderous sound clapped as the hay turned to ashes.

Oops!

Kyler pushed his tongue to his cheek, clearly stifling a laugh. He summoned a new target.

I looked down at my hands. A warmth filled my hand, and a ball of fire hovered around it. I shot the flames at the target and watched the smoke rise. Clapping my hands as if cleaning them off, I smiled at Kyler.

"I'm like the fucking *Avatar*!"

Kyler raised an eyebrow. "The what now?" He laughed.

"It's a TV show? Don't you watch TV? You don't know *Avatar*? Ugh, never mind! Did you see how cool that was? I'm so badass!"

Kyler swept me into his arms and kissed me.

"You are very badass, my Princess." Kyler gave me a simper.

"Princess feels wrong. I don't even know much about this world. How do witches move around? Plus, the werewolves can't phase." My mind drifted back to the world I lived in.

"There are portals all around Hell they can use. The ones in Lucifer's realm have guards, but everywhere else, everyone travels freely." Kyler waved a hand, and the targets disappeared.

"That's so cool. I can't wait to see more. To meet witches! God, if only I could share this with my friends." I leaned on my tiptoes and then backed down. A mix of giddy and sad festered. "Can they do everything demons do?"

"Not exactly. Witches, werewolves, and shapeshifters are considered lesser demons. They can summon things, but not phase or use elemental powers. It's how the creator wanted things to be."

"Creator? Another god?"

"Yes. I will explain The Eight to you someday. We should get back now, though. The sun will be up soon, and Ezra will be suspicious if we aren't there." He kissed the top of my forehead.

"Wait, can anyone phase into the throne room?" I raised an eyebrow at him.

"What are you asking for?" Kyler tilted his head at me.

"I'm just curious."

His eyes raised at me. "Only vampires, Lucifer, Ezra, and I can phase in. The wards don't block you because my essence tricks them. Anything else on your mind before we go back?" Kyler gave a quick laugh.

"When will the flashbacks stop?"

He stares at me, his lip curving in the corner.

"They never do, Fire. They never do."

Chapter Twenty

Sapphire

Kyler sat on the steps below the throne, his head tilted back, enjoying the warmth of the air. I leaned on the door to the outside, watching the colors in the sky change.

The sun had risen over the horizon by the time we returned. We didn't say much after arriving home. Many things continued flowing through my mind.

I could not shake the images of the demon collapsing after I took their soul. Nor the images of my friends and their laughter. Happy memories danced in my mind as much as the negative ones.

Taking a deep breath, I closed my eyes and imagined my life if I had never gone into the bar. What would I have done?

"Are you ready to see the kingdom I rule over?" Ezra asked me, placing a hand on my shoulder. I turned toward him with a sad smile.

"I am, Highness."

"Kyler, I think it is best if you keep your armor on in case someone wants to cause trouble," Ezra said in a cool tone, but I wondered who would cause trouble.

Aside from Ezra.

"Ready?" He reached for my hand.

As we headed towards the doors, Kyler fell in line behind us.

How lucky for him, he gets to stare at my ass all day.

I hid my smile at the thought.

The warm air of Hell hit my face. The feeling lingered like a much-needed hug. We traveled down gray brick steps toward a giant metal gate. A sentry stood on either side of it and bowed to us before opening it.

My eyes could not believe what they were seeing as we made our way through—sprawled out before us was an entire village. On either side were brick buildings, some shops with glass windows showcasing things like clothes or weapons, and others were eateries. The red and brown brick path we walked led us through the bustling town.

Emotions from vampires passing by would hit me and disappear as fast as they came. Nausea racked inside me. Absorbing a soul made the impact lessen but it was still there. I stopped walking for a minute and grabbed onto Kyler's arm, trying to get a hang of the emotions coursing through my veins.

"Everything okay?" Ezra deadpanned.

"Yeah, yeah. I haven't been able to get a grip on my empathic ability. Demon emotions are so loud," I pant and grip at my chest.

"Go on, Highness. I will bring her to you in a second." Kyler pleaded.

Ezra let out a huff and continued on. I watched as he made his way into the village, and demons bowed to him.

"Fire?"

"It's okay, really. I'm still adjusting." I let go of the arm I was holding and gave him a nod.

"Lead the way when you're ready, then, beautiful."

We began to walk toward the village's center. A big open area with a black marble fountain stopped me in my tracks. Three tiers of onyx ovals flowing with water and black rose heads floating in the water made it look like something out of a fairytale.

To my left, a few male demons came up to Ezra and bowed, then began conversing with him, laughing like old friends. With him distracted, I walked over to a small bakery and got a cinnamon bun. The demon at the counter refused to accept anything for payment. I continued to wander the village until I came across a small playground. Little demon children ran around, and their laughter echoed in my ears. A smile lit my face.

Even if I'd never have kids, the innocence of the demon children opened up a small happiness in my heart. Kyler came up beside me.

"You look wonderfully happy, Highness." Kyler's eyes met mine. The way he said it made my toes curl.

My excited nod answered him back.

"Oh, Kyler, this is nothing like I've ever seen before! It's magical, and it's going to be mine!" Grinning ear to ear, observing more of the playground, Kyler let out a soft chuckle.

"You're the most magical thing," Kyler whispered in my ear. His hand grazed mine, and that heat within me roared to life.

"Do all the realms have villages like this?" I motioned my hand outward to the children playing before us.

"Yes. Most kingdoms have a village just outside the castle where most of that faction stays. The only faction not in Hell are the shapeshifters. They prefer the mortal world," Kyler said as he straightened.

My gaze turned to a quaint jewelry shop nearby. Ezra seemed busy with his demons, so I wandered over. A bell rang as I walked in, Kyler in tow behind me. I walked around the glass display cases. He stood by the check-out display. Leaning on it, his eyes watched me. I stopped to look at the necklaces with sapphire stones in them.

"Kyler! What brings you into my shop, man! I'm glad to see you." A voice spoke.

I lifted my eyes for a moment to see a guy with yellow eyes and darker hair. I wondered what kind of demon he was. Kyler nodded his chin at me.

"I'm her sworn protector." He said, his eyes following my every move.

Protector indeed.

"You and I need to get together again soon, brother. Syl has a new cake recipe she wants to try, and you're the perfect victim." He patted Kyler on the shoulder with a laugh.

"Next time *this one* lets me free, I'll let you know, Zariah," Chuckles filled the store.

This must have been the werewolf he mentioned.

Looking out the window, I spotted Ezra staring at me from outside. He tapped his foot on the ground. I grabbed Kyler by the arm, pulling him with me.

"Guess that's my cue, man. See you later." Kyler waved at his friend, and they shared a laugh.

"You enjoy making me wait?" Ezra asked as he wrapped my hand over his arm.

"Mostly keeping busy while you talked to those vampires." My eyes drifted back to the beautiful fountain in front of us. "Where are we going now?"

"If you take the path to the left, it leads you to where the people of this village live. If you go right, that leads to a grassy park where the children can play," Ezra said as he placed a hand on the small of my back and pointed in either direction. "We are going forward, though, so I can show you more of the kingdom. Most places we have to phase to anyway." He led us onward as Kyler fell back in line.

"How's this in Hell?"

Ezra laughed. I huffed in response.

I swear if he laughs at me one more time, I will take his god-forsaken soul.

"Come, Sapphire, let me show you the rest of *my* realm."

He said it like I would never be a part of this world. Like I'd always be under his feet. It wouldn't stay that way.

Of that, I was sure.

Ezra wrapped an arm around mine. Every time he touched me, my skin crawled. His true colors made me hate his very existence. All I could do was hold a sword and shoot arrows in a general direction. One day, I'll be able to do something about him.

Once I could, there would be a dungeon with his name on it somewhere- and I'd have the only key.

Chapter Twenty-One

Sapphire

"You bury your dead?" I asked Kyler as we passed a massive cemetery.

Ezra continued walking. The headstones all stood in neat rows, with benches in random spots. Trees sat sparingly around the graves. A short stone wall outlined the cemetery's perimeter.

He nodded. "Yes, my mother is buried here." Kyler came closer to me, standing close to my side, our shoulders brushed. He pointed to the back corner, where a tall stone shaped like a column stood. "There." The word glided against my ear in one breath.

"Do you visit her often?"

Kyler's hand landed near my hip on the stone wall. His breath was warm against my ear.

"I try to." His voice dripped in sorrow.

"I'd like to know more about her one day." I turned and smiled up at him.

"You will," He nodded. "She was the only good thing in my life until recently."

"What happened recently?" I tilted my head.

"You showed up at the bar."

My cheeks burned, and I covered my face. Kyler winked and extended his arm, pointing to his brother.

"We should go before the Prince gets his panties wadded."

Ezra glared at me once we caught up to him. His eyes darted between Kyler and me before going back on his tirade.

"The true alpha owns this castle. I will introduce you one day. He is away on business in the Realm of the Damned." Ezra said low in my ear, "The next place I want to show you we have to phase to, but then you will have seen everything important." He wrapped his arms around me, and in a flash of lightning, we were in a new spot.

The training grounds Kyler took me to last night surrounded us. Only now, demons trained. Some were sword fighting, others used fists. I watched them for a moment as their leaders barked orders. My eyes went over to the bow. Its call to me was almost as strong as Kyler's.

I said nothing as my steps took me through the sparing demons. The fighting and training stopped as eyes followed me. Everyone was silent, even Ezra.

With the bow now in hand, pulling an arrow back, the edges were rough against my finger. A deep breath escaped my parted lips as I aimed for the target across the field. Letting the arrow go, it hit the bullseye, and the silence became roars and cheers. My pride took over as I held my chin high. I put the bow back down and turned to watch the fighting again as the demons returned to training.

"How did you do that?" Ezra's eyes met mine.

"I don't know. It comes naturally." I shrugged.

"That was impressive, Highness." Orpheus strode over to us. His armor showcased his defined muscles.

"Thank you, Orpheus. I prefer a sword, though." I gave him a small smile.

"Come train with me sometime, I'd love to see you in action." He bowed. "Sire."

"That will not be necessary, Orpheus. Let us get you fed, Sapphire." Ezra wrapped me in his arms, and lightning took us to the castle.

My shoulders drooped at my sides. Why did he pull me away any time someone acknowledged my existence?

"Kyler and I will be right back. There are two guards outside the door." Ezra said.

I sat down on the bed and pulled out my phone, looking at the lock screen. Pain seeped into my heart. I missed my friends so much.

This was my life now: fairy tale towns and thrones, with a jackass I couldn't escape.

When the guys returned, Kyler held a person wiggling. Their hands were behind their back, and a hood draped over their head. The shirt had stains and holes; it wreaked of cigarette smoke.

"Who?" I asked.

"A wife beater," Kyler said, shrugging.

I nodded and stepped closer. He promised only to give me people who deserved death. I bit my lip, flashing back to the first soul, the first life I took.

Pain shot through my stomach. I had no choice, and I knew it. This would be the only way to gain strength and become who I needed to be.

My arm extended towards the person, and my glow reached out. The soul came towards me in smoky blue swirls. The same as before, my power roared inside of me. Aching to be used. My breath caught in my lungs, heart beating at a slower pace. Taking the life of someone deserving sent a small thrill through me.

I enjoyed taking this soul.

Ezra's hands grabbed both sides of my hips. "Kyler, leave us."

Kyler looked toward me, concern etched across his features. I nodded to let him know it's okay. He bowed and phased away.

"You are the most beautiful creature I have ever had the honor of laying my eyes on."

Calling me a creature made my stomach turn.

I gave him the loveliest fake smile I could. His sudden turn in affection felt off-putting. My gut twisted with suspicion as he ran a hand over my arm. I took a step back, and his grip on my hip tightened.

A knock on the door turned Ezra's attention. He let out a low growl before going to the door. A ripple of relief came over me. Orpheus stood in the doorway. Ezra looked at me before stepping out of the room and shutting the door behind him. I flicked at my thumbs, waiting.

"Lucifer is summoning me. I have to go. Do not leave this castle, do you hear me? Orpheus went to get Kyler. I do not want to hear you disobeyed me again." Ezra stepped closer and gripped my wrist.

"Yes, Highness." I hung my head.

"Good." Ezra kissed my forehead with force and phased away.

Ezra would not have to worry about me leaving. I was too tired. The gears in my head continued to turn as my head hit the pillow.

The bedroom door creaked open, and footsteps made their way to me. I did not need to open my eyes to know it was Kyler. His pull tugged at me before he entered the room. He sat beside me on the bed and ran his fingers through my hair.

"I'll be right outside if you need me." He whispered into my ear.

The bed shifted as Kyler stood. I wanted to reach out to him, to tell him everything I was feeling, but words wouldn't escape.

Twice now, I'd killed.

But the second time, I enjoyed it.

And that scared me more than anything.

Chapter Twenty-Two
Kyler

Sapphire probably didn't realize I could tell she was pacing. Vampire hearing comes in handy during times like these, but she needed to process. I fought the urge to go into the room. I could recognize the look on her face anywhere. The look you make when you hold life and death in your hands. When you make a decision you regret forever. My own memories flickered briefly before footsteps turned my attention.

"Ezra is looking for you." Orpheus said, coming up the hallway.

"When's he not?" I groaned and pushed off the wall beside Fire's room. "Can you stay here? I hate leaving her alone."

"Yea, brother. I've got her."

"I owe you one." I nodded my head to him.

"You owe me nothing. She needs protecting. Go deal with your brother." Orpheus sat down by her door and summoned a book to read.

Begrudgingly, I phased to my brother. He sat at the bar counter talking to Kathy. As always, he didn't bother glancing in my direction. Instead, he was too busy making flirty eyes at the bartender. I wanted to punch his smug face.

"Ah, there you are. I am sure all that standing around doing... nothing has you bored. I have an assignment for you. With Sapphire still being defiant, I need more guards around the castle and realm. Everyone will do doubles from now on. I expect you to dole this out, Kyler." Ezra took a swig of blood and wiped his mouth with his sleeve.

Hard to believe this fucker was a prince.

"Of course, sire. As always, my devotion is only to you." I bowed and backed away into my flames.

He's lucky I didn't flip him off.

In the barracks, my men sat around the tables talking. A few slept in the spare beds to the right.

I ran a hand through my hair and groaned. They would hate Ezra for what I was about to demand of them. I knew they were loyal to me, but asking them for more when they already gave all made me feel like such an asshole.

"Amdis, can you gather everyone for me?" I asked my underling. He gave a quick nod and disappeared into the darkness.

I sat down on the top of the bench table and stretched my legs. One by one, the soldiers began to appear. The commotion within the walls amplified.

I stood and cleared my throat. Everyone fell into a stillness only vampire demons could manage.

"As you all know, our prince has decided the lost princess is his new toy. Due to this fact, he asks that we all do doubles." Groans and frustrated sighs bounced against the walls.

"I know what I am asking of you all is, well, ridiculous. However, I promise that once this is over, everyone will get extra time away from duties. You have my blood promise."

I lifted my hand and slit my palm open with my dagger. Drops of blood dripped onto the ground as I held it up.

"Blood for blood." I said to the room.

"Blood for blood." Echoed back.

The bonds were set, and I could at least get Ezra off my back over that. I sat back down and covered my face with my clean hand.

How much longer till my rage became deadly? Ezra's lunacy had escalated tenfold since Fire came to Hell. The invisible chains around my neck got tighter by the day. My anger only rose higher.

"You good, fang leader?" Amdis asked. "You've been under a ton of pressure lately. We all feel it, sir."

I rolled my eyes at the formal title. Fang leader is such a mockery of what we really were.

Of what I am.

"I am okay, Amdis. Heavy is the head that wears the crown, and his head is fucking massive." I stood up with a grunt.

"Let me know if I can help, sir."

I placed a hand on his shoulder, "Thanks, Amdis. I appreciate you," We exchanged a nod before I phased away.

"Back so soon? I trust that means it is done?" Ezra leaned over the bar counter with a mug in hand.

Kathy moved around the bar taking orders, and I grunted. Even the barmaid knows he's a piece of shit.

"Yes, Highness." I muttered.

"Good. Now I have one more thing for you to do. I know it is late, but this is of the utmost importance."

I'm sure it is, jackass.

"I am at your command, sire." I gave a short bow.

"As you should be. I need you to go to the Realm of Death. Lucifer has something for me. You will get it and bring it to my office. Show no one. Do I make myself clear?"

Me. Me. Me. Me.

That's all I heard every time he opened his mouth.

"Yes, sire."

I phased away before I had a chance to hear another ignorant comment.

It amazed me that we were even brothers. Long ago, before Dad really turned into a dick, Ezra and I got along great. That all changed when the pressure of the perfect prince hung over his head, but now? Now, he's a dick, just to be a dick.

Lucifer sat with one leg over his knee and a lollipop in his mouth when I arrived. The marble throne room, stained in blood, sat empty except for us. His eyes followed me until I came to the bottom of the dais and bowed. I didn't dare look up at him, not until he spoke. My palms were sweaty at my sides.

"Ah, Ezra's dog has come to fetch a bone." His thick British accent rang in my ears as I stood.

"My liege, I am here at Ezra's request."

"Yes, yes. Your prince is a handful these days. Such a thorn in my side." Lucifer stepped down until he stood in front of me. Static filled the space.

"You know, dear Kyler, sometimes dreams come true, and other times..." he pulled the lollipop from his mouth and twirled it in his hand, "other times, people find themselves in a grave they dug."

I swallowed and nodded. His presence filled the room as he walked around.

Ezra sent me to remind me how little I matter. I was sure of that.

"My liege." I said, opening and closing my fists.

"Come, walk with me. Tell me about this lost princess."

I followed Lucifer down a long corridor to his office. He took a seat behind the desk, and his red eyes fixated on me. He pointed at the chair for me to sit. It took all the muscle control I had not to laugh.

The devil asked me to come to his office.

"What would you like to know, my liege?" I sat.

"Is it her?" He asked outright.

I froze. My hands trembled.

He'd find out the truth one way or another. *Never lie to Lucifer*. That was Pop's number one rule. *Fuck*.

"Yes." I hated myself for answering. I balled my fists in my lap.

"Interesting. It would seem the Gods' plans are unfolding before our eyes."

He snapped his fingers, and a worn old book slammed onto the table. Lucifer brushed the dust away.

"Bring this to your prince." He lifted it, handing it over.

"Thank you, my liege." I stood and tried to take the book from him, but he held it tightly.

"Kyler, things will be changing soon. I suggest you prepare for the coming storm." He released his grip on the book, and a lump formed in my throat.

"M-my liege." I took the book as quickly as possible and bowed.

"You may go. Tell Ezra to leave me be a while." He waved his hand dismissively, and I phased away.

Ezra was nowhere to be seen when I entered his office.

Glorified coffee bringer slash Fang leader. I grunted at the thought.

I placed the book down and stared at the title. *Kings and Queens of Hell: A History.*

What could my brother have possibly needed the book for? I shook my head and bolted back to Fire's room.

"Holy shit, Kyler. You look like you saw a ghost." Orpheus said. He stood from his place on the floor and cocked a brow.

"Just a long day, man. You can go. Thanks for staying here."

"She stopped pacing an hour ago, from the sounds of the snores. I think it's safe to say she's finally asleep." He patted me on the shoulder and walked off.

I sat down on the floor and lay my head against the wall.

A storm was coming. How did I prepare for something I didn't understand?

I want off this ride.

Chapter Twenty-Three

Sapphire

As I tiptoed from the room, I saw Kyler sitting on the floor, head lolled to the side against the wall, sleeping.. I placed a small kiss on his forehead before phasing back to the mortal world.

I wanted to see my friends… to know they were okay. Sorrow filled my head. Would they even want to see me as this… this *thing*?

It didn't matter. My heart ached beyond repair.

When I phased, no lights were on in Emily's small brick townhome. Her car wasn't in the driveway, either. I stood outside Isabelle's house next. Her small two-story colonial, painted yellow, always felt too bright for her. My chest hurt thinking back on our memories.

The day we helped paint the inside of her house, she specifically asked for no light colors. '*I hate how bright the outside is*' she had huffed. Emily always teased her, saying she smiled on the outside but hated everyone on the inside.

I placed a fist over my chest, as if it would stop tears from flowing.

Standing in the yard, I spotted them from the window in the living room. They were sitting on the couch and laughing.

This was one risk my heart would ignore.

Suddenly, a hand landed on my shoulder.

Kyler's eyes met mine when I turned. The pain deep within me felt damn near impossible. He ran a hand up and down my back.

"I won't stop you from going to that door, but our world is dangerous, and people who want to hurt you could go after them. Ezra has threatened as much." His soft voice nestled in my hair.

"I want to say goodbye. Kyler. I can't live without them knowing I'm okay." Tears pooled..

"I know, I know. It's not safe to, not yet. It's a risk even being here now." He touched my face with his palm, and I leaned into it.

He was right, of course. I knew that, especially after Ezra, but I wanted to see them. Kyler and I walked away from the house for a moment of clarity when the door to Isabelle's house creaked open. Emily's face peered out from the door. Pulling Kyler by the arm, we ducked behind an SUV.

After she went back inside, Kyler took my hand. I didn't have anything to say. His soft eyes met mine, and I tried to muster a smile.

The beautiful night sky illuminated the ground. The chill of winter air danced on my skin, yet I didn't feel cold.

"Kyler, I need some time alone." I sighed. "Can you tell Ezra I'm sleeping or something? I don't want him to hurt me again." I rubbed my hand, thinking back to his grip.

"He hurt you?" Kyler growled and whipped his head toward me.

"It's not important. He was just being protective. Please?"

His eyes narrowed.

"I will always protect you. I'm your knight, but I swear to god, if he hurts you again, I will rip his head from his fucking body." He curved his lips in the corner, revealing a fang.

I blinked at Kyler. He went into protective mode over me? It made me feel a little better, but I needed to breathe, to escape everything.

"I'll see you soon." I whispered.

Black butterflies surrounded me as I phased away to the arena.

Grabbing the red bow and some arrows, I aimed for the targets surrounding the area. The rough string slipped past my fingers as arrows flew, one after the other, until my skin turned red.

With every arrow, the pain subsided, and determination replaced it. My only goal could be to hone my skills. To escape Ezra. To get away.

I put the bow down and looked at my hands. Mustering what energy I could, I tried to summon a fireball. The warmth didn't come naturally to me. The static didn't flow on cue. A guttural scream left my throat.

How could I ever escape Hell if I couldn't use my own God's forsaken powers? Why did it work some times and not others?

I felt a rage I had never experienced before; it was like a wildfire. I was forced to leave my life behind. Forced to give up my childhood home. To leave my friends behind. To kill. Forced to be a monster I no longer recognized.

The job at the bar had been a mistake. Bellowing into the sky, a ring of fire circled me. I didn't mean to summon it, not at that moment. Falling to my knees, my hand glided through the fire. It didn't hurt or burn. Instead, warmth danced on my skin.

Even after learning I was never human, it felt real. All the memories growing up, all the birthdays and holidays, they were etched into my brain.

They *were* real.

Not anymore.

My mortality had died in that bar.

I waved my hand, and the flames went away.

Closing my eyes, I focused on the sand below my legs and the warm air of Hell in my face. When I opened my eyes, the sun was rising—Hell's version of sunrise, anyway. The colors in the sky only mildly darkened or brightened, depending on the time of day. No sun physically sat in the sky.

Every year, my mother, father and I would take a road trip. The beach was Dad's favorite spot. Mom used to hate the sand, but she would always say I was a fish out of water. I could swim for hours and not get tired. I knew now that it had to be because of my demon. Sure, my muscles ached, but I never felt fatigued unless I used a lot of my elemental powers.

I'd have to return to the castle soon. It would only be a matter of time before Ezra came looking for me.

Kyler would cover for me. *My protector.*

I stood up and swept the sand from my legs. Beautiful butterflies whisked me away.

No one was in the throne room when I arrived. I wandered to look for them. I found an open door down the hall and poked my head in. Ezra sat at a desk, and Kyler looked over his shoulder.

"The witches' territory should be left alone if the treaty goes through," Kyler said, pointing to the paper on the desk.

"Whose the prince here, *me* or *you*?" Ezra snapped.

I peered over at his desk. A giant red book sat in the corner, covered in dust. I couldn't read the title. Ezra didn't have any clutter near it, like it was the most important thing in the realm.

I leaned against the wooden door frame and waited for them to notice me.

They glanced up. Kyler's eyes looked like he was asking if I was okay. Ezra waved his hand, and everything disappeared from the desk as he stood. I waved my fingers at them.

"Don't stop on my account." I shrugged myself off the wall.

"I am glad you listened to me," Ezra said as he approached me.

"I did." Anger came from my voice that startled even me. Ezra didn't react. Kyler eyed me, "I know you're keeping secrets about what I am and what you want from me."

Ezra's eyes widened as the weight of what I said hit him. I watched as his eyes shifted around; he wouldn't look directly at me.

"You are right. I have been lying to protect you. If anyone knew what you were, they would try to take you from me." Ezra placed a hand on the side of my neck, and I recoiled.

An accurate statement to a fault. He knew that, too, because under the surface of his calm tone, deceit radiated from him. He wanted to keep me to himself for whatever selfish reason.

"Fine," is all I said before returning to the throne room.

This was getting old. He lied to me and tried to use whatever false affections he had to keep me under his wing. I'd wait for the right moment, and he'd feel my wrath. If I were so strong that he wanted me as a weapon, to keep me to himself, then he'd learn the hard way what I could do.

Kyler came into view, his sword glistening against the light drew my attention.

"Are you alright?" He asked as he approached the dias.

Before I could answer, lightning swirled beside him, and Ezra appeared. His presence felt heavy.

Why couldn't he walk around like a normal demon?

"Kyler, leave us." Ezra said without looking toward his brother. Kyler bowed and left the room.

"You will learn your place. Do not disrespect me in front of anyone like that again." Ezra's palm came down hard on my cheek.

He glared at me with such intensity that my hands shook.

I nodded. The shock of the slap took away any word I would have spoken.

I needed to train more with Kyler. I had to get strong enough to fight back. Perhaps he would back down if he knew I had control over my powers.

Once Ezra was asleep, I'd find my knight and have him help me train again.

I refused to continue being a punching bag.

Chapter Twenty-Four

Sapphire

The following day, on my way to the throne room, I saw an open door in the hallway.

Peeking my head in, Kyler had his head in a book. He sat slumped in his chair, head resting on his fist as he read. I never took him for the reading type. A smile crossed my face as I watched him. The knowledge that this gorgeous man also liked to read caused flutters in my heart.

That pull from him called to me, and I shook my head, ignoring it. With light steps, I backed away. As much as I wanted to bother him, there would be no point. He'd be next to me soon for the meeting.

Ezra's throne remained empty as I sat in mine. Crossing my legs, I tapped on the arm with my fingers.

As soon as Kyler walked into the throne room, our eyes met. He gave me a bow before taking his place beside my throne.

Where he belonged.

"You seem happy," Kyler bent down and whispered.

"I'm starting to figure things out," I smiled as Ezra's lightning appeared before us. Kyler straightened immediately.

"Sapphire!" Ezra kissed my lips in his usual harshness before he took his seat beside me. "Are you ready?" He turned his head to me, and I gave him a quick nod.

His legion of vampires formed in front of us. I didn't know why Ezra had called a meeting. He didn't tell me anything about what happened in my own *supposed* kingdom.

I rocked my leg as he talked about a treaty with the witches. Something about not killing them for sport.

Orpheus appeared and bowed before us.

"May I approach, sire?" he asked.

Ezra gave a curt nod, and Orpheus approached, handing him a folded piece of paper.

Groaning at the letter now in his hand, Ezra cracked his knuckles. I turned to face him. He lit the letter on fire and whispered something to Orpheus, who then bowed and phased away.

As he stood up, Ezra announced the meeting was over and sent all the other vampires away. His face appeared bleak when he turned to me.

"Looks like you get to meet the true alpha after all. He reported problems in the mortal world."

A genuine smile crept across my lips.

I am going to meet a werewolf! Something exciting is happening, after all!

"Are you ready?"

"You have no idea!"

"You better not embarrass me." Ezra whispered low in my ear before he rose from the throne and extended his hand to me.

We made the familiar walk to the castle on the far side of the realm. As we passed the cemetery, I sighed. I didn't go visit my mother's grave nearly as often as I wanted to, and it became increasingly hard to leave Hell.

Once we reached the alpha's castle, his two guards bowed to Ezra before opening the large metal gate. We walked through, and I noticed the small village just beyond it. Just a scattering of small buildings huddled together.

A curvy woman gave a polite nod at the door to the castle. Her bright, emerald dress swayed behind her as she led us through the halls. The wooden walls showcased pictures of many wolves and a few assortments of swords.

The room we entered had bookshelves covering the walls and a couch in the center.

A tall man in a black shirt and jeans paced back and forth, reading something. He combed his hair to one side, and the muscles bulging from his shirt were twice the size of my arms. I walked into the room, standing in his path. He bumped into me as he paced.

"Sapphire, I take it?" He closed the book hard in his hand and raised a brow.

"Indeed, I am, and you are?" I mimicked his brow rise.

"Of course, you didn't even tell her my name." He gave Ezra a dirty stare. "Princess Sapphire, Alfonso, true alpha, at your service."

"She does not even have proper mannerisms in meeting a prince. I was hoping to wait to introduce her. What can we do for you, Alf?" Ezra chimed in.

"Let me get to know this lost princess before we get to business." Alfonso lifted my hand to his lips, pressing a gentle kiss on my skin. His touch lingered before he released it.

"I've never met a werewolf before, except in passing. You're much more handsome than I expected." I admitted, batting my eyelashes.

"You'll find lots of unexpected things about me, My Princess." Alfonso's lips curled into a wicked grin. A slight growl came from the doorway as my eyes met Kyler's.

"Like what?" I ask lightly.

"She is not a crowned Princess." Ezra gritted his teeth, interrupting us. He was so worried I'd embarrass him, yet here he is, reminding an alpha that I am not his princess.

He was so very wrong, though. I might not have been crowned, but I was a princess in my own right.

"Come, let's go to my office. Did you need to bring the attack dog?" Alfonso eyed Kyler as he walked past him.

"Please don't insult my knight." I pressed my lips into a firm line.

"Ah, the Princess's noble protector." Was all Alfonso responded as we made our way through his castle.

We followed him down a long brick corridor.

He was the second person to call Kyler a dog. I would have to ask him about that later.

We came to a room with a long desk and a couple of chairs on the side of the wall. I sat on a chair next to Ezra. Kyler stood by the door, not making a sound. I frowned at the sight of him in the background.

He mattered more than a watchdog, at least to me.

A slight tug came from his pull, and we eyed each other.

"Some of your vampires have been attacking my wolves, Ezra. It's becoming a problem." Alfonso gritted his teeth as he took a seat behind the desk.

"I will get them in line. That is not a problem," Ezra said waved Alfonso off. Alfonso shot him a glare as he folded his arms.

"I assure you, Alfonso, I'll personally see to it that it stops." As I smiled at the wolf, Ezra glared at me. I still had more to say that would annoy him. "Is there any way we could make it up to you?" I put my hands in a fist against my chest. Alfonso's eyes lit up.

"I like this one, Ezra. I appreciate your kindness, dear, but there is nothing to be done except getting the vampires to fuck off." He let out a roar of laughter, and I joined him.

"You heard him, Ezra. *Fuck off.*" A sly grin crossed my face.

Alfonso covered his mouth, trying not to laugh more. Kyler let out a quick guttural sound behind us.

"Now, Sapphire, that was uncalled for." Ezras' hand gripped my thigh firmly, voice cooing.

They began talking about ways to keep the vampires in line.

My eyes met Kyler's again. I wished I could speak to him mind to mind.Sometimes, it felt like I knew what he was thinking, and others, I had no idea.

Alfonso shot me a coy grin. They must have been talking about me.

I paid them no mind. My attention drifted to the souls I took as hunger twisted in my gut. Biting my lip, I tried to ignore it. Maybe a cheeseburger could still satisfy my appetite.

"Ezra, I need some air," I cut in. He just nodded and waved his hand.

Jerk.

I walked out of the office, and Kyler followed. I sagged against the castle wall outside and took in a deep breath. Kyler eyed me as my head tilted up at the sky. Many oranges were flowing above us like waves. It reminded me of home, not the color of the sky, but the warmth and the breeze.

"What do werewolves look like? Is it like the movies? Why are they in Hell? *How* are they in Hell? Do they change during a new moon? Well, that wouldn't make sense. There's no moon here." My voice trailed off as Kyler laughed.

His shoulders relaxed, and he leaned on the wall beside me.

"Werewolves that are Hell-born can transform whenever they'd like. The ones created in the mortal realm adhere to the moon's schedule; if they shift any more than that, it can kill them. Mortal bodies are very weak. As for how they look, it's like a bipedal wolf standing on two legs. There are doors, portals, to hell all over the world. My personal favorite is in Dubai."

"So, if a demon is a mortal first, not born here in Hell, is it a weaker version? Does that go for every Hell creature?" I asked.

He propped one foot against the wall.

"Yes," He raised his eyes, "Hell demons can give birth, with the exception of soul eaters and Knights of Death. Two mortal-made demons can not have a child."

"How come Hell born ones can have babies? Seems unfair, if you ask me." I pouted.

"Mortal bodies are too weak to contain the power of a full blooded demon." Kyler shrugged.

"Are all werewolves like Alfonso? He's very...*interesting*." I said with a half smile.

"You want a wolf more than me?" A smirk crossed his face.

Shaking my head, the red guitar keychain he once gave me appeared in my hand from my summon, "Never."

"You're something special, Fire," Kyler's eyes lit up.

"Why do people keep calling you Ezra's dog?"

Kyler paused and shook his head. A flurry of emotions crossed his face before he spoke.

"Ezra makes me do his dirty work. Any mundane task, any stupid errand. I'm also the one who deals with the prisoners or vampires who cause trouble." Kyler shrugged, but his voice was low, shoulders tensed.

"What do you mean?"

Kyler let out a sigh.

"I have to punish whoever Ezra deems necessary; there is a lot of blood on my hands, Fire." His voice cracked, and his posture crumbled before me.

"That doesn't matter to me. You're more than a dog. You're my protector, and with you by my side, being near Ezra is bearable." I placed a light hand on his folded arm. Although I doubted he even felt the touch through his armor.

"I appreciate that, Fire. More than you know." He gave me a warm grin. "During the war, Ezra hid in his castle, and I led the charge with the vampires."

"War?" I asked.

I thought back to Kathy's worry that Ezra might start another war. Why would he do such a thing if he didn't even fight in the first one?

"The seventy-year war. The previous Lucifer hid. He had all that power and locked himself away in his castle. Anarchy ensued in Hell, and war broke out. Some factions wanted democracy, while others wanted things to stay the way they were. The current Lucifer slipped into the castle and took his place. He gained control and wiped out anyone who opposed him as supreme ruler. Ezra was one who wanted things to stay how they were. While everyone was distracted, he planned to kill Lucifer, but it didn't work out that way." Kyler ran a hand through his hair.

"That explains his war room." I touched my lips and looked at Kyler with wide eyes. "Did I say that out loud?"

"Yes?" Confusion crossed Kyler's face.

"Ezra took me to his war room; he said it was enchanted, so I couldn't tell another soul about it."

"We share a soul, Fire." He pointed out. "This isn't good. It means he never stopped planning." Kyler's voice trailed off.

"He wants to rule Hell and use me to do it, doesn't he? That's why he showed me the room. Once I start *behaving*, he's going to try something shady."

Kyler nodded.

The world around me spun, and dizziness crept into me. A weapon. That's why he wanted me. More than ever, I needed to learn to control my powers.

"I'll never let that happen." Kyler closed his fists.

"*We* will never let that happen." I amended.

"They're going to be a while. Would you like to formally meet my best friend? Maybe stop thinking about what's to come for an hour?" Kyler pushed himself off the wall and reached for my hand.

"Absolutely!" I interlocked my fingers with his, and he led me towards the tiny village.

Chapter Twenty-Five

Sapphire

We ended up at a small house in the back corner of the village. Kyler knocked rapidly twice and then once more. Zariah opened the door and hugged Kyler. They laughed as they greeted each other.

His friend motioned us through the door to the living room with a couch and two chairs. I sat down on the chair by the window. A small woman with voluptuous curves came from the kitchen and stood next to Zariah. She gave me a wide grin before they bowed to me.

"Thank you for letting us host you, Your Highness. It's such an honor." Zariah interrupted my thoughts, and I smiled at him.

"I'm here as a friend. Please feel free to call me by my name." I said with a dismissive wave. I shifted in my seat at hearing him call me Highness.

"Oh, and this is my wife! Sylvie." Zariah said, motioning toward the woman beside him.

"It's nice to meet you both." I smiled with a nod.

We moved further into the house and sat on the couches in the living room.

"We were talking about some fond memories." Sylvie smiled at her husband.

"Yeah, man, you remember that time you kicked some kids ass for calling my mom a whore?" Kyler asked his friend, who nodded with a laugh.

"Dude had it coming to him long before he said that." They both shared a laugh, and I couldn't help but smile.

"This does not sound like an appropriate conversation to have in front of ladies. High-" Sylvie stopped herself. "Sapphire, would you like to join me in the kitchen?" She asked with a soft smile.

"I'd love to, but I must warn you, I can burn anything." Laughter echoed behind me as we stepped into the kitchen.

Sylvie had a pot of boiling water going on her stove and something in the oven that smelled of meat. I watched as she poured carrots and potatoes into the pot. She stared at me for a moment before finally speaking.

"I don't mean to overstep, but may I ask you a question?" Sylvie asked in hushed tones.

"Of course." I nodded.

"Are you going to save us? Save *him*?" She looked down at the pot of water and put a lid over it, avoiding my gaze.

"I'm not sure I understand the question." I said softly.

"From Ezra. He's evil. I know we're in Hell, but he lets his vampires kill whoever they please. He has no remorse. As long as he sits on that throne, no one is safe, not even Lucifer." She looked at me, and worried lines creased along her forehead. "I've lost family because of him, and Kyler? He's changed."

"I swear to you, I'll save all of Hell." I turned and showed her the crest on the back of my neck. She let out an audible gasp. "I'm the sword and shield."

"It's true, then. You're the lost princess. It's you." A tear rolled down her cheek. I placed a hand on her shoulder.

"I promise, things will get better. I need time to hone my powers, but once I do..." I didn't need to finish the sentence. Sylvie pulled me into a warm embrace. Although the action surprised me, I gladly returned the gesture.

To see her react that way only reminded me how much I needed to learn who I was. No matter how much I hated taking in souls, the reality was clear. I have to find the means to kill Ezra. I'd continue to let him believe he terrorized me, but when I was ready, he would learn the truth. He couldn't go on being able to do whatever he wanted.

I gave Sylvie a soft smile before returning to Kyler's side. I sat beside him on the couch, and he patted my thigh.

"Did this jackass ever tell you about the time he got me in trouble with the mortal cops?" Zariah asked as I gave him an intrigued look.

"Please don't tell her this story," Kyler grumbled, covering his face with his hands.

"Oh, now you have to tell me, Zariah." I laughed at Kyler, who gave me a begging look.

Now, I wanted to hear this story more. I leaned in as Zariah began.

"Kyler and I were at this mortal bar just drinking and having a good time for his 276th birthday, and there are these two beautiful ladies, I mean, drop dead, not as beautiful as your Highness," Zariah added, and I let out a little chuckle. "Anyways! This dumbass decides to hit on them, and when they say it costs money, he's like, yeah, that's fine, it's my birthday fuck it! Go to find out; they're cops!" Zariah burst into laughter, and Kyler continued to hide his face in his hands.

"Did you end up getting arrested?" I laughed so hard I thought I might pee myself.

"Nah, luckily, he's also a charming dumbass, and we got off with a warning." Kyler shot Zariah a death glare, and we started laughing even harder.

"You should have introduced me way sooner!" I laughed and leaned against Kyler.

"I'm starting to think I should've kept you far away," Kyler grumbled again.

"She is a spitfire, Kyler. You might need to watch out." Zariah winked at his friend.

"Oh, trust me, I know," Kyler smirked, and I glared at him. "We should get back soon. If we leave Ezra and Alfonso alone too long, they'll talk for days."

With a nod, I followed him towards the door.

"Bring her back soon, man. It's always a pleasure to see you." Zariah and Kyler slapped hands and gave each other a quick hug.

"Sylvie, next time we visit, Fire needs your pot roast!" Kyler waved to her. She gave him a warm smile with a nod, and we left.

I didn't want to spend more time with Ezra, but I knew it was inevitable. The gears in my mind began to turn. Ezra was harming other demons, and it would be up to me to stop him. I would tell Kyler about it later, and a real plan would need to be made. Behind closed doors, I would become who I needed to be. My mom believed in me, and now I needed to believe in myself.

I'd be the weapon he wanted, but couldn't have.

We wandered around the castle halls until we found the office again. As I stood in the doorway, they were still talking about random things. Alfonso looked up at me.

"Sapphire, if Ezra here doesn't frequently tell you how beautiful you are, my door is always open," He smirked in my direction. "Just like your legs could be."

"I suggest you keep your thoughts to yourself," Kyler growled behind me. "That is my Princess you are disrespecting."

Alfonso let out a laugh.

"Sit down, dog. I'm sure Sapphire here can appreciate a handsome man's advances." Alfonso's smooth voice filled the room.

"I'd appreciate it if you put your foot in your mouth." I tilted my head towards Alfonso with a wide grin.

"That is enough. I will handle what we discussed, Alfonso. Let us go, you two." Ezra stood up, his voice angry.

He rushed us out of the castle and didn't say anything the entire journey home. We got under his skin. Kyler making a stand for me the way he did made my heart race. He didn't even care that Ezra had been right there. The idea of someone else hitting on me made him so brazen.

"You embarrassed me today." Ezra turned on his heel, and his face was inches from mine.

"I dealt with a man who made me uncomfortable. Something you seem to keep failing to do." I kept my voice level but full of anger.

Ezra went to raise his hand, but Kyler shifted, drawing his gaze. Ezra growled and stormed off. Kyler looked over at me with a smirk on his face.

Ezra would lose his soul to me one day.

One day soon.

Chapter Twenty-Six

Sapphire

"Kyler?" I whispered, standing in the hallway outside my bedroom door.

He turned to me and raised a brow.

"Can I trust Orpheus?"

He paused for a beat, "With your life. What's going on, Fire?"

I pulled him into my room and shut the door as quickly as I could. Kyler looked at me with furrowed brows.

"I need him to cover for me, while we go to the mortal realm. I have to say goodbye to my friends. Things are going to change. Something is shifting inside of me, and I need to say goodbye before..." My lip trembled, "Before I'm too far gone. Please. I don't want them to see. To see the monster." I begged, voice breaking.

"Okay, Fire. Okay. I'll be right back." He rubbed a thumb over my cheek.

With no hesitation, Kyler phased away.

I sat on the edge of my bed and took in the love on my lock screen. It was a picture of Emily Isabelle and I at out favorite place, the fair. A tradition we'd kept every year for the past five. Emily always came home with a stuffed llama, and Isabelle only wanted popcorn.

It was now a shattered memory.

"Highness? You need me?" Orpheus whispered as he phased into the room.

"Can you cover for me? With Ezra for an hour. Please." I bit my lip to stop my trembling chin.

"You never have to beg me for something, Highness. Say the word, and I am at your disposal." He bowed with his torso. A sight I might not ever get used to.

"Thank you, brother." Kyler nodded.

"Go, but be quick. Ezra's patience is fickle at best these days."

"Take me where we need to go, Fire. I've got your back." Kyler extended his hand out to me.

"Wait. Change into mortal clothes. No sword. I don't want to scare them." I said, staring at his black armor.

He nodded and summoned a change of clothes. Once he got dressed, my butterflies wrapped around us and took us to Isabelle's home.

I stared at the black front door and chewed the inside of my cheek. My heart beat rapidly. I just had to knock, but my muscles locked up. My palms were sweaty. Kyler placed a hand on my shoulder.

I took a deep breath and knocked.

"Saph, what are you doing here?" Isabelle asked, opening her door.

"Is Em here too?"

"Yeah, come in. You look so thin, girl. What's going on? Hi, Kyler." Isabelle gave him a short wave.

He gave her a curt nod. She led us into the living room, where Emily sat on the couch. The smell of apple cinnamon hung in the room. Isabelle's favorite scent.

"What is going on?" She asked, her eyes roaming between us. "Where have you been? We've been worried sick!"

"I-I have to go away. I won't be back. I needed to... I needed... to say goodbye. To tell you I loved you both." My voice cracked, tears swelling in my eyes. They turned their heads toward each other and then back at me.

"I don't understand, why?" The whites of Isabelle's eyes turned red.

"I wish I could explain. Please just... don't come looking for me. Stay far away. I have to do this." I shook my head, tears falling uncontrollably.

"W-wait. I have something for you." Emily muttered.

After a bit of rummaging noises from her purse, she held a picture in her hand and passed it to me. Tears fled from my eyes at the sight. It was the picture we took in a photo booth at a carnival the first time we met. That day brought a smile to my face for the first time in months. We all clicked instantly, but we didn't form a regular friendship. We formed a family.

The second family I had to lose.

I fucking hate this!

They pulled me into an embrace. We cried into each other's shoulders. I crumbled beneath the weight of this farewell. My legs buckled, and we collapsed onto the floor.

The three of us knelt, huddled together like we were weathering a storm. My hands shook as I gripped them tighter.

All of their emotions mixed with mine made my body ache. Every inch of my skin felt like it was on fire. I couldn't shut out their sorrow when my own clouded my mind.

After a while, we straightened, and I backed away from them. Their faces turned pale. They stepped back and looked between Kyler and I with wide eyes. I knew before anyone spoke what had happened. My eyes turned black. I closed them, tears streaming even harder.

"Saph..." Emily took a step further back.

"Please don't hate me. I'll always love you guys."

My friends had tears streaming down their faces because Hell was taking something else from me. The gods had a cruel sense of humor.

Must I give up all of who I am for a life I didn't ask for?

I took off running out the door, Kyler following behind. Wind nipped at my cheeks as my pace quickened. The world around me turned into a blur. All of my energy was depleted, but I didn't care. Nothing mattered anymore. Not me. Not my life. Not the God's sick joke.

Since my parents died, all I had done was try to find some semblance of normal. Instead, the universe decided to trip me up at every angle. How much more would I give before I couldn't give any more? Pain seared through my chest as I ran.

"Fire. Stop." Kyler yelled from somewhere behind me. I ignored him and kept going.

"Fire!" He yelled again.

When I ignored him the second time, he phased in front of me. I slammed into him, punching his chest over and over again.

"Get out of my way!"

"I can't do that." He ran his hand over my hair and pulled me to his chest.

"What else will this life take from me, Kyler? What more could I lose? I'm a monster. I'm a killer. I'm all the things you're told to fear as a child! What happens when there is nothing of me left? When the demon I'm becoming takes over." I covered my face with my hands.

"That's it. I need to show you something."

Kyler gripped my arm and phased us off the street. When I uncovered my face, we were in the middle of my home. Everything remained just the same as I had left it.

"Kyler, did you do something?"

"Yes. I paid off your home. It'll always be here. Now close your eyes and listen to what I have to say very closely."

I did what he asked.

"Remember your childhood, the memories? Growing up, your mom and dad dying, all of it. Now remember what your mom's journal said. You have always been a demon, Fire. There is no 'what I'm becoming.' You are and have *always* been. If there's nothing left of the Fire I met in the bar, it's because you let your new life swallow you whole. Not because you're some evil thing. You. Are. Light. Fire. *Strength*. All of the things that are going to help you break free from your binds. Do you hear me? You're not a monster."

I sniffled and wiped my face with my sleeve.

"Kyler, how can I ever thank you for everything you've done and continue to do for me?"

"By proving everyone else wrong."

Chapter Twenty-Seven

Sapphire

"I told you before not to take off." Ezra spoke through gritted teeth.

I walked into the castle to see him lurking by the throne. His gaze pointed at me.

"And you said I wasn't trapped here. Kyler never left my side, so calm the fuck down." My growl surprised him enough to flinch.

"Do not speak to me that way. I am your Prince. I have something to do with the witches, and you are coming with me, since I cannot trust you to listen." Ezra grabbed my wrist hard and phased us away.

I found myself standing in front of a smaller castle. Kyler appeared behind us, and my shoulders relaxed. Ezra proceeded to knock on the door and released the grip on my wrist. I rubbed it and looked over at the pool of black water beside the castle.

A woman with a petite frame and long brown hair greeted us. She leaned one arm on the door, and I spotted her crest on her wrist: a Wiccan spiral. I met her contagious smile as she pulled the other door open. She wore a blue crop top and jean shorts, but the silver crown on her head made me think this had to be the Princess herself. Kyler had told me about her once or twice.

"Ezra, who is this?" The princess pointed her question at me.

"This is Sapphire." He said simply.

Vealla eyed us before leading us into her castle. The inside welcomed us with light blue walls and paintings of hell along them. The entryway led to us throne room, with two doors on either side. The small room had only a handful of guards. Vealla took her spot on the golden throne, and Kyler bowed before her.

"We can't have a treaty if your vampires continue to kill my witches." Vealla's voice rang with a sharpness that sent a chill through me.

"Your vampires seem to be bothering everyone," I murmured under my breath.

"It is not going to be fixed overnight, Vealla. It is unrealistic to expect otherwise." Ezra retorted, crossing his arms.

"Sapphire, what do you think? Is it unrealistic to expect my witches not to be killed?" She shifted in the throne, her legs crisscrossing under her. "Or is this murdering jackass wiser than me?"

"I don't think it's unrealistic at all. In fact, I believe it should have been dealt with as soon as it became a problem." I shrugged.

Kyler tensed behind me. We knew Ezra would be angry about this later, yet I did not care.

He'd reap what he sowed.

"She understands nothing of Hell. Her opinion does not matter." Ezra said. His eyes shifted to me briefly before he approached Vealla.

"Acting like your future Princess is an invalid is not a good look, Ezra. If she understands nothing, that's your shortcoming, not hers." Vealla gritted her teeth. "Why don't you leave her with me for a few hours? I'd love to get to know who she is." She hopped off the throne and wrapped her arm around mine. I gave her an awkward smile in return. Vealla gave off calming energy like I had never felt before.

"Give me one second." Ezra turned and pulled me off to the side by the arm. I shoved him off with a grunt.

"What?" I snapped.

His eyes narrowed in on me. I could feel the anger boiling over in his chest. Would he be dumb enough to try to do something here? In front of another prince of Hell?

"Do not talk to me that way! You are an ungrateful bitch. I can knock you down as easily as I can make you rise. You would do well to remember your place." He whispered aggressively in my ear. "If I leave you here, can you fucking behave?"

"Yes, sire. I'll be on my absolute best behavior. I wouldn't want you to knock me down." I fluttered my eyelashes. His nostrils flared.

"Fine, but Kyler stays to guard her," Ezra said, walking back over to Vealla.

"Yea, yea. I'll have her home for dinner. *Toodaloo.*" She gave Ezra a sarcastic wave of her fingers.

He huffed and phased away in his flash of lightning. The tension in the air faded out, and Vealla stepped back, giving me a once-over. Kyler came to my side and took my hand, surprising me as our fingers locked. I looked up toward him, and he gave me a smug smile.

"Thank you, Vealla." Kyler bowed his head at her.

"It is the least I can do for you. Ezra is becoming a problem for us all. I'm glad you sent word ahead of time. Why don't you get Dante? He wants to meet Sapphire, too." She gave me a warm smile.

"Keep her safe, Highness." Kyler let go of my hand and phased away.

"Come on, Sapphire, I'll show you what I do for fun. Perhaps you can help me with my current project." She took my hand to lead me elsewhere.

"Thank you, Vealla." I said behind her.

"Don't mention it." She turned and smiled at me.

We went to the door on the left and paced down the hall. She led me up a spiral wooden staircase. It took us seven stories before we came to an open room. The walls warbled a sheerness, and the hues of Hell's sky surrounded us. Only blue pillars in the corners of the rooms held the ceiling above us. Along the walls were blankets, crocheted and hanging in all arrays of colors. An audible gasp escaped my throat.

"This is amazing. My mom was really good at making wedding dresses. She tried to teach me, but I'm not good with a needle." I chuckled.

"One of the only gifts magic didn't give me. It's my guilty pleasure." Vealla shrugged, watching the amusement on my face.

"Thank you for showing me this. I needed it. Things have been hard since I learned what I am." I ran a finger over a pink blanket she had folded on a rack.

"You're welcome. I can always teach you if you'd like," she said.

"Really? I'd like that. Maybe I can make mom proud." I said, gazing at her shelf of crochet animals.

"I'm sure she'd already be proud." Vella smiled.

"I really want to believe that. She knew I was a demon the entire time. Somedays I wonder why she never told me." I sighed and looked out at the sky. My heart sank at her memories.

"I'm sure she had a good reason. I'm also sure whatever answers you're looking for, Kyler will help you find. He came to me asking for help when you first read your mom's journal. He's loyal; his devotion to you will never end."

I regarded her with a brief smile. He told me he'd ask for help, I never realized he did.

Perhaps I would be okay after all with him by my side.

Chapter Twenty-Eight

Sapphire

Kyler's fire appeared before us, and someone appeared in a blink beside him. The demon looked exactly as I expected it to look. Black horns with a slight curve inward sat on his head, and black wings folded against his back. Dante had muscles bulging on his arms. His hair was long, dark blonde, and he wore a black shirt and black jeans.

Kyler came over to my side, placing a hand on my shoulder. I tilted my head up at him before focusing my attention back on Dante.

"Dante? You're really hitting the nail on the head with that one," I laughed. "Can I touch your horns?"

"Of course!" He grinned and knelt on one knee, bending his head so I could reach. My fingers ran over his rough horns. They felt like a centipede's shell, rough and jagged.

"They feel weird." I said as Dante straightened.

"Yea, they take some getting used to." He nodded in agreement, running a hand over the left horn.

"Shall we show her our realm, Dante?" Vealla asked, turning my attention.

"Absolutely."

We made our way back down the swirling staircase and through the castle. Vealla led us outside and pointed at the lake.

"That is a magic spring. It holds healing properties. It's part of why we built the castle here." She said, kneeling down and touching the water.

The light from the sky glistened off the lake's black ripples. I dipped my own fingers in the water and gasped at the tingling feeling. Kyler gave me a smirk. I wondered how his face wasn't permanently stuck like that.

All three of them watched me with amusement on their faces as I took in the realm around me. The black water that heals, and the sky never really changing, amazed me. Even after being in Hell for weeks, the reality didn't stick in my mind. The idea of torture and lava had been so ingrained in my mind that none of this seemed real.

After a few minutes, I walked over to Kyler. He wrapped his arms around me while Dante held Vealla's hand. We phased to Dante's castle. It was built into the mountain, and small brick homes could be seen from where we stood. The platform we stepped onto had to be at least ten feet long and curved around the castle in a half circle. Vines and overgrown roots spread wildly on the walls. Battlements stuck out from the mountainside, with giant ballistas every few yards.

Dante pushed open the doors, and we made our way inside. The entryway was dark and musty. A lingering scent of wet grass followed us into an open room. Dante's stone throne sat in the middle of the space. Demons were roaming the castle, occasionally bowing. Slight rays of light from the cracks in the ceiling made the room a little brighter.

"Welcome to my humble abode." Dante motioned his hand to the throne.

"This is beautiful, even if it's gloomy," I walked over to his throne and placed a hand on it.

"You're welcome here any time." Dante placed a hand on my shoulder. "And I do mean anytime."

"Thank you, Dante." I smiled and went back to admiring the structure of his castle.

The inside had six floors, all with rails protecting stone walkways. Demons bustled about, roaming around every which way. Laughter could be heard down the hall, and the soft scent of meat rolled around the air.

"You okay over there, Fire?" Kyler asked, and I turned to the group.

"Sorry, I still can't get over how amazing everything in Hell is." I shrugged.

"Is there anything you want to know, Sapphire? Since we have the freedom to talk without Ezra up our asses?" Dante asked from his throne.

"What powers do you have?"

"Fire and Ice." He laughed and showed me a fireball and an ice spike in each hand.

"Odd combination for sure." I echoed his laugh.

"You think that's cool, check out witchcraft." Vealla handed me her black book. I flipped through the pages, but the words made no sense to me. It was all in a demon language. Kyler was quiet, for the most part, observing and guarding.

"You're going to have to teach me this." I said, running my finger along a symbol on the page.

"Done." Vealla nodded.

"I don't mean to pry too much, but do you guys have wives? Husband's? Seconds in command?"

Dante shifted in his seat at my question.

"I never found my mate. We were all occupied during the war, making it rare for many of us to find love. Those that did got lucky." Dante explained, tapping his fingers on the armrest of his throne.

"My mate spends most of her time in the mortal realm, since she's a mortal born witch." Vealla's eyes shifted toward the rays of light drifting into the castle.

"Do you visit her often?"

"I do when I can, but with me being a princess, it gets tricky." Vealla sighed.

"Can you have relationships without a mate?"

They shifted their eyes towards Kyler. I tilted my head and raised an eyebrow. Why did they look at him like that?

"You can, but the bond of mates is stronger than anything else. Our mates amplify our powers and magic. Most of us in Hell choose to wait. And if we lose our mate, we don't usually get into a relationship again." Kyler spoke this time, and I turned to him.

"I can't believe fated mates are real. What about the mortal-made demons?" I rubbed my arm.

"They do not get mates. It's Hell based only. Honestly, mortal-made demons get the short end of every stick." Dante laughed at his joke.

"What happens if you reject it? Does it hurt like in the shows?" Everyone exchanged looks before speaking.

"You have to accept the bond, too. If one person accepts and the other rejects, it still breaks the bond. Both have to accept. If both reject it, it doesn't hurt in the sense that your body feels like it's breaking, but more, you feel weaker overall. The creator made it so that you are powerful together and weaker apart." Vealla responded, but her eyes lingered on Kyler.

"The creator? What Gods do you... *we* have?" I asked, still unsure what to believe.

"There are the main seven, then the creator of all." Kyler responded.

"Atropos, Kai, Zephyr, Axel, Pax, Onyx, and Eden." Vealla chirped. "Here, I'll let you borrow this so you can read over it later."

She waved her hand and summoned a brown book. She handed it to me, and I read the title. *Gods for Demons*. At least it was in English.

"I'm sorry, Sapphire. There is so much you don't know about Hell. We've all been here for hundreds of years and grown up in this life. I promise we will help you learn." Kyler gave me a warm smile.

"Thank you, guys, for today and for answering my questions. I appreciate it," I said in a soft voice. "I hope this comes easily soon."

"Of course. If you want to train, you can come here any time. My demons would love to fight someone other than each other." Dante stretched his arms, groaning.

"You're welcome at my castle any time as well. I'd love to have a crochet buddy." Vealla bounced on her heels.

"There is one more thing," Dante said, and then all eyes were on me.

"Ezra may have misconceptions about who you are, but we do not. Dante and I, we back you. If you need us, we will go to war for you." Vealla's voice was firm. I looked around, and panic set in.

Should we be talking about this in public?

"Don't worry, my demons are very loyal to me." Dante said, watching my eyes.

"If I take over, what does that change? Lucifer seems unimportant. Ezra is a problem, sure, but I don't need to take over Hell to deal with him. I only need a good dungeon." I said.

A deep sigh came from Kyler.

"That is the problem. Lucifer does nothing. He allows Ezra to do whatever he wants. Rogue vampires kill mortals constantly. There are many problems in the human world that get left alone. He took over, only to hide in his castle, and kill demons for fun." Dante spoke with an anger I could feel in my core.

"Thank you both, truly. I don't even know how to control my powers yet or who I am. If I sent Hell to war again, I'm not exactly bringing on a golden age."

They turned to each other again, sharing a look I couldn't quite place.

"Why do you guys keep doing that?" I called them out.

"We're surprised. You haven't been here long, and already you're talking about making sure we don't go to war. You don't owe demons anything." Dante admitted.

"I owe Hell a great deal if it's to be my home. If I'm the lost princess, then it's mine."

My heart still ached at everything I had to leave behind in the mortal world. Yet, these three helped me smile today. They showed me their world with open arms. Vealla even showed me something special to her and offered to teach me.

Kyler showed me something I hadn't seen till now.

Hell is home.

"You're going to make an amazing queen one day." Dante bowed his head to me.

"We should get back, Fire." Kyler placed his hand on the small of my back.

"I hope to see you guys soon." I waved at them. Kyler took my hand and phased us back to the castle, and all the joy I held onto all day vanished.

"It is about time you got back." Ezra pushed himself off his throne and walked towards us. Each step he took felt more menacing than the last, heavier.

"Highness," I said.

"You will be crowned in a week's time. I will make arrangements for Vealla to anoint you. There is already a dress in your room. You are not to leave this castle until I deem you allowed after the crowning. A princess has duties to fulfill that do not require you bouncing around the realm." Ezra tapped his foot on the ground.

All I could do was nod at him. He could continue to expect me to stay put, but I would not. Kyler and I would continue to train until I could control my powers fully.

"Highness," I replied.

Little did he know that giving me a crown put me one step closer to reaching my goal.

Ending his tyranny.

Chapter Twenty-Nine

Sapphire

"I am going to Lucifer's realm. I will be back in two days. Kyler will stay with you, and the guards will check in around the clock. I expect you not to leave the castle or the village grounds." Ezra's stern voice sounded like nails on a chalkboard.

"When will I be allowed to leave Ezra? I hate it here."

His hand wrapped around my shoulder, fingers digging in. I kept my gaze level with his despite the anger at his touch. His need to control me both physically and mentally was exhausting.

"You are *mine*. You will leave when I say so, speak when I say so, and do as I say. If I never let you leave, it is my prerogative." His grip tightened, and I lowered my gaze. He needed to believe I was scared of him and vulnerable.

"Yes, Highness." I kept my voice low.

"Good." He phased away without another word.

Kyler had not been in the throne room. I didn't know where he was. I left my seat and wandered the halls of the castle. Quiet echoed in the halls more than usual as I roamed. There were not many guards in sight.

First, I went to the library, but there was no sign of him. With a small sigh, I made my way upstairs to Kyler's room. I pushed the door open, but he was not there either.

Where could he have gone off to? He was almost always by my side.

I thought of him, and my butterflies took me away. When I emerged in a new room, my eyes found my knight. He pointed to a map, hunched over a table. Two more men in full-blown armor were hunched over it as well. The fragrance of blood and iron hung in the room. My eyes wandered around to realize where I was: the barracks.

"Fire? Is everything alright?" Kyler asked once he saw me.

"I didn't mean to interrupt. Ezra left, and I didn't know where you went. I can leave if you're busy." I walked over to where he stood and gazed at the colored map on the table.

"You're not interrupting anything." Kyler shook his head.

"Ezra left?" The guard across from us asked.

"He said he was going to Lucifer's realm for the next two days," I said.

Kyler and the other guards exchanged looks.

"Odd. He did not mention this to me. Amdis, can you check and see if he's in Lucifer's realm? I don't want to leave Fire by herself." Kyler asked the tall guard across from us.

"At once, Fang Leader. Highness." The guard bowed to me and disappeared.

"I'm sorry, Fire. The Prince asked me to add guards for your coronation. I didn't mean to leave you alone with him.

Are you okay?" He brushed my cheek with his hand, sending chills down my spine.

"I'm fine." I tried my best to hide the sadness within me. If I told Kyler Ezra laid a hand on me again, he might try to kill his own brother. "You are allowed to be away from me. What's a Fang leader?"

Kyler ran his hand through his hair and groaned obnoxiously.

"Some title made by some prick ages ago. Now, I'm stuck with it. Essentially, it's vampire code for leader of the vampire army."

"But you don't like it?"

"God's no." He shook his head.

"Oh, captain, my captain?" I teased.

"Now who's being ridiculous? Want to do something?" Kyler tucked a stray hair behind my ear.

"Can you give me a tour?"

"Of the barracks?" Kyler asked with a raised brow.

"Yes. This is part of your world." I smiled up at him.

I looked around the room again. Demons bowed in my direction whenever they caught my gaze. I wondered what they all did during the day, besides standing around for Ezra's amusement.

"When you're thinking too much, your face squints. You look like you're trying to find a missing puzzle piece, and it's absolutely adorable." He grinned as my cheeks flushed. "Let's go on the grand tour then, shall we?" Kyler held an arm up, and I wrapped my hand around it.

We roamed through the big open room, and Kyler waved at his men when we passed by. He took me through a door that took us into what looked like sleeping quarters. Beds lay against the wall in neat rows. In front of every bed sat a wooden chest. We tiptoed through the room, so as not to wake the sleeping soldiers.

The next place Kyler took me blew my mind away. Beyond the barracks, a small garden sat outside. Plants with unusual petals and colors sat in dark soil. Stems were black, and the flowers ranged from light purple to teal. The vision before me looked like a fantasy.

"Kyler, what is this?"

"A remembrance garden. We plant a new flower every time we lose a large number of demons. To remind us that life is precious." His eyes lowered slightly.

"It's beautiful." I whispered into the wind.

"Yes, it is." Kyler whispered into my ear.

He wrapped his arms around me from behind. I pressed against him and relaxed for a few minutes.

Kyler was my home.

He still had his hands on my waist as I let my butterflies take us back to the village. I could have stayed in the garden forever, but I needed to train. We arrived in front of the fountain. Demons bustled about around us.

A demon phased before us, Amdis, the soldier from earlier.

"He is indeed with Lucifer. From what little I could gather, Ezra placed his claim on our Princess. Again." He bowed to me and then straightened.

Annoyance flickered through me.

"Thank you, Amdis," I said.

"Highness," he bowed his head at me. "I'll get back to my post, Fang leader."

"Take the night off, Amdis. Thank you for your intel." Kyler tapped his shoulder.

Amdis bowed a final time before leaving.

"Kyler, can I trust them? The other Princes and Princesses of Hell? I'm sorry to keep asking. You're the only one I really trust right now. Perhaps Orpheus, too."

"Yes. Dante and Vealla fight for a better Hell, and you, Fire, are the promise of one. Alfonso is a coin flip. He is friends with Ezra, but I think his wolves getting killed is making him change sides."

"Then we'll have to work on bringing him to our side." I said with determination.

"That's a good idea, Fire."

Kyler shifted his gaze toward the store his friend owned. I wondered how often he actually saw his best friend, but I doubted it was often enough.

"I'm letting you be free," I said, breaking the silence.

"What?" Kyler turned his head down toward me from where he stood at my side.

"Go see your friend. I'll be okay for an hour or two. I think I am going to take a nap so I have energy tonight." I smiled at him. Ezra's absence gave us both a chance to relax and not be on edge. Kyler should enjoy it, and I wouldn't be the reason he didn't get to see his friend.

"Are you sure?" He asked.

"I am. Go. Tell him I said hello." I motioned my hand toward the store.

Kyler reached for me but pulled away, remembering we were in the village. He gave me a half smile before walking off. I waited for him to go inside before I turned and headed back towards the castle. The walk gave me some time to clear my head. My friends had been on my mind whenever things got quiet. Even if I suddenly knew exactly who I was and how to use my powers, this was home now and no place for mortals.

Once I entered the throne room, the guards on duty bowed to me. I gave them both a warm smile before making my way upstairs. The room I chose to rest in was not mine but Kyler's. His space made me feel comfortable and warm. I closed the door behind me and slid into his sheets. The comforter wrapped around my body, and I closed my eyes. Thoughts still swirled in my mind about all that had happened.

I thought of my friends and our first time ever meeting. We played a few carnival games and ate cotton candy. Isabelle had been amazing at the balloon pop game. We had to keep hiding Emily from the clown walking around since they scared her. A tear slid down my cheek as I pulled the photo out that she gave me.

It was the first time since I lost my parents that I felt happy. An ache in my chest remained no matter what happened in the world around me. With time to myself, I let my tears flow freely. I curled in a ball on the bed and flashes of my life swirled in my mind.

A bleak reminder that I had to start focusing on training. My powers were still very much out of my control. Ezra thought he had me wrapped around his finger, but he'd learn.

Our little chess game would end, because *his* knight protected the queen.

Chapter Thirty
Kyler

"Sapphire must like you a lot. I'm seeing you all the time now!" Zariah jested as I walked into his store.

A few of his customers wandered around when the bell alerted him to my arrival. The store's small interior looked deceiving from the outside. Rows and rows of jewelry counters lined the interior. I never pictured my friend as the salesman type, but the way he stood, prideful at the counter, showed me he was in his element.

"Keep it up, Zariah." I teasingly threatened, waltzing over to him.

"You good, man? Every time I see you, the bags under your eyes triple."

"Wouldn't they be at my chin then?" I raised a brow at him. "I'm fine. Too much on my mind these days." I shrugged.

"Gonna elaborate or do I have to get Syl down here to pull it out of you?" He crossed his arms over his chest.

"God's no. I hate when Syl uses her mom voice." I laughed.

"Then spill, fucker."

"When I went on an errand for Ezra, Lucifer said there was a coming storm. Now Ezra is in the Realm of Death. I think something's up. I'm worried how it will affect my men, affect Hell, and affect Fire." I ran a hand over the back of my neck.

The last thing we needed was another gods-damned war. I lost enough of my friends and good men. Ezra's deranged behavior had me on edge already, but Lucifer and his riddle sent me spiraling.

"Lucifer also talks in riddles like he's in a green suit. You keep giving pieces of yourself to everyone, there will be no *Kyler* left."

"If only you understood how ironic what you're saying is. No one protects-"

A demon manifested before us. His face looked rough, with dirt covering his cheeks. The look of horror flashed in his wide eyes.

"FANG LEADER! Kyler, come quick! Please." Panting, the demon from the mortal world held his chest.

"What is it?" I summoned my armor and sword. Zariah stiffened beside me. We both knew this couldn't mean anything good.

"There are rogues in a human bar. Killing people. Please." The demon begged, trying to calm himself.

I gripped his shoulder, giving him a nod.

"We'll talk soon, man." I said to my friend, who gave me a knowing glance.

Too many times in our lives have I been called away for duty's sake. Even as a young boy, my father would summon me from playing to force me to watch him torture an undeserving soul. I pushed the thoughts down and phased away.

Chaos erupted all around me once I positioned myself inside the bar. Soft country music played over a radio, and a few patrons huddled in the corner in terror. Cigarette smoke lingered in a fog around the room. Empty glasses and red baskets of food were tossed every which way. Two vampires had mortals in their grasp, fangs dug deep.

A growl left my throat. Darting over to the couple, I summoned my firepower in my hand.

"Let the mortals go. *Now*." I barked, standing firm.

"Oh, look, Leslie, the prince's dog is off his leash." The man said, holding a limp body.

A man with a pale face and glossed-over eyes stared back at me from the demon's arms. He barely had a heartbeat. I knew what that meant. Heat gripped my chest. The vein in my forehead twitched. This was not going to end well.

For them.

"Ha! Come play, Kyler, the meat's fresh." The female vampire, Leslie, removed her fangs from the human's neck, and blood dripped down her chin.

Screams resonated behind me. Humans ran out the door. The cowardly demon patrons in the corner took the opportunity to run past me.

"You've got three seconds. Then the fresh meat will be from your heads rolling." I growled and put a hand on my sword.

The two vampires shared a look, then went back to their meal. One heartbeat stopped, and I flared my nostrils.

Fuck this.

Gripping my sword, I slid it with ease through the male vampire's neck. His head rolled, and the female screamed, dropping her human and running off. I phased in front of her and slid my sword through her chest. The sound of bones breaking drummed in my ears.

I dashed back to the human who hung on by a thread, my heart beating at an insane pace. There was no way to save her, and sirens blared in the distance. Time stood still. My chin wobbled at what I had to do.

Springing around the room, I grabbed every human left in the bar and took them outside. They were dazed and confused, walking in circles and gripping their heads. Hopefully disoriented enough that they forgot what happened and forgot me.

Back inside, I threw fireballs everywhere. Exhaustion snuck in from depleting all my energy, but it didn't matter. Every last bit of evidence had to be destroyed. Once the building had billowing smoke, I hovered in the tree line, watching. Dozens of firetrucks and ambulances barreled down the road.

This was one part of being commander I'd never enjoy.

Death.

Even lurking in the shadows, it was hard to miss the body bags. To know I was partially at fault. I closed my fists and gritted my teeth.

I hated myself.

This wasn't the first time, nor would it be the last, where I had to take a life because I couldn't save them. It used to be dad's torture victims, but in my recent years, it's been shit like this.

No matter how dark Fire thought she became, this was true darkness.

I looked at my sword, blood still dripping down the edge. I wanted to scream, to yell, but I had to make sure no one else got hurt because of me. Once the fire died out, I let out a breath.

"I know that look, how many?" Zariah asked when I phased back to his shop.

"Two."

"You did what you could, man."

Zariah was right, but I couldn't speak. I didn't for a long time. My palms were sweaty. My head pounded as I rubbed my temple.

"Ezra needs to go." I gritted my teeth. "I'm done with the bullshit. I'm done losing innocent people."

"What do we need to do?" Zariah asked without skipping a beat.

"Train Fire and hope she accepts who she is."

Chapter Thirty-One
Sapphire

"You are early, Highness." Dante bowed to me.

He stood on the balcony outside his castle. We arrived shortly after my much needed nap. The wind whistled through the air. Down below, the village buzzed with demons. I placed my hands on the railings and peered past the horizon. Black shadows swirled along the edges of the realm.

"Ezra is away; the princess will play." I teased, turning back to them.

"I'll go get Vealla." Kyler said, placing his hand on my shoulder.

"Can I hang out here while he goes?" I asked Dante.

"Of course. Highness, would you like to see the top of the mountain?" He asked me, offering me his hand.

"Absolutely! Hurry back, Kyler." I smiled at him. He nodded and phased away.

Dante, holding my hand, took us to the peak. The grass beneath our feet swayed in the wind. My eyes went wide at the view before me. The clouds floating through the sky looked close enough to touch. The sky was brighter here. I could see the entire realm's flowing hills. Dante extended his wings out, causing a push of wind. Hell had a beauty to it that nothing could compare to. From where we stood, I could see the shadows. They swirled around, clashing against an invisible barrier.

"Dante?"

"Yes, Highness?" He responded. My gaze stayed locked on the shadows.

"Why are the realms separated? Also, please stop calling me *Highness,* are we not equals?" I asked.

"The very first Lucifer, Samael, did that. He decided to separate the realms by class. Originally, the witches and werewolves were together, but the second Lucifer, Apollyon, wanted to change it. He could not figure out the magic that divided the realms, though, making the shadows continue to divide us." Dante stood next to me and looked out at the shadows.

Apollyon.

Mom mentioned him in her journal. How did I end up so many millennia into the future? How was time traveling even possible? I had so many questions and still no answers.

"Are you that old?" I asked, rejoining our conversation.

"Oh," He ran a hand over the back of his neck, "I'm not that old no, I'm only six hundred and thirty two. I read a lot."

My mouth gaped open.

"Six hundred and thirty-two? I'm only six hundred years younger. Not bad." I laughed.

"Oh, Kyler is back, ready to go?" Dante's gaze shifted down toward the castle patio where Kyler stood with Vealla.

I gave him a quick nod. He wrapped a hand around my waist and jumped off the mountain. Wind whipped around us, and adrenaline kicked in; my heart felt like it could leap from my chest. A scream wanted to escape my lips, yet no words came out. His wings extended out, and our fall turned into a gentle glide.

"Could you show off just a little less?" Kyler remarked once our feet were back on the ground.

"Where's the fun in that?" Dante shrugged with one shoulder.

"Fire." Kyler opened his arms, and I wrapped mine around his neck, leaning my head against his chest. He phased us away.

The arena here looked much more extensive. The sand had brown thin logs outlining it. Seven racks of weapons fell in line to the left. Three alone had swords, two had bows, and the last two had war hammers and axes. There were still tents in the back corner, and a few benches sat sparingly around the oval.

"Let's start with elements," Dante said. He and I walked into the middle of the arena. "What elements do you have?"

Vealla sat down on a bench to the left. She summoned her black book and flipped through the pages, eyeing us occasionally. Kyler sat on the opposite bench, hunched over. He twirled his sword in the sand but kept his gaze on me.

"Lightning and fire." I opened both hands, sighing. I couldn't summon my power at will even now.

"Good. Throw them at me."

I blinked at Dante.

"You won't hurt me, Saph." He added.

"I don't think I feel comfortable throwing my power at you, Dante." I shook my head. "Plus, I can't summon my powers on cue. I don't know how." I kicked the dirt in frustration.

"I will heal him, it's ok." Vealla gave me a warm smile from the bench.

Kyler's eyes met mine, and he nodded. I gazed down at my open palms. I wanted to be able to do this with ease.

"It's connected to our emotions, to our magic energy. Close your eyes and find your center. You didn't grow up in this world. No one expects you to get it right away." Dante stood in an iron cross formation waiting for me.

Closing my eyes, I felt the world around me. I imagined my magic power flowing through me like a river. With a gasp, one arm tingled with static, and the other warmth of my fire power. I threw the fire at Dante, and it fizzled out in the air. I tried the lightning and he didn't flinch at the impact. There weren't even burn marks on his clothes.

"You need to put your back into it now." He said. Again, I blinked. "Your power is as strong as you want it to be. Don't be afraid of it. Try again. Vealla can heal me. Be the queen of Hell you are meant to be." His words rang in my ears.

The queen of Hell had a nice ring to it.

I formed the fireball again in my hand, this time focusing all my energy on it. Dante groaned, and a hole burned through his shirt. Vealla walked over, and her hand had a white glow as it hovered over his shoulder. The burn mark went away but the hole remained. He nodded at me and waited. I summoned the lightning power and threw it at him hard. The blast pushed him back in the sand, and he moaned out in pain. Vealla quickly came over to heal him again.

"Oh gods! I'm sorry, Dante!" I panted.

"No, no, that was amazing!" He boasted with a smile. Vealla nodded in agreement at my accomplishment.

"That was good, Fire." Kyler cooed from the bench.

"Thanks, it's all in the wrist." I laughed, swirling my hand around.

"Oh Gods, she's been spending too much time with you, Kyler." Dante gave him a side eye.

"I hope there's enough room in this party for two more."

Everyone turned to see Orpheus and Alfonso standing by the tents. Kyler and I shared a look before I stepped over to Alfonso.

"Whose side are you on?" Kyler asked, stepping beside me.

"*My* side. Ezra isn't the winning horse anymore. If *she* is what I have to rely on to make sure my wolves don't die, then I'm going to make sure she can fight." Alfonso turned to me. "Prove you're worthy and I'll be loyal to you. Falter, and I'm taking matters into my own hands."

"What do you want from me?" I pushed my hands out from my chest in anger.

I'm getting sick of men demanding I prove my worth.

I gritted my teeth.

"I want a better world. My spies tell me you want something different than murder and war. I want that also."

"Then give me your loyalty, Alfonso. You have my word that I will make things better."

"Let's see how you do today. Then I'll decide."

"You've been my brother's friend for as long as I've been alive. Why the sudden change of heart?" Kyler gripped his sword and came to my side.

"Calm yourself, dog. Friends aren't the cause of things you love dying. Yet, Ezra lets vampires kill my pack." He walked past me into the arena and stood beside Dante.

"I'll follow your lead, Fire." Kyler whispered in my ear.

Orpheus gave me a slight nod, then sat on a bench where Kyler joined him. I pulled in a breath and held my head high. A new feeling, something I didn't recognize, washed over me. I looked out at everyone. Weeks ago, I walked into a bar as a mortal.

Now I was a princess with people who wanted me to win, to be something bigger.

To be me.

Chapter Thirty-Two
Sapphire

"If we are going to do this. I want to do it right. I want all of you to fight me, except Vealla. We will need your healing, I'm sure." I walked over and grabbed a black sword from one of the racks.

"Fire, you sure? You've only managed to control your powers once. Five minutes ago." Kyler ran a nervous hand over his cheek.

"I'm sure. Kyler, you and I know how ugly the truth is. If I wait until I'm perfect, it'll never happen." I shuffled to the middle of the arena.

He let out a long breath and nodded.

"Please, don't hold back."

Everyone came to the middle of the sand and took a stance.

Alfonso shifted before my eyes. He went from handsome guy to giant dire wolf in seconds. He stood on his two hind legs.

Dante nodded at us, and it was time to fight. I felt static charging my lightning with my hand. Dante threw ice at me, and I dodged. He still clipped the side of my shoulder. Everyone froze waiting for my reaction.

"Don't do that. I'm fine." I groaned.

Dante nodded and continued to throw ice and fire at me, while I danced around. I got hit a few times. My clothes looked war-torn, but I didn't care. Alfonso came at me with his claws extended, and I backed away from him. Dante was at my back with fire in hand. He went to hit me with it, and my back stung with pain before I healed.

I couldn't stop; I had to figure this out. Ezra would never go down without a fight. His fragile ego couldn't handle that.

Alfonso came from behind me and swatted again. I moved my feet to avoid being hit and tripped over the sand, falling. My hands caught me before my face planted down. I stared at the ground and took a deep breath.

Princess and future queen, I reminded myself.

The guys waited for me to get up. I stood and swiped the loose sand off my legs. Kyler eyed me, and I gave him a nod. I'd continue to fight them and learn to handle myself.

Hell depended on me.

They depended on me.

I grabbed the sword and twirled it, ready to fight again. The guys all took seats on the benches. Orpheus and Kyler sat on the one closest to me, and Alfonso sat alone, ogling me. Vealla began speaking the demon tongue, summoning a giant monster. The black sand swirled around until a creature that stood seven feet tall roared. It had thick arms and legs, with a round belly.

Woah.

I made a new lightning bolt, shooting it at the beast. It did not do anything except agitate the monster. It roared and charged at me. The monster pushed me into the terrain, sliding on my back. It scratched at me as I covered my face.

Time slowed down, and I took a breath.

You can do this.

Finding my center, warmth filled both arms. I blasted the monster with fire. The rough sand turned into glass and shot everywhere. The shards sliced my body all over, and blood dripped into the sand. I healed slower than I usually did. Hunger pangs twisted in my gut. I took another deep breath and stared down at my hands. Flickers of the demon I killed flashed in my mind again. I pushed the memory down and dug my teeth into my lip.

I stood panting and sore. My muscles buckled, and sweat dripped from my forehead.

But I did it.

"You did well, Sapphire. You'll need more training, but that was amazing for someone who only had a few sessions with a vampire." Dante boasted and clapped his hands.

"Hey!" Kyler huffed. "Let me remind you, I'm the fucking Fang leader."

"But you hate that title." I reminded him.

He crossed his arms over his chest, "That's besides the point!"

I rolled my eyes at him, and everyone laughed, except Alfonso. He sat on the bench, clearly lost in thought. He gandered toward the sky and took a deep breath.

"Do you need healing, Saph?" Vealla trotted over and placed a hand on my shoulder.

"No, no. I'm okay. I need a shower, though." I placed my hands on my knees, catching my breath.

"I'm nothing if not a man of my word." Alfonso stood before me, giving me beady eyes. "You have my loyalty. Don't make me regret it." He said, extending a hand to me.

"You won't." I gripped his hand tightly and released it. "I need to figure out how to deal with Ezra. He's been visiting Lucifer a lot as of late. Something doesn't sit right with me."

I found myself pacing in the sand. The indent where my feet continued to walk got bigger and bigger. I rubbed the bridge of my nose, thinking of all the times Ezra had threatened me or randomly disappeared.

"How many times has he gone?" Vealla asked.

"At least three since Fire got here. Not to mention sending me for some book about Hell's history. This last time, he claimed her as future Princess." Kyler's eyes followed me while I continued to pace.

"He's making sure Lucifer knows he has a weapon against him now," Dante said.

I stopped in my tracks and met his eyes.

"If I killed Lucifer, his soul would be mine. Ezra is playing the wrong hand."

Kyler raised a brow at me.

"Fiiiire?" He asked, elongating my nickname.

"I have to ascend the throne. Ezra thinks he holds the key to Hell. If I continue to train secretly and let him feel I'm scared of him, he won't see me coming. When I have full control, it'll be something he can't plan for. I won't get anywhere with him in the way. I have to be strong enough to keep him in prison. To keep him under *my* control."

Again, all four of them stared at me. Then, bowed.

A shiver slid down my spine.

I didn't know what the future would hold. But I did know I wouldn't face it alone.

Chapter Thirty-Three

Sapphire

The dress Ezra picked for me hung on the back of my closet door. A soft sigh left me as I sat on the edge of the bed. At least with this coronation, I'd be crowned. Ezra made sure I knew being a princess involved being stuck in this castle. He wanted to keep me under lock and Key. It didn't matter since he left so much; it made it easy to get away.

I walked over to the window, pushing the curtain aside, my eyes peered down below. Demons were gathered and talking around the village. Everyone would be here to witness my official rise to the throne. It seemed like hundreds of demons came for this.

My stomach sank.

What if I didn't live up to what everyone expected? What if I wasn't the princess everyone thought I would be? My palms were sweaty, and my head pounded.

A tap at the door turned my attention. Vealla slid through and bowed before shutting the door and walking deeper into the room.

"Highness, I need to tell you something urgently." She said in a whisper.

"What's wrong?" I asked and took a step towards her.

"Ezra is not just crowning you; he's binding himself to you."

"What?" My body went stiff.

"He put it in the ceremony. It's all in the demonic language, so that you wouldn't know. If he binds to you, you are trapped. Until one of you dies, you'd be his subservient. It would mean he could do whatever he wanted and the rules of Hell would no longer apply." Her words came out rushed. She bit the corner of her lip.

"Meaning?"

"Meaning, Sapphire, that he could bring you to the brink of death if he so chooses to, and no one could intervene. The magic that binds can not be broken. Not even by Lucifer. Only death."

"How does it work?" I asked her, and sat on the bed.

She sighed and looked outside before answering. "It would mean he could call upon the bond, and it would force you to obey him. Bonds like that are ancient witchcraft that no one truly uses anymore because of how violent demons were getting, and that's saying something."

I paced. Vealla stood by the bed watching.

If we were bound until death, would I have to kill him? No. *No*. It didn't matter. I wouldn't take a life unless deserved. Kyler told me not to let the evil win, and I wouldn't.

"This does not change anything."

Vealla turned to me with wide eyes. "But Highness-"

"I need you to trust me. You said yourself, it is only until one of us dies." A plan began rolling around in my head. "Does Kyler know?"

"No, Highness." She shook her head.

"Don't tell him, please."

"We said we would follow you, and we will." She bowed to me then and explained how the coronation would go. "I will see you in an hour, then, Highness."

She bowed her head and walked toward the door.

In only an hour, I'd hold this part of the kingdom in my hand. Ezra was giving me a power I'd use to my advantage. A chance to do more, and it started here, with a red satin dress.

Kyler and I would need to amp up our training sessions. I opened my hand, and that tingling sensation slithered through it as a ball of lightning formed. My hand closed, dispelling the elemental power.

I needed to figure out how to harness it and control it without it controlling me. The power deep in my bones yearned to come out. What held me back?

When I took the dress down, it felt heavy in my hands. The satin slid over my fingers like waves. I laid it on the bed and slipped out of my clothes. In my mind, I pictured my life to be different and filled with people I loved. Instead, it would be full of demons, and my friends would forget me in time. My new family became the only solid piece of hope I held onto. I slid the dress over my body and shifted it a little so it sat perfectly against me.

In the bathroom, I stared at myself in the mirror. Tears swelled in my eyes. I tried to cling to my mortality as much as possible, but Hell kept throwing things at me. I barely took in souls and could feel the weakness inside because of it. Syl's words kept coming back to me, though, and I knew I needed to save them.

I needed to keep pushing forward.

I phased to Kyler, who waited for me. He wore his armor with his sword strapped to his back. His eyes scanned my body, and sadness filled them. I bit my quivering lip and ran a hand over my dress.

"You look like an angel." He said, taking a step closer to me.

"A Princess." I smiled at him, and he mirrored it.

"Are you ready?" He asked.

I moved closer to him and touched his arm. The static I had grown to love tingled between our skin.

"Things are about to change, Kyler; I need you by my side now more than ever." He laid a hand over mine and his other ran over the back of my hair.

"I've been by your side since you walked into the bar. I refuse to leave it now." His words filled my heart with warmth.

"Let's do this," I said with a nod.

Kyler nodded back and then headed inside to tell Ezra and Vealla I was ready. I waited for my sign to make the grand entrance. The doors opened, and I entered the throne room with a deep breath. My heels clicked against the floor with every step, making the only sound. All eyes were on me, but I focused on what stood before me: Ezra holding a black crown.

The room full of demons stood and watched me. Alfonso and Dante stood in the front by the dais. Vealla stood beside Ezra in front of the thrones, her black book in hand. The closer I got to them, the more I wanted to run away.

He would try to control me more than ever if I were bound to him. My throat closed at the thought. There would be no running, no turning back. My fate was sealed when I walked into the bar, yet I wanted to escape it all, if only for a moment.

Kyler stood beside his brother, his eyes never leaving me. He didn't know what was going to happen, and it would crush him. I couldn't deny our feelings for each other.

Not anymore.

Once I stood before them, Vealla began to recite the words in her book. Demon language sounded guttural and aggressive as she spoke. I turned to the room of demons, whose eyes were still on me. Dante gave me a subtle head bow.

Suddenly, thunder cracked through the room, and a black tornado of smoke surrounded by lightning spawned in the walkway. The demons stepped back, getting closer to whatever wall was close by. Tension filled the room as a tall demon with red eyes stood in the middle of the room.

Lucifer.

"Did you really think, dear Ezra, that having a coronation without me would go over well?" He took long strides towards me.

He kept his head held high. Every step he took was one long stride. The British accent and lollipop in his mouth made my head spin. My heart beat at an alarmingly high rate.

The room bowed before him, except me. I stood, staring into his eyes.

"I am sorry it has taken so long for me to meet you, Sapphire. It would seem congratulations are in order. I do hope that, in the future, we will spend more time together. Please continue, Vealla." Lucifer walked past all of us and sat on Ezra's throne, crossing a leg over his knee. A far away stare sat firm on his face.

I tried to feel Lucifer's emotions to no avail. A small smirk crossed his face as he eyed me. Power and dread radiated from him.

Ezra placed the crown on my head, everyone bowed, and for a split second, pride shot through me. Even with Lucifer here, all attention turned to me.

Vealla then began to say the next set of words. From the sly smile on Ezra's face and the pain shooting through Kyler, I knew what she was saying: Ezra and I were bound until death. Lucifer plopped another lolly in his mouth, but his gaze never left me. Curiosity coursed through my veins.

"Your new Princess." Ezra took my hand, and we faced the demons.

Invisible chains wrapped around my body at the binding. Opalescent bindings drifted around my wrist until they snapped into place. Air couldn't escape my lungs, but I smiled. He would not win.

Not now.

Not *ever*.

The room took a second bow. Ezra waved, allowing them to leave, but the princes and Lucifer stayed.

"Congratulations, Highness." Dante bowed his head.

"Thank you, Dante," I smiled, shifting the crown on my head.

"Kyler, you are her high knight now. Orpheus will take over your duties as second." Ezra said in a stern tone. "You will still keep your duties to the legion as Fang leader."

"Yes, Highness." Kyler bowed to him, but his expression stayed flat.

"Now, now. Let me have a word with our esteemed Princess." Lucifer stepped down and leered over me.

With every move he made, everyone moved away from him. Only I stayed in his orbit.

"My lord." Ezra bowed his head.

"You're taller than I expected." I blurted out. An amused smile crossed Lucifer's lips.

"Ah, how little you know of Hell and our traditions, I see. Come visit me whenever you please, Sapphire. It would be my greatest pleasure to have you." Lucifer bowed to me, and in a whirlwind of black smoke, was gone.

Fire wrapped around Ezra's hands. Anger shot from him into me as a volcano erupted. My heartbeat became painful.

"Take her to her room, Kyler," Ezra growled. His lips twitched in the corner.

"No, I don't want to go," I said, shaking my head.

"I demand you go." Ezra's face turned into a sly grin. My feet started moving without me wanting to. The bond.

God's damnit!

Kyler followed behind me to the room upstairs next to Ezra's. I waved my hand and summoned a new outfit. I didn't want to be in that damned dress one more second. I sat on the edge of the bed and laid eyes on Kyler. He stood against the door with his arms crossed.

"He bound himself to you," He said after a long silence. "And Lucifer bowed to you. Ezra will be angrier than ever."

"Yes, he did. It changes nothing. We'll continue to train and work on my powers until he can be dealt with." I crossed one leg over the other. "Ezra won't be a problem for long."

"It changes everything, Fire. If we get caught, it would be a death sentence." He came to my side and knelt at my feet.

"It was always a death sentence." I ran a thumb over his cheek.

"For us both now, before, it was only a death sentence for me." His eyes were darker than usual as he spoke.

"Kyler, I need you to trust me." I pressed my lips to his.

"You might as well rip my heart from my chest and put it in yours. It only beats with you. I am at the mercy of your will, Princess." He pressed his lips to mine, and all my worries fell away.

Chapter Thirty-Four
Kyler

R^{age.}

That was the only emotion that burned deep in my chest. Sapphire was bound to my prick of a brother, and time was running out. Sure, she told me to trust her, and I did. It's Ezra I didn't trust for shit. The bond took, and he knew it. If Sapphire had any inclination of how bad it could be, she didn't let on.

My arms were crossed over my chest as I leaned against the wall. As guards roamed, they would bow their heads to me and move on. I took deep breaths, hoping the anger would subside with no luck.

"Fang leader," Amdis came up to my post outside Fire's room. "Ezra is looking for you. Silas requests an audience."

"Who will guard her?" I nudged my chin toward the door.

He just stripped my title of second to watch her, now he's pulling me away? I balled my hands into fists. I was sick of his fucking games.

"I will." Orpheus phased into the hallway as if on cue.

"You need a bell or something, man." I shook my head.

"It would take away the mystery. Go, she'll be fine."

"I owe you a drink or something, brother." I tapped his shoulder with my palm, and he shook his head.

"Nah, it's for our princess." Orpheus bowed his head.

I pushed the bedroom door open to see Fire staring out the window. Her black hair hid in a bun under her crown. She held the picture of her friends in her hand. When she turned to me, her hazel eyes puffed with red lines. Before I could say anything, Orpheus stepped into the room beside me.

"Fire, I have to go do something with Ezra, but Orpheus will stay with you, alright?"

She looks so worn out. Ezra is taking too much from her. Orpheus murmured in my head. I wasn't sure if he meant to say it over our vampire connection or not.

"Orpheus, you're a good friend." She gave him a light smile, and he nodded. "Don't be gone too long, my knight."

The way her eyes lit up when she called me her knight gave me a slight hope that things would be okay.

With Orpheus on duty, I took off down the hall to Ezra's room. I could hear the smoke coming out of his ears from anywhere. When I opened the door, he paced in front of a window, vein twitching in his neck.

"Silas wishes to see me. You will guard us at his home. He requests only you." Ezra turned to me. I simply bowed my head.

Since Silas was our alpha, there was little room to argue. How he's managed to live since creation, I'll never know.

Aside from the true alpha of the werewolves, all the others had died or been killed off.

We phased to Silas' home, and I instantly became nauseous, scrunching my face. The smell of sex and cigarettes filled the air of his den. Underneath it, though, ancient evil lazed. Vampires of every kind hung on furniture, making out, some mid sexual encounter. Silas sat on a black couch in the back of the room. Only in boxers, with a cigarette in his hand.

Fucking pretentious prick.

He and Ezra were made for each other.

"Ezra, Kyler. Come, I wish to discuss something." Silas jumped from his spot and led us into his room.

I grunted at the array of sex toys lying on his bed for everyone to see. For a split second, I imagined using a toy on Sapphire and shook my head. Now was not the time. The image of her curvaceous frame in my bare hands lingered in my mind.

"What is it, alpha?" Ezra asked, instantly helping me go soft.

"Kyler, it is you that I require." Silas turned to me, taking a puff of his cigarette.

He walked over to his bed and sat down. He bent forward slightly, and a coy grin crossed his face.

"Me?"

"There is a vampire I need dealt with. Ezra is merely here to keep me company. I cannot wait to hear all about your new plaything, Prince. Oh, the ways I would make Sapphire squirm for me." Silas' words rolled off his tongue and into the pit of my stomach.

Ancient magic flowed through his veins. Ancient and reverent. I couldn't kill him.

But fuck did I want to.

"Dealt with, sir?" I asked, already knowing the answer.

"Yes. He needs to die. I am sick of him sleeping with my woman. His name is Jones. Oh, and Kyler? Because I know every good dog needs a treat, do this for me, and I will release one of my mortal cattle. I know how much you love humans."

More blood. That's all they craved. To carve me into a killing machine that's been used for hundreds of years. He played on my urge to do better. No matter how many lives I saved, it would never make up for the permanent stain of blood on my hands.

"Okay." I left without another word.

The house I arrived at seemed abandoned. The windows were falling down, parts of the roof were missing, and the stairs creaked with every step. When I pushed open the door, a breeze bellowed out. Cobwebs lined the walls. No one could be living here.

"Hello?" I called.

Only ghosts whispered back.

I walked around the house, looking for this dude. The living room had blankets covering furniture. Upstairs, a bathroom had no tub or sink. The bedrooms were a mix of spiders and shadows. Standing in the kitchen, I ran a hand over my face. Another game. That's all this had been. A mission to send me away to talk about whatever they wanted. I wasn't actually needed.

My eyes burned. Worthlessness crept inside of me.

I'm a dog.

Laughter soon bounced off the walls. I peered up to see Ezra and Silas. They stood by the archway to the living room, both dressed in fine suits.

There I was in my armor and angry. Angrier than I had ever been. The laughter continued to ring in my ears.

"I told you, he does everything you tell him to! *Everything.*" Ezra's laugh shook me.

I took one deep breath, my chest rising and falling. My hand gripped the hilt of my sword. He wanted to embarrass me. Childhood games played by elders. Silas whipped his back from laughing so hard.

My entire core shook with anger. My vision blurred with fury.

"You can go back to guard duty. You're a good sport." Silas waved me off.

There was only one way my torture could end.

With Fire.

Chapter Thirty-Five

Sapphire

I stared out the window, watching the black clouds float across the sky. The silence meant Ezra could not terrorize me, due to his not being here. Orpheus had been outside my door for hours. I wondered where Ezra made Kyler go. The creaking of the door to my room took my gaze from the window. He walked in and shut the door. His eyes were puffy and red.

"Kyler? What's wrong?" I darted to him and held his face in my hands.

"There's somewhere I want to take you. I only have a few good things in my life, especially you. Right now I need...I need hope. Please let me take you somewhere quiet." He said, but his eyes didn't meet mine.

For the first time in a while, I opened myself up to feel his emotions. A tear fell down my face. Guilt. Worthlessness. Self-hate. All of it hit me like a truck. Something happened to him, and I couldn't let it go.

"Kyler, what happened?" I demanded this time.

"Please, Fire. Let's get out of here first." His voice cracked, and his eyes finally met mine.

My heart broke. He was begging me.

"Okay, Kyler. Whisk me away." I wrapped my arms around his neck.

He buried his head against my shoulder and phased. We stood before a dark wooden cabin. A small porch wrapped around the front and back. The cabin's bottom floor rested just above the body of water it rested against. Wooden stairs to the side led down a hill to a small boat ramp. Flowers on vines covered the outside of the building. The beauty touched me as I placed a hand over my mouth.

"Kyler, what is this place?" I asked.

A light breeze rustled the leaves in the trees. He released his grip on me, and his eyes scanned the scenery before us.

"My mother's hiding spot. When my father was in one of his moods, we would come here for a few days." He took me by the hand and led me down to the water.

He sat criss-cross on the floating wood dock, and I joined him. Taking off my shoes, I dipped my feet into the water. The moon reflected against it, the light moving in ripples. Little fish swam around and jumped out of the water occasionally. Crickets chirped off in the distance.

"You hid here? Why?" I kicked my feet back and forth.

Kyler took a deep breath, "My dad used to beat me. Everyday. I never understood why. He loved my mom unconditionally, but Ezra was his golden child. He could do no wrong. It didn't matter how well I could handle a sword or how little help I needed blending into the mortal realm to do his bidding. I was never good enough." He looked out at the moon, his voice breaking.

"What'd your father and Ezra have you do?" I turned to look at him, but his gaze was focused far away from where we sat.

"I don't want you to look at me differently if I tell you. You're the only person in my life who doesn't take more than I can give. You don't look at me like I'm beneath you. I don't want to lose that."

After pulling his hands into mine, he turned towards me. A bird chirped off in the distance, and the sound of crickets echoed around us.

"I'd never treat you differently, Kyler. In the short time I've known you, you've helped me more than anyone. Learning I've been a demon my entire life, and knowing I have parents in a different time, has taken a piece of me. Yet, when I look at you, that piece isn't missing. It's with you."

He pulled me into his lap in one quick motion, and our lips met. I held his face in my hands and kissed him as if it would be our last. Static shot through me in a way that made my entire body fill with static. His warm tears slid down my face. I didn't know what happened, but I did know it would never happen again.

Or I'd kill someone.

"My father had me infiltrate the mortals often. He would ask me to find one who would do well as a spy for him in Hell. Sometimes he'd come to the mortal world and ask me to kill, for the sake of watching me take a life. If I ever disobeyed him, he would threaten to torture Zariah." Kyler spoke, but his eyes saw through me. Pain slammed into me, taking my breath for a moment.

"Did he ever?" I asked. I didn't want to upset Kyler, but I needed to know.

"Only once. My father took him from his bed one night, and I could hear his screams in the castle. When I found him, he was covered in whip marks on his back. He still has the scars. I vowed never to let that happen again."

I pressed my forehead to his.

"I've had to burn dying humans to cover our existence. Kill mortals for someone else's thrill. Run errands that anyone could do; that was embarrassing for my station."

The more he spoke, the faster my heart beat. Pain radiated off of him and into me. I didn't care. Not if it meant he hurt even a fraction less.

"Ezra is no better. He's beaten Zariah, too, just to get to me. I have so much blood on my hands, Sapphire. It never goes away. I've tried to clean myself of the evil, but I will always be a demon. I'll always be a killer."

His tears continued to fall. His pain ached in my chest. I tried my best to bear the weight for him, while he let his world crumble into my arms, I held his head against my chest.

"Kyler, I don't see you differently. You are a piece of me. Nothing will change that." I said, and his grip on my hips tightened.

"The fear stays inside of me." Kyler pulled away and looked me in the eyes.

"Let's do this scared then, together. You'll never be alone again. We need to make a plan. He has to die." At that moment, nothing else mattered.

Ezra's reign of terror would end.

"Fire, no. You are good and light, and killing him would go against everything you've been fighting so hard to protect." He argued.

"You're wrong, Kyler. I vowed to protect Hell and those who can't protect themselves. You may not be able to take Ezra's life, but I can. Especially knowing who he is now. He may not have blood on his hands physically, but everyone who does, because of him, deserves better. No more games."

Kyler's eyes met mine. The tears stopped flowing, and he shifted slightly under me. His blue eyes, red from the tears, changed to black. He took in a deep breath before kissing my lips. His hand wrapped in my hair, and he held me against his body. I felt his chest rise and fall against me in a slow rhythm.

"You need more training, and then we'll make a plan, not a moment sooner. We'll only have one shot, and I won't risk your life." Kyler spoke with more determination now. The spark in his eyes returned. I'd protect him with my life.

"Then it's a plan, to make a plan." I smiled at him.

"My mom used to sit out here and read while I swam as a child. When I got older, we still came here, but she and I would sit by the fireplace and play chess." Kyler pushed a stray hair from my face.

"Are you any good?" I asked.

"Have you seen how good I am with my hands?" He waggled his eyebrows, and I laughed.

"You're so arrogant sometimes," I said with a shake of my head.

"And yet, the hottest demon in all of Hell is sitting on my lap." He said with a wide grin.

"You've been by my side since I got to Hell. What did you do before becoming my keeper?" I wrapped my arms around his neck, enjoying our closeness.

For the first time, it genuinely felt safe to be in his arms. The weight of everything lifted, and we could just be. It wouldn't last, but for this brief time, I'd absorb every lingering moment.

"I spent a lot of time with Zariah when I was not at Ezra's beck and call. He and I love to cause trouble, as you heard." A wide smile crossed his lips. "I also used to visit my mom's grave more often, but since you appeared at the bar..." Kyler stopped talking then. I tilted my head.

"What?"

"Nothing, nothing. You just gave me a reason to want to be around." His thumb brushed my cheek.

"I'm glad," I smiled. "What about when you aren't by my side now?"

"I have been spending a lot of time doing Ezra's dirty work and taking care of my men. Fang leader things." He grunted and ran a hand over my arm.

"Kyler, how does being Lucifer work? He is not the original, Ezra told me. If I take over Hell, I would have to take his life, wouldn't I?"

He pondered the thought for a moment, his eyes never leaving mine. The serenity around us made talking about killing almost peaceful. This might not be who I expected to be. Yet, now, I didn't hate who I became.

"Yes. You will. Whoever holds his soul holds his power. However, Lucifer's soul gets weaker with every transition. I hope you're the last one Hell ever has. It breaks into war every time someone tries to take over. The last one had been especially bad. Hell lost half of its demons. Brothers killed brothers. It was not just a move for Lucifer, but a move to change Hell." Kyler shifted under me and pulled me closer to him.

"Changing Hell, how?"

"Demons wanted more voice, more chance at living peacefully. Having one king is fine, but we want to be heard." He bit the corner of his lip.

"And you fought in the war?"

"I did. I led the army, while Ezra sat on his throne in the fortified castle. I killed demons I had known my entire life so he could have the comfort of controlling a legion that hates him."

Kyler's gaze shifted toward the cabin, and he stood with urgency, placing me on my feet beside him.

"What is it?" I asked, my eyes scanning the woods surrounding us. Static filled the air, and I didn't need him to answer.

Ezra was coming.

I found a tall tree hidden further in the woods and phased behind it after grabbing my shoes. Looking past the woods, I could see Ezra walking down the ramp to Kyler.

"Where is she?" Ezra flared his nostrils and snarled.

"I do not know, brother. Try the library in the castle." Kyler said with a shrug.

"You are a fucking liar," Ezra grabbed Kyler's shirt by the collar. "I find you here, at your whore mother's cabin, alone? And I am supposed to believe you left Sapphire all alone with no guard?"

"Call my mother a whore one more time, brother. I dare you." Kyler spat at Ezra's feet.

Ezra landed a punch against Kyle's nose. I covered my mouth to stifle the noise. Kyler let out a laugh and wiped the blood from his lip.

"You are lucky I need you alive." Ezra let go of Kyler and backed away a step.

"As I said, check the *library*," Kyler said, the word sharper than the others.

Reluctantly, I phased away to the castle library. Once there, I opened a book and acted as if I were reading it. I lay on the couch, looking as relaxed as possible. Ezra's lightning formed in front of me, and distaste filled his features.

"You have been here since I left?" He growled.

"Yes?" I asked, laying the book down beside me.

"Do not lie to me, swear on our bond!" Ezra demanded, tapping his foot.

"I swear, I've been here since you left!"

The cabin that is.

Ezra said nothing else. He stormed out, slamming the door behind him.

I didn't know I could lie like that, even with his call upon our stupid bond. I hoped that would make the coming storm much easier to handle.

More importantly, I hoped Kyler knew how much he meant to me. Not even the blood on his hands would scare me away.

I looked at my palms, and the reminder of the life I took stung. He wasn't alone, even in killing.

Chapter Thirty-Six

Sapphire

When my eyes opened, the sight before me took me back. I circled to see nothing but a vastness of white. Where I stood had no doors or walls, nor sky or ground. My body felt light, being surrounded by the emptiness, and all the pain and sorrow I had been holding in felt nonexistent.

"Ah, there's my beautiful goddess of power." A deep voice echoed in my ears. The figure of a man made his way towards me.

"Who are you? Where am I?" I asked as the figure got closer.

"This," He gestured around us, "will make sense when the time is right. I am Zane." The figure now appeared in my view. He was tall, with thick muscles all around his body. He wore a black leather vest and black skinny jeans. His long brown hair was an undercut and tied in a small knot, while most of his hair lay below his shoulders. Tattoos covered his arms.

Zane.

"Am I dead?" I asked. He let out a boisterous laugh that shook me to my core.

"No, my sweet jewel, you are not dead. I wanted to give you a message, one that was only safe to give in your mind." Zane spoke as if we were familiar. He stood closer to me, and a warmth crawled along my skin.

"A message?"

"Yes. I need you to know that everything will make sense when the time comes. For now, remember that you are powerful, more so than anyone could imagine. Do not let that lowlife vampire take one ounce of who you are, mighty Queen." His words slid into my head like velvet. My body tingled from his presence.

"Are you the angel my mother saw?" Her last words to me sat in my mind.

An angel told me he would guide you when the time was right.

"Something like that, my jewel, something like that. You need to wake up now; we would not want poor Kyler to think you are dead in your sleep." Zane ran a smooth hand down my arm, and electricity tingled my every bone.

"Zane, wait!"

"Yes?" He raised an eyebrow at me.

"Can I do it? Can I rule Hell?"

Zane paused for a moment and studied me. His eyes roamed my body before he stepped closer and pulled me against his chest. His hand lifted my chin so our eyes could meet. My entire body felt like it lit on fire.

"You will be a goddess amongst them all."

He pressed his lips to mine, and something inside me ignited. My power roared to life, and fire and lightning swirled around our bodies.

"Until we can meet again, my beautiful jewel."

I woke up with a startle. My body had been covered in sweat. After sliding out of the covers, I looked around. My room had an eerie quietness to it. A slight tingle remained in my body.

That was an intense dream.

Kyler sat by the door when he noticed I woke up. He pushed himself off the floor with his arm and stood.

"He didn't touch you again, did he?" Kyler's growl surprised me.

"No. Not this time." Kyler and I walked towards each other, and he pulled me into his embrace.

He didn't have his armor on. The clothes on his back were his typical black shirt and ripped jeans. The warmth from his skin radiated off him and slid along my body. The surge of life he gave me with every touch brought me back to a place of happiness. A place I longed for.

"Let's go train. I sent word to Dante that Ezra needed a distraction. I don't think we have much more time before he tries to harm you in irreparable ways. I can not live with the idea of not training you enough. You are the light to my darkness; without you, I don't think I could survive." Kyler's soft murmur brushed against my hair.

My body ignited at his words. Yet, what I clung to was Ezra hurting me. It would be a matter of time before he tried.

I can be a goddess amongst them.

The words stumbled through my mind.

I could do this.

"Take me away, my knight." I looked up and met his eyes. A warmth filled them as he phased us to the arena.

The night sky around us thickened with clouds. To my surprise, Orpheus was sitting on a bench, cleaning a sword. He looked our way and bowed his head to me.

"Highness, Brother." He said.

"Want to make good on your offer to train with me, Orph?" I asked.

He seemed to pop up any time I needed him around.

"Of course, highness." He smiled and stood, twirling his sword around with ease. I gulped.

Kyler handed me a sword and took his own. We moved to the middle of the arena and began our dance. The swords clashed into the night. Orpheus' sword went low, and Kylers went high, tripping me into the sand, and getting a mouthful. I stood and spit it out, wiping my tongue off. The two of them burst into laughter.

"Sure, make fun of the girl who's been training for five minutes." I pouted.

"Sorry, Highness," Orpheus said, still laughing.

"Let's go again," I said, holding up my sword.

Our swords hit and smacked hard while we shuffled our feet in the sand. I swung hard and caught Kyler off guard, tripping him. A giggle echoed, and his eyes shot to me. I turned and pretended to look elsewhere, causing Orpheus to laugh. Even with the reason for training lingering over our heads, Kyler made me smile.

Orpheus moved swiftly over the terrain. He never lost focus as our swords continued to slam against one another. He and Kyler both aimed for me, and I jumped out of the way, sliding back.

We fought for what felt like hours. My muscles began to ache all over. No amount of training felt like enough, though. I put my sword pointy side down and took a few deep breaths.

"I should get going, Highness. I need my beauty rest." Orpheus gave an exaggerated yawn and stretch.

"Hey Orpheus, thank you for having my back." I smiled at him.

"Always, Highness." He bowed and phased away.

Kyler and I went back to practicing with the swords. Every so often, Kyler would catch me, and I'd trip, or he'd accidentally cut my arms or legs. Aside from needing new clothes, it didn't matter. I had to practice till my bones couldn't handle the fatigue.

"This is where you have been." Ezra's voice boomed as a ring of lightning formed around him. His gaze shifted from Kyler to me, to the sword in my hand. My smile instantly faded, and my heart began to race.

"I can explain, brother." Kyler took a step closer to me.

"I do not want to hear a word from you, and it is *Highness*. My father may have slept with your whore mother, but do not mistake that to mean anything to me. I am your

Prince." Ezra said with harshness. Something flickered in Kyler's eyes, and he shifted. I could feel his own anger rise, but ultimately, he bowed to his brother.

"Highness," I interjected, "My knight is simply helping me train my power. Is that not what you want?" I stepped closer to Ezra and placed a hand on his crossed arms. The movement sent a different kind of chill down my spine.

He took a deep breath before responding. "Very well. If you insist on training, then I will do it myself."

Kyler hesitated before he handed Ezra his sword and stepped to the side of the arena. My grip on the sword tightened. Ezra's black eyes watched the motion before he stepped forward.

I expected him to swing his sword hard. Instead, he threw a fireball at me. It hit me square in the shoulder, causing me to flinch. I looked at the burn and then at him.

Was this another fight to teach me? Or punishment for leaving the castle when he thought I couldn't?

Ezra's fireballs continued to come at me fast and hard. His sword also came at me. I used my sword to fight them off, shifting around the arena. Blast hit me over and over. I tried to dodge as much as I could. His black eyes followed my every move. With the swing of his sword, another fireball came my way. Ezra drilled into me.

As we moved around, the sand kicked up in our wake. I'd pull back ever so slightly when he pushed forward. He stuck his sword out at the right moment. I tried to avoid a fireball and tripped, landing on my hands and knees. The sand dug into my skin, causing a sting of pain briefly before I healed.

I panted and looked down at the ground. It became obvious he was trying to break me. Wiping my face, a layer of dirt covered my hand. Blood-stained sand surrounded me.

Kyler went to step closer, but I put my hand up. I would not back down from Ezra. It was evident I'd have to control myself and show him my real place, and that wouldn't be a timid princess sitting on the sidelines. Once my breathing calmed, I stood up and retook the position.

I summoned a second sword and met Ezra's eyes. A flare of anger came at me in the form of multiple fireballs. As I fought him off, exhaustion entered my bones. My muscles began to buckle with my movements. My body fatigued, something I never expected to be a problem as a demon. I needed more souls than I took in, but I refused to have that on my conscience.

Kyler's worried eyes met mine for a moment before I began to swing my sword again. My feet crossed in an X pattern while dodging another fireball. Ezra's eyes followed my footwork—a grin formed on the corner of his mouth. I shielded my face from his sword as it came down. A fireball then came at my foot, throwing me off. I tripped forward, and Ezra's sword slid into my lower left rib cage. My eyes shifted down, then back at Ezra, who grinned fiercely.

Everything came to a screeching halt. My body shook intensely, not from pain, but anger. I balled my fists, and fire shot out in every direction from me.

"That's enough, Ezra! She is going to need a—"

Both of them shifted their gaze to me.

I pulled the sword from my body and watched as the skin closed and healed before the sword was even fully out. Gripping the sword, I glared at Ezra.

Kyler placed a hand on my shoulder, and he said something to me, but I did not hear it. The world was fading into the background. A ringing filled my ears. Ezra stabbed me and smiled. Did he know I wouldn't die? My breathing quickened, and fury took over. My eyes shot to the vampire Prince. The man I once adored vanished, and this monster took his place.

Tears began to stream from my eyes. Kyler took a step closer. I continued to shake, and fire wrapped around me. My emotions and power ran wild with my rage.

Ezra stood there with that smug look.

"You stabbed me." My voice shook.

"You healed instantaneously," Ezra said callously with a shrug. My anger continued to rise.

"You. Stabbed. Me."

"Yes, yes, and now we know how quickly you can heal." Ezra rolled his eyes before turning away from me.

"You stabbed me!" I yelled this time, and lightning shot out, hitting Ezra.

He came up to me fast, fingers wrapping around my neck. His grip was tight, and the look in his eyes was menacing. Kyler stepped closer to us with his grip on his sword. I knew things would get ugly if Ezra did much more.

"You are lucky I found you. If anyone knew what you were, they would be far worse than me. Be thankful and shut up," he released my neck. "Now go home!"

My eyes darted between the brothers. There was only one way out of this.

"You will regret ever trying to lock me away, Ezra." I grabbed Kyler's hand and let my butterflies take us away before Ezra could use the bond against me.

The games were over; it was time to say hello to the King of Hell.

Chapter Thirty-Seven

Sapphire

"Ah, Sapphire. You have decided to come to your senses, I see." Lucifer leaned against a black skeleton horse.

"I'm just here for the pancakes." I walked over and touched the horse's face.

Real bones, a Hell horse. It neighed and bobbed its nose into my hand. Lucifer had a sly grin on his face. We stood on white sand against an endless black beach. Lucifer had a new lollipop in his mouth. How did he not get cavities? Kyler bowed at his feet, but I looked out at the water.

"Pancakes? You do realize who you are talking to?" Lucifer rubbed the furrow of his brow and sighed.

"How could I forget? You interrupted my coronation." I pointed out. I ran my hand over the horse's mane. Silky hair slid below my fingers as the horse gave another calming neigh.

"If anybody came to my realm, especially unannounced, they would be dead." He wrapped a hand around my neck and studied my face. Flames rose from Lucifer's eyes.

"Well then, I guess it's a good thing I'm not just anybody. Might I point out, you did invite me."I said with a snarky voice.

"Clever girl. Ezra has come here multiple times to proclaim you as his. Rather annoying. He's lucky I did not have his head for trying to crown you, without me present. Would you like some tea?" He let go of my neck, still studying me.

Did the king of Hell ask me for tea?

I blinked at him for a second.

"Always knew the Prime Minister of Hell would ask me for tea." I snickered again.

"You have got spunk. I like that. Let us go back to my castle and chat. I know you have questions." He smirked, and my eyes rolled. "Did you have to bring the bodyguard, though?" Lucifer pointed his lollipop at Kyler.

"He is my protector," I said, glancing toward my knight.

"Very well, but he is walking." Lucifer popped a new lollipop into his mouth- cherry this time- and jumped on the horse.

I grabbed his extended hand, and he lifted me onto the horse. I sat in front of Lucifer while he kept a hand on my hip. As we took off, I watched as we sped past the beach. I remembered it from Ezra's elaborate map. The black water clashed against white sand, glistening in the light. The sky's pinkish red filled dark clouds. Lightning occasionally bounced between them. Even a cool breeze hit my face as we rode. The Realm of Death appeared more magical than I could believe. If my memory served me right, we'd ride north to Lucifer's castle. Kyler zipped next to us with his vampiric speed, staying close the entire time.

We eventually arrived at a beautiful black castle. The tall stone walls had four different towers. Guards lined the walkway between them. Battlements encompassed every roof, and vibrant stained-glass panes formed most of the castle's windows.

Lucifer snapped his fingers, causing a drawbridge to come down. The horse trotted through the gates. Kyler came to a slower pace beside us. As we passed by, all the demons and similar beings backed away and bowed.

Here, Lucifer had buildings like townhouses, market stands on the street, and black grass everywhere. The horses' hooves clicked on the brick pathway. A faint aroma of fresh meat filled my nostrils. Children laughed and ran around in the distance. A few demons whispered as we strode by.

Once we got to the stables, Lucifer swiftly got off the horse and grabbed my hips, picking me up with little effort. He was strong and handsome, not the scary thing I had pictured. His eyes never left mine while wrapping the horse's reins on a wooden post. Kyler crossed his arms over his chest at the sight.

"Do not worry about the whispers." Lucifer groaned a little. "Come," he took my hand and led us through the castle doors.

My jaw dropped, and I couldn't believe what I saw. The doors opened up to a heart-shaped staircase with gold rails and marble steps. A beautiful oak wood floor rests under our feet, and golden chandeliers hang throughout.

Lucifer guided us over and allowed me to go up first. At the top of the stairs, a long hallway came into view. Lucifer took us to the black double doors at the end. He waved his hand, and the doors swung open. Yet another unexpected scene amazed me. My face must have given away my awe, as Lucifer laughed at my reaction.

His large black bed sat in the middle of the room. A gigantic TV had been mounted on the wall. Floating shelves held every gaming system you could think of. Blood red walls showcased swords and banners with his crest. My jaw hit the floor.

As I walked into the room, Lucy snapped his fingers, and I realized he had changed my clothes. Thanks to his magic, I now wore a black and red lace-up corset and a pair of black skinny jeans. Lucifer watched me as I admired myself in the mirror by the closet door.

"Bloody clothes do not suit you. You are exceptional, Sapphire. I can feel the power radiating off you. This necklace will help you focus your powers. You are a pure-blooded soul eater. One of one." Lucifer slid a red heart necklace around my neck. Looking at it in the mirror, I realized it had a burning flame. "When you absorb a soul, a small piece will be here, just in case. If you smash it, the souls will flow out." Lucifer popped another Lollipop into his mouth. "Each Lucifer inherited it, keeping it safe, until the lost princess appeared, and here you are." He gestured a hand toward me.

"You killed the last Lucifer. How did you know about this?" I raised an eyebrow.

"His previous second told me before I killed him too." Lucifer shrugged. A small tingle shot down my body.

"Lucy, I don't understand. Why are you telling me any of this?"

I glanced at him as he sat with one leg over the other. His arm stretched over the back of his chair. Kyler came back over to my side. The hilt of his sword stood out to me, noticing the new sapphire sitting on it.

"I am sorry, did you just call me Lucy?" Lucifer raised an eyebrow as an amused smile crossed his face again. "You realize I am the most feared thing in all of Hell?"

"Only because no one knows what I can do yet." I gave him a flattering smile.

"Touché. I am telling you this because I know more about you than most. Every Lucifer since the beginning of time knows you. I know you will want my throne, but I think we can come to a better arrangement. I want you to join me. Sit by my side for a few days and see if you want to rule with me. I am well aware Ezra has laid claim to you, but I couldn't care less. He has been plotting to kill me since the moment I took the throne." He said with a hint of annoyance in his voice.

"He will come looking for her, Majesty," Kyler took a step forward and bowed his head.

"It will be dealt with when the time comes. Let me bring you to my library. I have a book with information you might seek. Learn more about who you are, and tomorrow, you can sit on the throne by my side." Lucifer popped up from his seat and walked out of the room.

Kyler and I followed behind as he descended the stairs and went down the right hallway. He waved his hand, and thick brown double doors creaked open. His library was two stories tall, with railings lining the walkway to the second floor of books. Lucifer walked up one of the spiral stairs and found the book he was looking for. He jumped over the railing and landed before us, shaking the room.

"Here, this should answer most of the questions you have." He handed me a thin book with frail bindings. "You may take the first door on the left in the hall upstairs. We have already prepared your room; I expected Ezra to anger you eventually. I have some business elsewhere, but consider my castle yours while I am away." Lucy put a new lollipop in his mouth and waved as he disappeared.

I looked down at the black leather book in my hand. Did it have the answer I so desperately wanted?

Can it tell me who I am?

Chapter Thirty-Eight

Sapphire

Kyler and I sat down on the bed in the room Lucifer had made for me. I flipped open the book, scanning the handwritten notes covering the pages. The first few chapters talked about the link between soul eaters' powers and the strength of the souls they consume. The stronger the soul we took in, the stronger we would feel.

One of the handwritten notes said:

We do not consume powers of souls unless it comes from Lucifer or a higher entity.

-Apollyon.

What was a higher entity than Lucifer, aside from the Gods?

I stared at the name written beside the note. Flutters danced in my chest.

Apollyon.

The man mother mentioned in her journal. The second king to Hell. His name held a power over me that I couldn't explain.

The rest of the book was vague. It mentioned we have two or three elemental powers, the ability to absorb souls, and a select few in the alpha bloodline who can move things with their minds.

Apollyon wrote another note:

Alpha line can have up to four elementals.

Kyler read over my shoulder. His eyes scanned the page at lightning speed. A vampire power I currently felt jealous of. The last page of the book only had handwritten notes.

Soul-eaters can not have children. I don't know if this applies to the girl. She is the only one in existence. We must hide her in time.

- Apollyon.

The soul-eater necklace was given to me by Lucifer's previous wife. She claims to help pureblood in a way she could as a mother.

- Drax

The pureblood is favored by the Gods. Her angel protector hides amongst us. He thought no one could see when he extended his wings, but I did. The rumors of time are true. She is the savior.

-Alberta

I am the only soul-eater left. The pureblood never showed; she hides amongst the stars. If she reads this: Only you can save us all from the gallows. May the Gods favor you more than they ever did us.

- Scarlett.

The last page held a note I stared at for a long time. My hands began to shake. An unmistakable message from Lilith.

Sapphire, I don't know when you will see this book, or if you ever will. I need you to know something important. Read these words out loud, and a truth will be revealed to you.

Your mother.

Lilith.

I looked at the scribbles on the bottom of the page. Ancient demon language that I didn't understand stared at me. I ran my fingers over the words. A spark ignited in me. Whatever it said, Lilith wanted me to read it. Could this lead to answers to my past?

I took a breath and read the words out loud.

Kyler tried to speak, but I couldn't hear a word. The world in front of me shifted and contorted until I stood somewhere I had never seen before. Looking around, I was surrounded by a garden of black roses. The reds in the sky told me I was somewhere in Hell. A gray brick patio rest under my feet, and stairs led down into the garden. I turned around to see a black castle towering behind me.

"Apollyon, I can't do this. I can't give her up."

A voice pulled me to a woman with long black hair who held a baby tightly in her arms. Tears rolled down her cheeks.

"Lilith," He placed a hand on the baby's forehead, gently rubbing it with a thumb. "Sapphire will never be safe here. He will come for her. If she goes, the angel can watch her. Maybe she can do for Hell what we never could. She can bring on a golden age. Love demons with a passion and not shun them as Sameal had." Apollyon's eyes had bags under them. He looked tired, wary even.

I watched as Lilith's legs shook below her. The tears in her eyes made my own burn. In real time, I watched them choose to give me up, and my heart ached. Apollyon and Lilith had a pain in their eyes.

"She's our daughter. She shouldn't even exist! She was a gift from the Gods, only for them to take her away again!" Lilith wailed into the sky.

Apollyon placed his forehead against hers and held them. A tear slid down my cheek. Anna and Owen loved me with all they could. Lilith and Apollyon made an impossible choice over their love for me. I balled my hands at my sides. Two sets of parents I've lost to this life.

"Sapphire will know who she really is, someday, somehow, she will know. She will be loved across the ends of time. But we must let her go." Apollyon's voice cracked as he spoke.

I touched my face, my own tears flowing. My parents had to let me go. Who was the he coming for me? What was so great an evil that they had to send me to a different time?

"Okay. Pray to Axel. I'm ready." Lilith sighed and looked down at the baby with a sad smile.

Axel. I remembered the name from the book Vealla let me have. He is the God of time. The evil coming for me was so powerful, the Gods agreed to keep me safe. I swallowed at the thought.

Apollyon nodded and walked away. Lilith sat down in the grass and began to whisper demon language to the baby. The spell that kept me locked away.

"Sapphire, I know you are watching. My spell worked. I can't see you, but I feel you. I feel your power." She turned and looked exactly where I stood.

"Lilith? Lilith, I'm here." I cried.

"I'm sorry, but I could only make the spell powerful enough for you to see and hear me, not the other way around. Listen, my sweet daughter, no matter where you are, when you are, or who you are, Apollyon and I love you. Evil is coming, but you are strong. Stronger than even the original Lucifer. You were never meant to exist. I may never find out why the Gods gave you to me, only to take you away. But I promise, we will meet. One way or another, I will find a way to you. Remember who you are. Daughter of Lilith and Apollyon. Princess of Hell. Gift of the Gods." Lilith's tears came again as she kissed baby me's head.

"Lilith! Lilith, please, I don't understand! What evil? Who is it?"

The world blurred until I sat next to Kyler, in my own time. I touched my face to find dry cheeks. The tears I had cried never happened. My ears rang.

"Fire, Fire!" Kyler shouted, shaking my shoulders.

I turned and looked at him, dazed and confused. "I'm still here?"

"Yes? Are you okay? You started staring off, and then your eyes turned white. I kept talking, but it was like you were in another world." Kyler patted my cheeks a few times.

"I'm okay, Kyler. I'm fine." I touched his cheek and gave him a soft smile.

"Fire, what happened? What did you see?" He held my wrist, checking for a pulse. I looked at his chest, rapidly rising and falling.

"I know who I am now."

Chapter Thirty-Nine

Sapphire

The next day, I wandered through Lucifer's castle, but felt like a ghost. I stopped in the middle of the hallway and leaned my head back against the wall. No matter how hard I tried to focus on the world around me, I couldn't. Only Lilith's words rang in my mind.

I'm a gift from the Gods.

With a deep breath, I continued through the halls. I had to come back to reality. Whatever was coming, I had to be ready.

The throne caught my eye as I walked between the staircase into the throne room. Skull and bones made out the main part of the seat, with sword hilts as legs. Lucifer sat with his legs extended out with yet another lollipop in his mouth. Kyler followed behind me, and we made our way to the bottom of the dais. Lucy pulled the lollipop out of his mouth and twirled it in his hand, meeting my gaze.

"If you are going to stay, you might as well be comfortable." Lucy gave a half-shrug as he waved a flat hand to the duplicate throne next to his.

"Thank you, Lucifer." I bowed to him.

He gave a slight bow of his head. I took my place beside him and admired the room around us. Marble columns lined the sides, and a black carpet led to the dias.

I am a Princess of Hell.

Kyler's hand touched my shoulder, and I turned to see his face. The weight of this seat meant more somehow. It was always meant to be mine.

"I am going to summon the other Princes and the Princess, along with my two officials. You will be seeing them a lot if you choose to stay. Ezra included." Lucifer said in a whisper.

I gripped the arm of the throne and took a deep breath. Ezra would not be stupid enough to try to hurt me in a room full of people, let alone Lucifer. The last thing I needed now was Ezra making trouble.

"I have four Knights of Death as well. Asmodus, Alaric, Belial, and Drexon, but you won't meet them. They are…hidden." He added, studying my face.

I inhaled slowly, "Okay, I'm ready."

Lucifer waved his hand, and a few familiar faces appeared before us. Dante, Vealla, and Alfonso stood to the left. Ezra stood in the middle, meeting my gaze, but his face stayed flat. Beside him was a female with a bob cut.

With her lingered a demon who wore red demon armor, aside from the helmet he held at his side. His broad shoulders showcased his firm build. He did not have wings, yet he still had curved horns like Dante. Everyone bowed to us before Ezra opened his mouth.

"I see you are getting comfortable, Princess." His cool voice reminded me of when we first met at the bar. The mask hides who his true self is. I gritted my teeth.

"Oh, yes, you may never see me again." I cooed and leaned my chin on my hand.

"She will stay with me until she decides to leave. She is the key to our golden age of Hell, yes?" Lucifer questioned Ezra.

"Of course, Sire," Ezra said through his teeth.

"This is Esme, a powerful witch, and Blade, my strongest demon warrior." Lucifer pointed to the girl with the bob cut and then the demon beside her.

"Hello to you both." I gave a small smile.

Blade grunted in response to me, and I took it as a hello.

"Are the problems in the realms getting sorted, Esme?" Lucifer turned his attention to the witch.

"As well as they can be, my Lord." She nodded her head. Lucifer stroked his chin.

"Very well. Any other issues I should be aware of?" He asked everyone in the room.

"I would like to stay here with my Princess," Ezra said, taking a step forward.

I kept my face flat and gripped the throne a little harder. Kyler shifted beside me, but I didn't dare move to look at him.

"And leave the vampires with no Prince?" Dante asked, turning to Ezra with a raised eyebrow and his lips curved in one corner.

"Kyler could go back. I can protect my Princess." Ezra said with a shrug.

"No," All eyes turned back to me as I spoke. "The vampires need their Prince."

Lucifer took the lollipop from his mouth, twirling it around, "I have to agree with Sapphire. The vampires need their Prince, considering they are causing problems everywhere." Lucifer's voice filled with annoyance.

"She is my Princess and needs to return home." Ezra gritted his teeth.

"I refuse." I said outright.

"There you have it, Ezra. She made her choice. Unless you wish to call upon your bond?" Lucifer raised an eyebrow, and I swallowed. Would Ezra call it? Force me to return home against my will?

"No. Of course not." Ezra gritted his teeth and fell back in line. I let out a sigh of relief.

Lucifer and the others began to talk about politics. I should have listened, but my mind decided to think about everything I've lost in life. My parents, both sets, and my friends. I hadn't even had a chance to see my childhood home. I closed my eyes for a second and blocked out the world around me.

"Princess, are you okay?" Esme asked, pulling me from my thoughts.

I turned to see everyone staring at me. I looked down and realized my body had blue static flowing over me. My lightning magic. I took a deep breath and let the static die out.

"I think Sapphire needs space. You all may go. And I do mean all of you." Lucifer's eyes narrowed on Ezra as he waved a dismissive lollipop.

One by one, everyone left the room until only Kyler remained.

"Thank you. I didn't mean to cause a fuss." I looked to Lucifer, who raised a brow.

"No fuss at all. They are a boring group." He gave me a cunning smile and popped his lolly back in his mouth.

"Lucy, what are you?" I asked.

He rubbed his chin before answering. "Please do not call me that in front of anyone. I am still the Lord of Hell. I'm a shapeshifter. It is why Ezra detests that I became Lucifer. We are considered lesser demons."

"No demons are lesser." I bit the corner of my lip.

"You feel very strongly about that, do you not?" Lucifer stood up and stretched his arms.

"I do."

"There is hope for Hell yet. I need a nap. Being this powerful is tiring. Consider my castle yours." Lucifer bowed his head to me and phased away.

"God is he arrogant," Kyler grunted beside me.

Chapter Forty

Sapphire

We had been with Lucifer for a few days. Things stayed quiet for the most part while Lucifer continued to have me by his side. Most demons did not bother him, and he usually dismissed those who did.

I sat on the drawbridge that led into Lucifer's village and kicked my dangling legs. Kyler stood behind me, just watching. The noise from people bustling around the village echoed in my ears as my eyes closed. The warm air sent a calming wave over my body. There had been no word from Ezra, which kept me on edge. He had to be planning something.

Lucifer embarrassed him when we held the meeting. I knew enough to know Ezra would not let that go. He was still a problem I had to take care of. Once I got more comfortable being by Lucifer's side, I would test the waters. Until one of us died, the bond would keep me tied to Ezra.

"Ah, so this is where you hide from me." Lucifer's voice came from beside me.

"Not hiding, per se. Avoiding? Yes." I turned my body and pushed myself up. Lucy popped a new lollipop in his mouth and smirked.

"Have I scared the most powerful demon alive? What a feat." He let out a boisterous laugh.

"A feat indeed." I echoed his sarcasm.

"You are more powerful than you understand." He extended a hand to me, which I reluctantly accepted. We started heading towards his castle through the village.

"Then explain it to me." My tone went flat.

I was getting so sick of hearing people tell me how powerful I was. My magic sat below an invisible barrier. I could tell I had it, and I could feel it in my veins, yet it seemed dull.

Had Lilith's magic been holding me back still?

"There are the legends, then there are the true stories passed down only from Lucifer to Lucifer." Lucifer said.

Kyler made a low grunt behind us. As we walked through the village, people backed away from Lucifer and turned away.

"You are a pureblood, sure, but soul eaters are still demons. You need to understand that if you do not find your strength, find the power you possess, you will be dead or far worse."

"Are you not the worst of the worst, my Lord?"

Lucifer stopped in his tracks and turned to me. He held out a hand, and shadows danced around us, hiding away the world, including Kyler. I met Lucy's red eyes with confusion on my face.

"There is a great threat beyond even what the Gods can foresee. *You*, Sapphire, have to become the worst of the worst."

Lucifer took a step back, and the shadows fell away. Kyler looked at me with a raised brow. I bit the corner of my lip and tilted my head at Lucy.

"I am powerful," I whispered and glanced down at my hands.

"Prove it. Let us go to the arena. I will only use a fourth of my power. You know, to be fair." A smirk slid across Lucifer's face.

"One condition," he and Kyler faced me. "No more fighting after this. No more training. I want to see how to rule Hell, not fight against it. I never want to rule by fear."

"I accept your terms, Princess. Shall we go?" Lucifer grinned.

I nodded, and the three of us phased into the arena.

I found myself in the middle of an amphitheater. A wall at least eight feet tall surrounded us, with only two gates for escape. Above the wall, concrete stadium seats curled all around. To the north was a platform with a black throne perched high. Kyler leaned against the wall by the left gate, his leg bent with his foot flat behind him.

Lucifer stood parallel to me. He bent his fingers in a let's go motion. I felt the warmth in my arms as fireballs formed in both hands. Lucifer's sly smirk didn't leave his face as the fire hit him.

"You are going to have to try much harder than that, Princess." He mused.

My hands opened, and that static tingle filled me. I threw two lightning bolts at Lucifer. This time, I made sure I willed it to hit harder. He shifted backward and then came at me with lightning twirling in between his fingers. He threw a continuous lightning rod while I dashed across the arena. A bolt hit me and sent me flying to the other side. That did not feel like a fourth of his power.

I glared at him and rose, wiping dirt off my legs. Kyler had a look of panic, but I shook my head. Lucifer would see I am a force of the Gods.

I threw a fireball again, only this time with more determination. His shirt lit up, and pieces of cloth fell to the ground, causing holes with burnt edges. There was no sign of pain on his face. Once again, I failed to inflict any real damage. Then, words echoed within my ears.

You are more powerful than anyone could imagine.
Princess of Hell. Gift from the Gods.

The voices rang in my head as loudly as when I dreamed them.

My power filled me. I summoned my fireballs and threw them at him, over and over. It pushed him further back in the sand. His shoulder would knock back with every hit. I didn't give him a chance to fight back. Anger flickered in his eyes. He ran at me and aimed his shadow power at me again. Dark clouds blasted my chest. I kept walking towards him. A growl escaped his throat.

We ran at each other, throwing our powers back and forth. Fire, lightning, and shadows clashed against our bodies. The echoes from our growls and moans bounced off the walls of the coliseum. Kyler dodged occasionally when an element came at him. I threw one more lightning bolt Lucifer's way with all my power. Smoke rose from Lucifer's hit shoulder, and his eyes darkened as he glared at me.

Lucifer's body straightened for a second. The lightning left a mark on his exposed shoulder once the smoke died down. His gaze shifted to Kyler and then to me.

He ran at Kyler, who pushed himself off the wall to dodge the impending attack. Time slowed to a screeching halt. My heart began to race. Something came over me, a rage I had never felt before. I cracked my knuckles and ran at Lucifer. With all the force I could muster, I pushed him away with wind power. He slid in the sand and put a fist in the ground to stop himself from moving.

"He's not a part of this," I growled. My nostrils flared, my chest heaving.

That sly smirk crossed Lucifer's face. He straightened himself before snapping his fingers and summoning a new shirt.

"You are indeed a powerful thing." He nodded once at me. "The Gods were right to choose you."

Kyler's eyes bounced between Lucifer and me.

"Will you teach me to rule now?" I spat blood from my mouth into the sand.

"I will hold up my end of the bargain. Starting tomorrow, I will show you what it takes to be Lucifer." He turned to Kyler, "You are a good sport. Get some rest, both of you." Lucifer bowed to me and then disappeared.

Kyler came to me in three long steps. He put his hands on my shoulders, and our eyes locked. My breath was starting to even out while we stared into each other's eyes. The world fell away, and all I could see was him. When I watched Lucifer head for Kyler, my heart fell in my chest. The idea of anyone hurting him angered me in ways I didn't know I could be angry.

No one would take Kyler from me.

No one.

"Fire, you ok?" Kyler asked, breaking the silence.

"Yes. I needed a moment to calm down. Fighting Lucifer is intense. Can we go back to the bridge? It's peaceful." The rumble of hunger waved through me, and I pushed it away.

"Your every whim is my command, My Liege." Kyler did his exaggerated bow, and a small cackle escaped my lips.

Chapter Forty-One

Kyler

I sat on the pier at my mom's cabin. The night air smelled like fresh rain, while the moon hung lower in the sky. I ran a finger over the water and watched the ripples move. I closed my eyes and envisioned her long blonde hair draping over her face as she laughed. The warmth of her body when she held me. Her angelic voice soothed me when I cried.

Fuck. I miss you, Mom.

"How can you stand the mosquitoes?" Zariah's voice came from a few feet away.

"Vampire blood isn't as tasty." I shrugged, facing his direction. "What're you doing here, man?"

He took a seat next to me and dipped his hairy legs into the water. Fish swam off at the sudden change, and I grunted.

"You think I'd forget your mom's birthday?" He raised his brow at me.

I shook my head. Mom's birthday used to be a big thing when Father was alive. Every year she would throw a party. It was damn near the only time I saw Father smile. Thinking of better times caused pain in my chest.

I summoned a bottle of her favorite whiskey and two glasses. Zariah and I toasted, then I drank the shot.

"You didn't want to bring Sapphire with you?"

"She has enough on her plate. She doesn't need to deal with my brooding ass for one night." I poured another shot.

"Can she do it?"

He didn't have to elaborate; I knew exactly what he meant. Fire was coming into who she was in such a majestic way that it kept me in awe. But it also meant the coming storm would be rapidly approaching. Being at Lucifer's side caused an uneasy twist in my gut that I hated.

"Yes. She fought Lucifer, managed to scar him."

We both took another shot, and Zariah nodded. The noise of the night pulsated around us. My muscles tensed, and I threw my head back.

"Mom spent her entire life fighting for me. She taught me to fight back. To be a man. When she died, Ezra and Father got mean. I think it's time I started standing up for what's right. If Fire can accept her fate, so can I." I chugged the bottle of whiskey and jumped to my feet.

"What are you doing, dude?" Zariah rose beside me and furrowed his brows.

I pulled him into a hug and handed him the empty bottle.

"Gonna go do something stupid."

Phasing away, I had a giant fucking grin on my face.

Ezra's castle had a chill in the air as I stomped my way to my jackass brother's throne. He looked up at me with a raised brow. Orpheus hovered beside him. Ezra handed him the Cursed King book, then walked down the steps of the dais.

"Brother. What brings you here? Did you bring me my Princess?" His voice was filled with sarcasm.

The smug look on his face pissed me off. How could he sit in this room and not even celebrate the woman who raised him? How could he be so fucking heartless? I balled my fists and flared my nostrils.

"She is not yours. She will never be yours. You will stay away from her, and you will leave me the fuck alone." I growled.

"You might be my brother, but Dad made sure to tell me exactly where you belong. *Dog*." Ezra's lips curled in the corner, nostrils flaring.

"I am done being your dog. You can take everything Father said and shove it up your fucking ass. You do not deserve your God's damned throne!"

"It is so sad to see what you've become. If your mother were alive, she would still choose me. You are weak and a disgrace to our kind. Pathetic." Ezra took a step closer to me.

"The only disgrace here is you!" I pointed an angry finger at his chest.

"You are drunk. Go back to Sapphire. Never know who might try to get a taste of her when she is alone." Ezra let out a wicked laugh, and his eyes darkened.

I dashed at Ezra with fire in my hand, but got stopped by a wall named Orpheus. He shook his head at me with pity in his eyes.

"I will remove him, Sire," Orpheus spoke.

He quickly dragged me from the throne room. I made sure to give my brother a fat middle finger.

"I will see you soon, Kyler." Ezra smirked, and a shadow glossed over his eyes.

I kicked up the dirt outside the castle doors. Even the sky appeared darker than normal. Letting out a guttural, I turned back to Orpheus.

Fuck this. Fuck all of this.

"Not yet, Kyler. His time will come soon, brother. Go back to our Princess. Ezra will get what's coming to him, but you're no use to anyone if he kills you." Orpheus whispered low enough that I could barely hear him.

"He's going to kill her, Orpheus. He's going to kill the woman I love!" I shouted in a loud whisper.

"How do you know that?" Orpheus asked.

"Because that's what he does!" I snapped.

"We won't let him, but you need to get back to her." He placed a hand on my shoulder. "You reek of alcohol. I know today is hard on you. We all loved your mother greatly, but doing something stupid won't honor her memory."

"You're a good friend, Orph." I patted his hand that sat on my shoulder.

"Go." Orpheus egged me on with a tilt of his chin.

I pushed my tongue into my cheek and balled my fists.

My smug shithead of a brother will die, and it will be by my hand when the time comes.

Phasing back to Fire, I vowed to protect her with my life.

No one would get in the way of the future she promised to build.

Blood for blood.

Chapter Forty-Two

Sapphire

When I crept from my room, Kyler was not standing outside the door. I wondered where he was. I didn't like it when he was away, but I wanted to have a private chat with Lucy anyway. I went down the stairs, only to find an empty throne room. As I continued to wander the halls, I found an office at the end of the east wing. I knocked three times, and the door swung open with a creak.

Lucy sat at a mahogany desk, his hands held his head. I watched as he let out a sigh and threw his head back. I cleared my throat, taking him from his trance. A heaviness filled his eyes when he looked at me.

"Sapphire, is there something you need?" He asked, summoning a new lollipop. His demeanor changed back to the arrogant Lucifer I knew.

"I need answers," I said.

"Shut the door, and take a seat." Lucy motioned for the chair in front of his desk.

I did as he requested and sat down. He waved his hand, and all the papers that were piled up moments ago disappeared. He leaned back in his chair and waited for me to speak.

"How did you come into power? If shapeshifters are lesser demons?" I asked him. He leaned his elbow on the desk and eyed me.

"You know, if anyone but you asked that question, I would kill them where they stood," Lucy smirked, pulling the lollipop from his mouth. "It was easy; anyone could have done it. My predecessor stayed hidden in this castle, and I shifted into a guard, snuck in, slitting his throat open in the middle of the night. I know that is not what you are here for, though, is it?" He stuck the lollipop back in his mouth.

"No. I need to know more about Apollyon, Lilith, and about me." I shifted in my seat.

"Apollyon was the second Lucifer. Lilith was the original witch. You are a soul-eater. Any other questions?" Lucy twirled his lollipop around, with boredom plastered on his face.

"Look, Lucy, I need real fucking answers." I slammed a hand on his desk, and he let out an amused chuckle.

"Now that is the kind of attitude you will need to rule Hell with. Weak demons die quickly down here." He gazed over at a picture on the wall of a tree with black leaves. His feelings shifted to guilt before he turned back to me.

"I don't understand the first thing about ruling Hell," I admitted with a sigh.

"The burden of the throne is heavy, Sapphire. Keeping it, and keeping people scared of you, it is not an easy task." His gaze drifted past me towards the door.

I turned my body to see Kyler standing in the doorway. The look of relief crossed his face once he saw me. He had bags under his eyes, and his forehead creased. I was starting to know that look well. A feeling of sorrow came radiating from him, along with the smell of alcohol.

"Ah, the ever faithful knight." Lucifer sang.

"My Liege." Kyler bowed.

"Tell me, vampire, do you know the burden being a king carries?" Lucifer stood and walked towards Kyler.

"Only stories, my Lord." He responded.

His answers were short, and I could hear the cracking in his voice.

Damnit.

"Is there a point to this?" I asked with a bit of annoyance in my voice.

"Kyler, leave us. I need to have a few words with Sapphire." Lucifer said, towering over me.

His close proximity to me sent my nerves to the edge. There was a presence about him, something more than the cowboy facade. Kyler bowed to us and walked away.

"Why did you send him away?" I asked, looking towards the now-empty hallway.

Lucifer took a step closer, and the feeling of guilt surrounded him. A lingering emotion of dread filled the space between us.

"The throne will take every drop of who you are and corrode it until nothing is left. I do not envy what your future holds." He said so low, I don't know if he spoke or I imagined the words. "Now then." Lucifer straightened and took a step back. "Let me show you a little secret."

He began walking down the hall, and I darted behind him. He waved his hand, and a new hallway appeared. Lucy led me down a corridor, and the darkness of it sent an uneasy chill through me. We came to a door draped in webs, and he pushed it open with a creak.

The room we entered was as dark as the hallway. Lucifer clapped his hands, and light filled the room. A few bookshelves sat along the wall. A desk sat by a window caked in dirt, and a bat flew past us.

"I think this will answer the question on your mind. It is the most kept secret among the Lucifer line. This is the final answer I can give you. Tomorrow, I will start teaching you how to truly rule." He turned to leave.

"Lucifer, what is this room?" I asked.

"Your father's old office, hidden behind magic." Lucifer didn't turn to me as he spoke. He gave me a final nod and walked away, leaving me alone.

I peered at the rows of books and tomes lining the shelves. A small purple book caught my eye. Pulling it out of the shelf, a photo fell to the ground.

I picked it up off the ground and wiped the dust off it. A man and woman stood, holding a baby. The caption read: *Apollyon and Lilith holding baby Sapphire.*

I ran my hand over the picture as a tear fell. Lucifer gave me something to hold onto.

My parents.

I folded it, slipping it into my jeans pocket. Placing the book down, I sat on the chair caked in layers of dirt. A small black widow crawled up my arm. With a raised brow, I laughed as it bit me.

"Sorry, friend, that won't work the way you hope." I placed the spider down on the ground.

Looking around the desk, not much had been left. A frame with a worn picture I couldn't make out sat on the corner. I opened the drawers one by one, digging through notebooks and random parchments. Something shining in the bottom drawer grabbed my attention.

Moving around the papers, I pulled out a dagger. The silver blade and Sapphire pendant in the hilt looked untouched by time. No dust or webs. A small inscription burned and etched itself into the blade before my eyes. I let out a small gasp and read the words.

May this dagger protect you from harm, dearest Sapphire.

My parents both left something behind for me. I never believed in fate before, but somehow, breadcrumbs of my past kept appearing when I needed them. I slid the dagger into my belt.

"Is this your doing?" I asked the Gods.

A new question slid into my mind.

What evil awaits me?

Chapter Forty-Three

Sapphire

The following day, Kyler stood at my side as I took my spot on the throne. Lucifer was not there yet, giving me time to relax. I tilted my head back and closed my eyes. Anna and my friends would be proud to know I got here.

Soon to be Queen of Hell with Lucifer, my kingdom in sight.

Would my birth parents also be proud?

Everything led up to this, to me being on the throne.

Footsteps echoed in my ears, causing me to open my eyes. Lucifer walked into the room. He wore a black velvet suit, vest, and pants. The shoes on his feet were as shiny as the floor, and suddenly, I felt underdressed. He bowed his head to me and sat on his throne. The lingering feeling of dread crept into me.

How did I not notice before?

"In a few moments, demons will start entering to tell me their grievances. There are typically not many because I do not care. My high officials will be here, too."

I nodded at Lucifer. He snapped his fingers, and his guards walked from the room.

After a moment, I discovered why: to let demons into the castle. The line was not long, but longer than I expected. Demons, witches, and even a few vampires stood waiting. The first one in line looked like Dante, with those black wings and horns. He was smaller, though. Lucifer motioned with a finger for him to approach. The demon walked to us with hesitant steps.

"Lucifer, my merciless Liege," the demon bowed. "I come to you today because it has come to my attention that someone is stealing my weapons." After straightening, the demon still did not make eye contact with either of us. His entire body shook, and his voice wobbled. I didn't need to feel his emotions to know how he felt.

"You have come here to waste my time over some weapons?" Boredom filled Lucifer's tone.

"Dante has been busy dealing with other things, and I well… I…" Lucifer walked toward the demon, who was clambering up. Fear shot through him.

"I suggest you run," Lucifer said, towering over the demon.

Panic filled the demon's wide eyes as he took off. Lucifer snapped his fingers, and the demon burst into flames. I covered my gaping mouth. Lucifer came back to the throne and sat with a groan. He rubbed the furrow of his brow before turning his attention to me.

"Most of these grievances are problems for the princes. Hell needs to fear you, or they will beg for everything. If you give one some, then they will demand all you have." He motioned for the next person to come in.

I sat there and thought about what Lucifer said. The demon's request for help did not seem unreasonable to me, especially if Dante had been busy. As a ruler of Hell, didn't Lucifer want to know his people were happy and taken care of? How could he kill so easily? This world was nothing like I expected. The demons were not all assholes out to get everyone. Most of them only wanted to be left alone; there was no reason to be such a hard ass. Lucy's true colors were coming through, and I didn't like them.

At all.

When I ascend the throne, things will be better.

A plump blonde demon walked into the throne room next. She felt scared as she approached us. Her outfit was a pale, thin dress, and dirt covered her body. She bowed before Lucifer, waiting for him to say something.

"What is your grievance today, Seraphim?" Lucy said with an eye roll.

"Rex killed my son!" Her nervousness turned to anger and sadness. Lucifer shifted slightly in his chair. "He said it was because he stole something, but my boy didn't take a damn thing!" Her voice turned to wails of agony, twisting in my gut. Lucifer went to speak, but I placed a hand on his shoulder. My gaze shifted momentarily to Blade and Esme, who stood against the left wall.

"Let me, please? I'm hungry." I said low in his ear. Lucy pointed his new lollipop towards Seraphim; I had the floor.

"Blade? Can you get Rex, please?"

Blade grunted and uncrossed his arms before phasing away. What could this woman's son have possibly done? I noticed a few demons had gathered in the back of the room to watch what was happening. Dante and Vealla had arrived at some point as well. They dwelled against the wall with Esme.

Blade returned with his arm around a demon's neck. He pushed Rex forward before stepping back to his place beside Esme. I eyed the demon before me. He had on clanky black armor but no helmet. His black hair flopped on his head to one side. He looked a mess.

My movements were uncaring as I played with a nail and walked toward the demon. My heels made a tapping sound with every step I took, getting closer and closer to Rex. I studied his face momentarily, and his eyes flicked between Lucifer and me. He did not feel scared.

But he should be.

"Hello, Rex. Want to explain to me why you killed this poor woman's son?" I sang, pointing my dagger at Seraphim, as I stepped in a circle around him.

"I don't have to explain a damn thing to you, little girl." He spat at my feet.

"Oh, but you do. See, Lucifer here would kill you before you could even plead your case. I, however, am willing to give you a chance." I let a wicked grin cross my face. My power roared inside of me.

Before Rex could speak another word, Lucy stood and bounced a fireball in his hand. Fear shook Rex's body.

"Now, would you like to try that again? Because I have to tell you, I have no control over the king." I laid my hand over his shoulder, using the other to point the dagger at Lucifer.

"Her son. . . stole...my...my...dagger." he could barely speak.

A dagger. This waste of space killed a boy over a dagger.

"Do you have proof of this?" I turned towards Lucy. Kyler watched with a smug face I'd never seen before. Lucifer eyed me intently but gave off an uncaring posture.

"N-No," Rex said, but kept his head down.

"Very well. What does it look like?"

"Silver, with a red line on the blade," Rex said quietly.

"Kyler?" Irritation filled my voice. "Could you please search his residence, and hers, for said dagger?" Fear spread through Rex like wildfire. That was my answer. Kyler nodded and bowed before disappearing.

I walked back up the dais and sat on the throne. Everyone watched me move, and whispers filled the room. I could feel the fear filling the air around me. Excitement tingled within my body.

How dare he kill a child? Even a demon child is still a child.

Kyler appeared again and walked over to Rex, stabbing the ground in front of him with the dagger.

"It was in his house," Kyler said, with little excitement in his voice.

I didn't say a word; I walked to Rex as Kyler stepped aside and gave a slight bow. My glow pulled the demon's soul to me from the finger I placed on his chest. A thud echoed as the lifeless body dropped. My powers purred from the strength of the soul I consumed.

Only this once, did I not regret taking a life.

"I'm sorry for your loss, Seraphim. I know this changes nothing for you, but he'll no longer be a problem." Kneeling, I gently touched her shoulder as she looked up at me. Her eyes were bloodshot from tears. Feelings of relief came from her, even though beneath it, a great pain lingered.

"I will never forget this," she said, her tone light. I gave her a soft smile.

"I think that is all for today. We will hear any other grievances tomorrow." Lucifer gave a dismissive wave of the hand. Once the room cleared out, he laughed. "Seraphim comes in here every day complaining that Rex killed one of her sons," he continued to laugh.

I turned to Lucy. Kyler watched my every move as his hand slid to the sword's hilt on his back. I took a deep breath and calmed myself. No matter how mad I may be, Kyler was ready to fight the devil for me, and I could not let him. After watching Lucifer charge for him yesterday and feeling that anger rattle me, protecting Kyler became more important than fighting battles I couldn't win, yet.

"Why did you let me do that, then?" I snapped.

"You said you were hungry." Lucifer's laugh was dismissive. "You will need to learn to deal with problems in ways that suit the situation. Let this be lesson number one. Demons lie. Often. Rex is proof."

"That was uncalled for, Lucy." I grit my teeth.

"I am the king of Hell. I do as I please, and you should too if you are going to have a chance as Queen of Hell." Lucifer stood and walked past me to Blade and Esme, who bowed to him. "I need to go back to the mortal world for a few days. Please help our dear Sapphire keep Hell in check, hmm?" He turned his back to me, and his red eyes narrowed.

"Don't worry, highness, we will be here to help, too." Dante bowed to me. With everything that had conspired, I had forgotten Vealla, and Dante stood in the room as well.

"We will guide her to where she needs to be." Esme bowed to Lucifer.

Lucifer grunted and phased away, leaving me standing at the bottom of the dais surrounded by demons.

Feeling lost.

Chapter Forty-Four

Sapphire

I couldn't sleep. I kept picturing Lilith and Apollyon saying goodbye to me. Pacing my room, my legs felt numb. This had become a nightly thing. I would pace for hours, trying to calm the visions in my head. Opening my left palm, I summoned my lightning power and watched little blue lines of electricity dance between my fingers.

I could feel a surge of power after taking Rex's soul, yet I couldn't tap into it.

Lilith's magic had to be behind it, but there was only one person I trusted enough to seek answers from. By the looks of the sky, it was the middle of the night. Deciding not to wake Kyler, I phased to Vealla.

"Highness? Is there something you need?" A guard stepped forward from the castle door.

I appeared outside of her castle. I didn't want to startle her if she had been asleep. The black pond glistened against the dark sky. The realm felt extremely still.

"I need to see the Princess," I said low.

The guard bowed, "At this hour, she is likely in the tower."

He opened the double doors for me, and I wandered in. The halls were silent as I stepped up the winding stairs to her knitting tower. When I arrived at the top, she was sitting on the floor surrounded by needles and thread. She had a crochet needle sticking out of her mouth while focusing on a knotted ball of yarn. For a moment, I flashed back to Mom sitting on the living room floor with a wedding dress.

"God's be damned! Stupid yarn!" Vealla cursed and tossed the ball to the floor with a huff.

"Need some help?" I walked over and sat on the floor across from her.

"Highness? Why are you here? It's awfully late." She picked up the ball she threw and handed it to me. "Think you can get it out?"

"I'm no good with a needle, but removing knots is my specialty." I gave her a faint smile. "I really came because I have a question and I only trust you to answer."

"I'll answer as best I can."

Vealla and I sat in silence for a moment while I untangled her knot of pink yarn. The sheer walls occasionally rippled, blurring the coloring of the sky briefly. It was a welcome distraction while debating how to ask the question.

"And... there!" I pulled the last part out of the ball and shoved it towards Vealla, who laughed.

"Thanks, highness, that was impressive." She smiled.

"Vealla, when I read my Mom's, well, Anna's, journal, she said Lilith had magic protecting me. Is it still? I can feel my power, but it's faint, like an echo." I held out my palms and summoned my fire and lightning. With a sigh, I closed my fist, dispelling the magic.

Vealla reached over and placed a hand on my leg. "I can try to see, but Sapphire, if it is her magic, I won't be able to reverse it."

"How come?"

"Lilith is the original witch. The alpha. She found a way to tap into the natural magic within the world and convert it to her will." Vealla turned her gaze to her project, not meeting my eyes.

"She's an alpha witch and soul-eater?"

Vealla nodded.

"I'm the daughter of two alphas. I feel like being a gift from the God's is an understatement." I laughed.

Vealla looked up at me with a smile. I found myself thankful for her friendship. Although I longed for my mortal friends, I didn't feel so empty.

"Will you try?" I asked.

She sighed but nodded and summoned her black book. After flipping pages, she murmured and found the spell she needed. Vealla began to whisper the demon language, and my body tingled. As she continued the words, a light shot from me, throwing her into a wall. I shot up and ran over to her.

"Are you okay?" I asked, shaking.

She rubbed her head and stood up. Her gaze met mine, and her face paled.

"Vealla?" I whispered.

She shook her head. Her cheeks turned pink again. I chewed on the inside of my cheek.

"That was... You are... *Fuck*."

"What? What happened?" I pleaded.

"That isn't Lilith's magic protecting you. It's the Gods'."

I froze where I stood. Lilith's magic didn't hold me back; the Gods did. Closing my eyes, the world around me fell away.

Why am I so important?

"Are you okay? I'm so sorry. I shouldn't have asked you to do that." I shook my head.

"It's okay, Highness. You couldn't have known. I hope it at least answered your question a little." She glanced at me with a softness in her eyes. It wasn't a look of pity, but kindness.

"Thank you, Vealla. I need to go do something. I appreciate your help." I gave her a quick hug.

"Anytime, Highness." She bowed her head.

I phased away to the only place the angel ever spoke to me. The moon lit the cemetery, and shadows swayed in the light breeze. Standing in front of my mortal parents' stone, I didn't even know what to say or ask. Visions of the last time I came here danced in my head.

Ezra had threatened me; I never thought I'd get a chance to return here. Chances are, if he knew I was away from Lucifer, he'd certainly come for me. My heart beat quickened at the thought.

"Uh, dear angel guy, are you around?"

I waited for what felt like years, but probably only lasted a few minutes. My heart beat quickly, and my palms were sweaty.

"It's dangerous to seek me out in the open, Sapphire."

"I'm sorry. I didn't know how else to find you. Why are the Gods protecting me?" I whispered and sat on the grass.

"I can't answer that. I can only say all things will happen how they are supposed to in time."

"That's such a cop out. What can you tell me? Please, I need something." I begged as tears formed in my eyes.

"Your destiny is far greater than you know. One day, you will rise above all. For now, know that I am watching and with you. Even if it doesn't feel that way, I am never far."

"Can't you show yourself?" I asked the wind.

"You know me very well, Sapphire. I can't reveal my face to you. Not yet, anyways."

I didn't answer the voice. I tried hard to think about anyone in my life who seemed like an angel or a guide, to no avail. The voice I recognized but barely. Like the name was on the tip of my tongue, but I couldn't quite reach it.

"I should get back. Bad things happen when I'm in the mortal realm." I rose from the grass. The sun started to rise, and that meant someone would come looking for me. I shuddered when I thought of Ezra finding me.

"I will be at your back, even if you don't realise it's me."

I wanted to take comfort in the voice, but I had lost too much to believe that it was true.

Chapter Forty-Five
Sapphire

The next day, I woke up earlier than usual. My hunger sat in the pit of my stomach. Grumbling, I forced myself to sit up. I tried hard not to take in souls, but after Rex, I felt power hungry.

After getting dressed in a black corset and jeans, I summoned my black crown. I hadn't worn it since the coronation. Learning I was a Princess of Hell made me want to show everyone who I was. Kyler did not stand by the bedroom door when I opened it.

I found him stretched out on the steps below the thrones. He had his head in a book, and I watched him. He looked so peaceful. I didn't want to disturb him. Dante and Vealla talked against the wall. Blade stood with them, occasionally grunting. Kyler's eyes shifted up from his book to me in slow motion.

"You're wearing your crown." He made his book disappear and scanned me with his eyes.

"I am the Princess of Hell." I smiled.

"It looks perfect!" Vealla boasted and came over to us.

"How's your head?" I raised a brow at her.

"The perks of being a healing witch mean I don't hurt for long." She laughed.

"Do I even want to know?" Kyler asked, with his arms folded over his chest.

I shook my head. Vealla gave me a quick bow of the head and walked back over to Dante. Kyler's eyes drifted between Vealla and me for a moment before he spoke.

"You're hungry."

"Yes."

"Will you be okay if I leave you for a bit? I won't if you need me here." He said softly. I gave him a small, sad look. I wanted nothing more than to reach for his hand. We had little opportunity to be close in the time we've been with Lucifer.

"I'll be okay. Go." I nodded my chin upward.

"Kyler, take me with you. We can get her what she needs from my castle." Dante walked over to us. His black shirt and jeans showcased his large muscles. I averted my eyes, hoping no one noticed me ogling him.

"What do you mean?" I asked, confused.

"You'll see when we get back. I promise." Dante gave me a warm smile.

"After you, then." Kyler motioned a hand for Dante to lead the way.

They bowed to me and were gone in a swirl of fire and a blink. Lucifer's guards lazed around while Vealla and Blade continued to chat. My thoughts wandered as I sat, looking out at the room. My friends would have loved this castle, especially Emily.

I pulled out the pictures of my birth parents and my friends. My eyes drifted between the two. A part of me yearned so desperately for my old life. It felt like a hundred years had passed since my interview. I wondered how Kathy was doing.

I rested my chin on my fist. My companions now sat on the stairs of the dais, playing a card game. My eyes moved to a body that walked towards us. Not just anybody, Ezra. I gritted my teeth. He gave me a low bow, and then his eyes met mine. Blade shifted his body, and he focused his eyes on us.

"My Princess, I would like you to come home." Ezra said in a calm voice as I walked down the steps till I was inches from him.

"I am home." My words came out in a sweet song.

"No. Home is with *me*." Ezra stepped closer, and my rib cage bucked at the remembrance of his sword sliding through me. Blade moved a step closer, and Vealla's hands were in fists.

"I'm not leaving, Ezra." This time, my words were a harsh boom. I would not be his little puppet.

"You are, or there will be consequences!" Ezra went to put a hand on me when Kyler's sword came down between us. Ezra took an unbalanced step backward. Dante moved to the other side of me, keeping me guarded.

"She said no," Kyler roared.

My hand lay on my chest as shock flooded me. He stood up to his prince, his brother, for me. He used to back down and fear his brother, but there he was, threatening him for me.

"I am your prince, and you will stand aside." Ezra's heavy voice threatened.

Kyler shifted his body between us, sword still in hand. Dante took my hand and pulled me back a few steps. He then moved beside Kyler and flexed his wings, hiding me from Ezra's view.

"I am her knight, which you assigned me to be, brother. That means I will protect her from any threat, *including you*." Kyler stood his ground, and my heart fluttered. Rage burned in Ezra's eyes as I peered over Dante's shoulder.

"I'm here at Lucifer's behest. If you'd like to fight the King of Hell for my hand, then by all means, *my love*, go for it." I sang, stepping between them.

Kyler stiffened beside me, but I wouldn't back down.

"I call upon our binds. You will come home." Ezra said to me.

A firm pull came from my chest. Without wanting to, my body began to move towards him. My breath quickened, and my eyes met Kyler's. The look of horror spread across his face. Ancient magic that no one could stop controlled my movements.

My mind wandered to my conversation with Vealla. Lilith was the original witch; her magic had to flow through my veins. *Ancient magic.* I got a few steps toward Ezra and roared.

"No. I refuse our bindings. I refuse you, Ezra."

The room went silent. All eyes were on us. The weight of invisible chains snapped, and Ezra turned pale. Blade grunted behind me.

"I'll never be your pawn again. I'm not yours. I'm no one's."

"Who do you think you are to deny *me*?" Ezra snapped, taking a step closer.

"I am Sapphire. Daughter of Lilith and Apollyon, Princess of Hell, Gift from the God's and you, Ezra, are a *speck. You are nothing.*"

Ezra roared from deep in his throat, and his nostrils flared. It was a fight he knew he could not win. He didn't expect his brother to choose me over him. Nor did he expect me to be able to break his binding. I doubt he calculated for all my friends to be here to protect me. I met Ezra's eyes and gave him a wide grin.

"You will regret this, Sapphire. You will get what is coming to you." Ezra hissed before turning on his heels and leaving.

My body shook. A heavy weight was lifted, and I could breathe. After my time in Hell, I knew not to be naive. Ezra had a plan. It would have to wait. Something stirred inside of me.

I grabbed Kyler's hand, ignoring everyone around us, and dragged him through the castle. After shutting the door to my room, he took off his sword and looked at me.

"You fought for me," I said quietly. "You stood up for me."

"I'm your sworn protector," Kyler shrugged nonchalantly as if what he did was some job.

I pulled him to me so our lips could meet. His hands wrapped around my waist, and he deepened our kiss. Sparks tingled through my body. The electric charge between us ignited my powers. Every time we touched, static filled my body. He made me feel safe. I took a step back and met his eyes. Tears began to swell in mine.

"You're my mate," I whispered.

"Yes."

"When did you know?" I bit my lower lip.

"I knew the second I saw you at the bar. You called to me, and I wanted to reach across the bar and kiss you right there. You thought you were human, though, and the bond felt weak. It took that bastard telling me about your birthmark to realize who you were. I wanted you to accept the bond because you wanted me, not because fate decided it would be so."

He tucked a hair behind my ear.

"That's why I show up every time you need me. I can feel your call to me in your darkest moments. When you came to Hell, I told myself there was no way the most powerful being in creation would want me. Ezra had his claim on you, and I thought you wouldn't risk that. Yet, you showed up in my room, you sought me out. It felt like I had been asleep for three hundred years, and you woke me up."

I rested my head against his shoulder. My throat tightened from the words.

"You have become my reason to breathe, to continue to fight for what matters, to fight for you. For the first time in my life, I can stand up for what's right. I need to be close to you more than anything else. I need to know you're safe. My life is forever yours, Fire. If you accept our bond or don't, it doesn't matter. I will follow you to the void. My life's not worth living without you. Blood for Blood."

Tears fell my face while I listened to his words. My entire body filled with something beyond warmth.

Love.

"I knew too, I think. When you first showed up at my house, there was this pull. I couldn't explain it, but I couldn't breathe. When I thought I was dying, it was your name I called. It's been there this entire time. When Lucifer charged at you, I was going to kill him right there. The idea of anyone taking you from me angered me more than you could imagine. You've been my guiding light, my knight, since we met. When you stood up to Ezra, I realized you were choosing me over the possibility of death. I am yours forever, Kyler."

He pulled me against his chest and held me there. It could have been only a few minutes or a few hours. Time stopped, and everything faded away.

"I, Kyler, accept our mating bond. Now and always."

"I, Sapphire, accept our mating bond. Now and forever."

"Forever with me being a cocky asshole, you sure that's what you want?" Kyler's smirk lit up my world.

"I've never been more sure of anything in my life." Our lips met again.

My arms moved around his neck and pulled him down closer to me. I was happy for the first time since coming to Hell. Things were going to change, and with Kyler at my back, I could take on the world.

LEXI CARON

Blood for blood.

Chapter Forty-Six

Sapphire

The next day, I peered out the window and watched demons bustling about below in the village. A plan rolled in my mind. With Ezra gone, I could sit beside Lucifer uncontested.

A knock at the door turned my focus. With a sigh, I walked over and opened it to see Lucifer's assistant. I never did catch the old man's name.

"Lord Lucifer requests your presence in his room," The gray-haired demon said in his raspy voice. Then he turned on his heels and walked away before I could answer.

I took a deep breath, shifting the crown on my head, and headed to Lucifer. Before I could even knock on the door, it swung open. I curved my lips to one side.

Alright, Lucy.

I laughed to myself. Stepping into the room, I saw him sitting on his chair again, his customary lollipop in his mouth.

He is awfully relaxed for a ruler of Hell.

It made me wonder even more why he helped me. This man was sneaky and took over Hell while the rest were at war. He carved his place with pain and fear. I wanted the opposite of all that he stood for.

"You wanted to see me?" I raised an eyebrow. He looked up at me and had a wicked grin on his face. I hated it when he smiled like that.

"You really should start addressing me as the Ruler of Hell. Other demons will think I have gone soft. Nonetheless, how would you like to help me kill a prisoner?" Lucifer raised a brow at me.

"What'd the prisoner do?"

Kyler leaned against the door frame. Our eyes met for a second, then my attention returned to Lucifer.

"The prisoner is rather dangerous. I sentenced her to death for killing one of my top demon warriors. I do not take kindly to that."

"Who is this prisoner?" I ask, as if whatever name he gave would make sense to me. An amused smile pursed his lips.

"Morgana. She comes from a long line of powerful witches. Not as powerful as your mother, but a fairly close second." Lucifer stood and eyed Kyler for a moment.

"She's a Thorne witch," Kyler said, to which Lucifer nodded.

"What was Lilith?" I asked no one in particular.

"She was a Nightshade witch." Lucy said, "Now, let us deal with her, hmm?" Lucy motioned for us to follow him.

Kyler walked behind me, and Lucifer descended the stairs to his throne room. He spoke to the gray-haired demon in whispers. They both nodded, and then Lucifer was on the move again.

We went to a door behind the stairs. At the bottom, a guard bowed to Lucifer and opened it. The cold stone helped trap the dampness within the walls. Metal bars acted as doors to the prisoners' cells. One of the full steel doors sat at the end of the hall, and we went down another set of stairs. Lucifer allowed me to go first.

In front of me, a female demon with short, red hair gave me an unreadable look. Thick metal cuffs around her wrists and ankles chained her to the floor. She eyed me and smirked at Lucifer.

"Is this the one who will kill me? She doesn't look like much." Morgana's voice had a soothing undertone. She took a step forward, and the chains rattled.

"She is the lost princess." Lucifer walked further into the room and leaned his back against the far wall, crossing his arms.

"I doubt you waited 20 years for her to arrive to kill me, Jason. Did he tell you what I did?" She spoke to me now.

"No."

Jason?

It occurred to me at that moment that Lucifers had names. They had identities before taking the soul. Jason, the shapeshifter, became Lucifer.

"I killed his brother, my mate, in the war. You see, Jason's brother wanted Lucifer to rule. He didn't want democracy. He helped Jason gain the throne. I'd kill him too, but you see my predicament." She raised her hands, and the chains rattled.

"Let us make this more interesting." Lucifer snapped his fingers, and her chains were gone.

My eyes shot to Lucifer briefly before Morgana came after me. I moved to the side.

"He's the one who has you in chains!" I shrieked, dodging her attack.

An evil chuckle escaped Lucifer's lips, and anger filled Kyler. Morgana threw a fireball at me, and it nicked me in the shoulder. It burned, but only for a moment before I started to heal. Kyler spun around me as he pulled the sword from behind his back.

He swung it at her hard. I tried remembering what everyone had taught me. If I could absorb her soul, this would be over. She wouldn't go down without a fight; that much became obvious.

Could I do it without touching her?

Another fireball came my way. As I ducked, Lucifer clapped his hands. He was definitely on my shit list now.

Why did he do this?

Because he was Lucifer, and could do whatever he wanted. He said as much. The anger in my bones tried to take over. Static engulfed my body, and lightning tingled over every inch of me.

Kyler punched Morgana hard, and she flew back into the wall. His strength surprised me; I'd never seen him use it like that before.

I took the opportunity to call her soul to me. She fought it as she stood up, and her hard steps came my way. It was harder to pull a soul when I had no physical contact and the target moved. Kyler punched her down again while I continued to summon her soul.

"Take my hand." Kyler's voice echoed in my head.

My eyes shot to him, and I took his hand. Her soul came to me with ease at our connection. After she fell to the ground, my eyes locked with Kyler's.

"That was impressive." Lucifer came off the wall and stepped over the demon's body. "Shall we?" He motioned for the door.

"What the fuck was that?" I yelled at him. Kyler tensed beside me. He moved his body, putting himself between Lucifer and me.

"A lesson, and you learned." He shrugged with one shoulder.

I was getting sick of people doing whatever they wanted when it came to me. With the gods as my witness, this would end.

"She is my Princess, and you will treat her like one from now on," Kyler growled, standing up to Lucifer just as he had with Ezra.

"Such a good attack dog you have, Sapphire. Now let us go." Lucifer walked out of the room. Kyler went to swing his sword again, but I put a hand on his shoulder.

Kyler turned to me, and my head shook. It was not worth losing him to the literal devil. We left the dungeon, and Lucifer went back to his throne. I was angry at him. I was angry at Ezra. Both of them played me, and it was getting on my last nerve. My feet stomped the entire way up to the room; I slammed the door. Kyler watched me pace. A part of me was ready to storm through the castle and take Lucifer's soul. This needed to end.

I didn't expect Lucifer to be decent and become my best friend, but to let someone attack me, or possibly kill me?

"You spoke in my mind." I stopped pacing and turned to Kyler.

"We are mates," He shrugged.

"So we can talk into one another's minds?" His never-fading smirk filled his face.

You can scream my name in here any time you want.

At that moment, something came over me.

How about now?

Kyler picked me up in one smooth motion and laid me on the bed, my head resting on a pillow. He hovered over my body and leaned down. Only then did I realize he was no longer in his armor. My heart raced, and the world stopped as soon as our lips touched again.

Nothing else mattered. The heat from his breath as our lips touched sent shivers down my spine. His legs rested on either side of mine as he held my hips, his body tight against mine.

"No!" I whispered as he pulled away.

I wanted more, needed more. He ignited something inside of me. He ran a hand up my thigh over my jeans, and I let out a small gasp. He pulled the holster, holding my dagger down, sending chills down my spine.

"I've loved nothing more than watching your eyes light up just now." He smirked as he laid the blade on the table beside the bed.

He slowly traced kisses from my lips to my neck. His hands explored every inch of my body he could touch. I instinctively arched into him. My body craved his every movement more than the last.

He lifted my top over my head, taking my bra with it in one quick motion, revealing my naked breasts. I could feel my cheeks redden. His lips trailed down to my left nipple. His tongue lapped in tight circles while he rolled the other between his fingers. A light whimper escaped my throat as his eyes shot to mine.

He was enjoying what he was doing to me, and I was helpless to it. He moved his lips down to my hip line and pulled my jeans and panties off with his teeth in one smooth motion. I could feel myself dripping. My hunger for him grew as I panted. I wanted him, here and now, more than I've ever wanted anything.

Kyler smiled at me as he pulled his pants off, revealing his hard member. I didn't even have time to react before he was on top of me again. His finger lightly ran along my wetness. With a growl, he licked his finger.

He craved me just as bad as I did him.

He went down my body, reaching my wetness with his tongue and beginning to lick in slow, long motions while a finger on my clit rubbed in gentle circles. My body shook. He continued and made faster motions with his tongue until I let out a scream as my body exploded in orgasm.

I lay there panting, still dripping onto the sheets. His eyes met mine as he came for a kiss—my turn to play the game. I pushed him off me and rolled, pushing him down. I straddled his body and lowered myself onto him. We echoed each other's moans as he slid inside of me. I leaned down and met his lips with mine as my hips moved against his.

He wrapped his arms around my waist and pulled me harder onto him, causing me to let out a low groan of pleasure. Kyler thrust his hips below me, and I could tell we were both close to complete ecstasy. I bit his neck, and hunger took over. He flipped me onto my back and slammed his hips against me. His warmth filled me. Letting out a moan of his name, I, too, exploded against him. The passion between us, overwhelming. My body still shook as Kyler slid out and lay beside me.

"That was mind-blowing," He panted out.

"Agreed." I breathed.

After a period of silence, I spoke into the room, "Do we go back to Ezra?" My words came out in a low breath. "Is he the lesser of two evils?"

"I think that's up to you, Fire." Kyler ran a hand up and down my arm in smooth movements.

"I want them both dead," I spoke in a whisper.

Ezra would get everything he deserved for every moment he hurt me. Lucifer had to die no matter what. It had become clear he would never let me rule equally. He watched as we got attacked. It made no sense that Morgana attacked me and not Lucifer. The anger that Kyler took away rose back to the surface.

"We'll make a plan, then." Kyler kissed my forehead. "It's time you took your throne, My Queen."

We both got off the bed and cleaned off before changing our clothes. Kyler put his armor back on. The idea of going back to Ezra made me sick, but after what Lucifer did, I had to choose until we had a plan in place. After we were ready, Kyler pulled me back and kissed me.

"I knew something was going on between you two! We do not steal what is not ours, Kyler." The bedroom door burst open, and my heart dropped as Lucifer's words boomed in my ears.

Kyler squeezed my hand tightly.

I watched as a devilish grin slid across Lucifer's face.

Chapter Forty-Seven

Sapphire

Lucifer snapped his fingers, and we appeared in the arena. He and I stood on the platform with the throne and a chair on either side. My eyes moved to Kyler, who stood in the middle of the oval below us.

My heart sank. My breaths became slow and shallow. Time moved slowly. I tried to move my body, but I couldn't. My legs wouldn't move from under me. Pain rippled through me. Demons filled the seats as dread washed over me in a wave, gripping my chest.

Kyler! I shouted as loud as I could into his mind.

God's! Where is my angel now!

"Sit," Lucifer said, and a force pushed me down. "It would seem this knight does not know how to keep his hands to himself, trying to steal the Princess from Ezra. Let us invite him to watch his brother's demise, shall we?"

Tears swelled in my eyes.

He was going to kill my Kyler.

No! He couldn't do this. No, no, no!

This was all my fault. I should have never let my guard down. Touching the necklace around my neck, I closed my fist around it. I was supposed to be powerful and a fucking gift from the Gods. I had broken an ancient binding, but now I was useless. My power sat below the surface, but I couldn't do anything, no matter how hard I tried. Kyler's eyes met mine, and fear filled his bones as much as mine.

It'll be okay. He wanted to reassure me, but we both knew the truth.

"Sapphire?" Ezra looked past Lucifer to me. "She finally accepted her mate's bond?"

My fingers gripped my neck.

Ezra knew?

It was that precise moment that I realised this was all a trap. Every moment since Ezra took me to Hell. He knew, they both knew. Lucifer was working with Ezra all along. All those meetings...

"Ah, nice of you to join us, Ezra. I am about to punish your knight. See, we have strict rules here in Hell Sapphire. One of the big ones is not taking a princess from her prince when she is bound." Lucifer sat down and let out an evil laugh. That wicked grin crossed his face, and anger filled me. Tears streamed down my face.

I will kill him for this.

With the wave of a hand, Lucifer summoned a group of demons. They were all tall and built like football players. The armor they wore was that of Lucifer's guard. The demons attacked Kyler with swords and fireballs. Kyler swung back at the swords as they came down towards him. Effortlessly, he avoided the fireballs.

He can do this. He can live. He has to.

All I could do was watch in horror as they took turns beating him down with their swords. Kyler spat blood from his mouth and continued to fight them off.

A tightness wrapped around my chest. The air in my lungs felt trapped. I wanted to yell. To scream. But nothing escaped me.

Kyler swung his sword and cut the head off one of the demons. My hand covered my mouth as I watched in horror. He killed the other demons in the group as he danced around with a dangerous beauty.

Lucifer roared and summoned another group of demons, only this time, there were more. At least twenty. I tried to speak to him but couldn't find my voice. Lucifer looked over at me and laughed. He was enjoying the pain he caused us.

Ezra watched with amusement on his face. That feeling of deceit again radiated off him. He wanted to use me. Lucifer was giving Ezra precisely what he wanted. I was not ready to take him on alone, and with Kyler dead, he knew I'd be powerless against him. Ezra would trap me in his castle with no escape.

How could I be this thing of legends when I didn't even know how to control my hunger?

Nausea twirled in my stomach at the thought.

Kyler phased but hit an invisible barrier and fell to the ground. It looked like he could only move within the arena. There was no way out of this. He tried to run, using lightning speed. As he did, I watched Lucifer summon a wall that Kyler crashed into. He fell to the ground and spat blood out of his mouth. Everyone in the stands laughed and cheered as he tried to stand back up. Lucifer and Ezra echoed the laughter, and anxiety filled my body.

This was an unfair game. Kyler would lose no matter what he tried.

There was nothing I could do but watch as the demons in the stands roared with cheer every time Kyler went down. A demon slid his sword through Kyler's heart. The sound of the sword squishing it echoed in my ears. The noise of the world faded away, and everything went still. An eerie silence shifted into the air. Pain shot through me as Kyler fell to his knees. Blood poured from his mouth, and he fell to the ground.

As he crumbled down, the crowd roared with cheers.

No. Get up, Kyler! Get up!

I screamed in my head, hoping he could hear me. Lucifer clapped at a steady pace and turned his head to me.

"Anyone else want to win the Princess's heart?" Lucifer and Ezra laughed in unison as Lucifer pointed to me. I couldn't breathe. The world spun around me.

"No!" I roared.

Looking around for familiar faces, for help, I spotted Orpheus, who looked like he was mouthing something. Vealla hid against Dante's chest. We were all helpless.

I used everything inside me to phase to Kyler and my power shot to life. Every ounce of my energy was used to get there. Weakness consumed my body as a tear fell my face. I couldn't lose him.

"Please don't go, Kyler." I cried as I pulled his head into my lap, not caring that I was sitting in a pool of blood. "Please, I love you! Don't leave me."

Why did I wait so long to tell him? My heart felt like it was ripping in half as that pull between us weakened.

"I love you, Fire. Forever."

Kyler's last words seeped through his bloody lips as pain and rage filled me. The pull disappeared as I shot my eyes to Lucifer and Ezra. My chest heaved. I let out a roar of pain, and fire skidded across the sand.

"I knew who you were and sent that vampire to attack you. I thought you were hiding who you were, but it turns out there was a spell keeping you hidden from everyone, even yourself. Now, here you are, crying in a pool of your mate's blood. Let this be a lesson, Sapphire. You are the one who is nothing." Ezra's words sat in my mind like bricks.

"You could never take over Hell. You cannot even save your mate." Lucifer's wicked laugh echoed in the arena.

Flames consumed Kyler's body, and he disappeared from my arms.

No! BRING HIM BACK!

FUCK THE GODS. FUCK THIS LIFE.

"I would like to take my Princess home now," Ezra smirked at me, and I threw up from the cascade of pain inside of me.

My reason to live was gone.

Kyler was gone.

"Very well," Lucifer snapped his fingers one last time.

Chapter Forty-Eight

Sapphire

The dark orange sky lit my room in Ezra's castle. I sat on the bed, staring out through the curtains.

An ugly emptiness filled my body. There was no eating or sleeping, only this quiet, empty room. I had no reason to move. To live.

Ezra would have Orpheus come get me every day. I'd sit on that stupid throne in silence. There was no point in living without Kyler. There was no point in trying to go on. The only thing I had left in this gods-forsaken world, taken from me in an instant.

The call from him used to keep me sane. No matter where I was, I knew he was with me somehow. Now, the call never came, and a vast emptiness replaced it. My cheeks burned from the trails of tears that had long since dried and hardened.

Days blended together. It could have been years or hours. I stayed in that spot, staring at the sky. Nothing pulled me from my trance.

The image of Kyler dying in my arms played over and over in my mind. His last words echoed in my head like a broken record player. There were no more tears left for me to cry. I don't think I could even if I wanted to.

With a sigh, I looked down at my hands. At least he died knowing I loved him.

A knock came from the door—my companion of the day, I'm sure. My body didn't move. Weakness sat inside me since it had taken all my power to phase Kyler. I had not taken in a soul, and the idea of dying became a silent promise that I could reunite with my love.

The bedroom door opened, and Orpheus walked in.

"Princess, I know you don't want to leave, but it's time to go to the throne room. Perhaps take a soul?" He came closer to where I sat, but no words left my mouth. "I'm at your service if you change your mind." A low sigh escaped his throat. "When you're ready, I'll be outside the door." Orpheus left the room, and the noise of the door shutting again turned my head.

I would have to face Ezra again. There would be no escaping the prison in my mind, but I could at least escape the room. Stretching and groaning, I got off the bed. All I had to do was make it through another day. My body didn't want to move, to see the man who helped this emptiness engulf my heart.

I walked into the bathroom and stared at myself. Bags hung below my eyes. My hair became a knotted mess. I lifted my brush, and every stroke through my hair felt like the hardest thing I'd ever done.

As I pushed the bedroom door open, Orpheus leaned his back against the wall with his arms crossed. The idea made me feel sick, but Ezra would no longer let me be alone.

Once Orpheus noticed me standing beside him, he bowed.

Did he see me as the Queen of Hell? Did anyone? How could they after watching me fail to protect my mate?

A goal I once had no longer mattered. It crumbled away as soon as it clicked that Ezra and Lucifer had played me. Orpheus and I moved through the castle to the throne room. I couldn't bring myself to make eye contact with Ezra.

He sat on his throne, talking to one of his subjects. No words escaped my throat as I sat beside him. I no longer bothered to put on my crown. Ezra turned his head to me and then went back to his conversation.

The warmth from outside crawled over my skin. It felt nice to feel it after being in my room.

"I see you came out of hiding," Ezra said, reaching for my hand.

I didn't move or say a word to him despite knowing his anger would turn into a beating later. The physical pain felt trivial compared to the pain that shredded my heart into pieces.

What could I say to the man who ripped my world from me? He was the reason that the vampire attacked me. He was the reason Kyler died.

I bit my quivering lip to hold back the tears. Our people would come in and out of this throne room all day. I couldn't let them see how broken I became.

"You want to ignore me? Okay. Then let me tell you how I knew Kyler was your mate. I overheard him tell Amdis the day he met you at the bar how beautiful you were to him. Oh, and the way he sang your praises for being able to banter with him. He was so in love. It was so easy to play you right into my hand. Now my worthless half-brother is dead, and you are mine."

He paused for a moment, his lips curling in anger from my lack of reaction.

"Did you know I pulled him from your date on purpose? I have eyes everywhere. I knew exactly what he was doing. I did not even let you get to the main course. He was so mad! Not as mad as when I reminded him how worthless he was. Silas and I made him cry. Such a Pitiful. *Dead. Dog.*"

My heart and my body ached.

Why couldn't I just die?

Why does death not beckon to me?

Where is my angel? The Gods? They never cared.

Never.

Kyler was my peace, the quiet I could tolerate. Tears began to stream down my face again as Ezra let out an evil laugh. I lowered my head and tried to pull myself together. The other princes were due for a visit, and they could not know how many pieces I broke into.

What a disappointment I became. They promised to go to war for me, and I couldn't even save Kyler. I couldn't save my mate. Hell deserved better than that. Hell deserved better than me.

Fuck destiny.

I took a deep breath, trying to push out the agony in my soul. Alfonso, Dante, and Vealla walked into my view. My shoulders straightened at the sight, and I wiped the tears from my face. Another group of friends I failed. Visions of all the things I lost ran rampant in my mind. It took whatever sliver of sanity I had left to keep from collapsing into nothing.

"Highnesses." Alfonso bowed to us.

I mustered a small smile for him. The worry lines forming on Dante's face told me I had not convinced them.

"May I borrow her Highness? I could use help with a private matter." Vealla stepped forward.

"No. She is to stay here until she is better," Ezra said simply.

No one had to ask what that meant. They watched me lose Kyler and heard Lucifer and Ezra's betrayal. Ezra would never let me leave again. It would be a waste to try. I couldn't die, and no longer wanted to live.

The idea of killing myself slithered into my mind: an escape from this Hell. My body would simply heal if I tried. There was no escaping. Dante gave me a sympathetic look. A tear fell down my cheek. Alfonso and Vealla turned their attention to me.

"Your vampires are still causing issues, Highness. What happened to personally taking care of it? Or did that go away when I forgot to put my foot in my mouth?" Alfonso chuckled, trying to pull a response from me. I shrugged.

"I think the Princess should be alone. She obviously cannot handle the company right now. Orpheus, take her back to her room." Ezra insisted.

I walked down the steps. He would not get a fight from me. Everyone bowed as I made my way past them. My legs wobbled when I went up the stairs. The weakness in my body grew with every passing day that I did not consume a soul. Orpheus shut the door behind me, and I found my spot on the bed.

The light from the sky reflected on the walls, making the room brighter.

My prison cell.

I curled into a ball, holding my knees against my chest. Anxiety pulled at me, my racing heart beating hard. My hand gripped my chest, trying to stop it, trying to calm the beating. To stop the beating.

This was my life now.

At least my mortal friends were safe from all of this.

I wished I could talk to them. They pulled me from my depression years ago. Isabelle especially would understand this hurt. There was no way to leave this castle, let alone Hell, without Ezra finding me. It would be pointless.

Oh, Kyler, I'm lost without you.

A walk in the warm air might help. When I had lost my parents, Isabelle told me it helped her clear her mind. Orpheus stood outside my door as usual. He leaned on the wall with his arms crossed. His black shirt gripped his muscles as he shifted his body towards me. No words left my mouth as I began to walk away. He followed in line behind me.

I ignored Ezra as he called after me. Orpheus continued to follow me as I walked out of the castle. The warm air hit me harder and I closed my eyes.. Where was the greatness in me now? I made my way to the village, and demons bowed to me. Polite smiles crossed my face as much as I could muster. I went to the park, where I could hear children's laughter. A small smile curved on my lips at the sound. There was an empty park bench by some trees, and I sat down and watched the kids play.

Sometimes, a demon would come up and bow to me and say how glad they were to see me, and I'd give more gentle smiles. The emptiness still sat inside me, but my broken heart felt a minuscule amount better to see my subjects happy.

I stayed on the bench for a few hours. A fresh pain twisted in me at the thought of Kyler and me never having this. I couldn't have kids as a soul eater, but we still could have been a family one day. We would have taken over Hell together. We never talked about our future; we didn't have a chance. I was stupid and waited till he was dying to tell him the truth, to say I loved him.

Standing up, I looked at Orpheus and nodded to let him know I was on the move again. After all, it wasn't his fault he got stuck babysitting me. The walk back to the castle was torment. I knew every step closer was a step to Ezra and whatever anger he had from my leaving the castle. Orpheus followed behind me and placed a hand on my shoulder. My eyes met his as I turned around.

"I know your depression is telling you that life is not worth living, but Kyler and I knew each other well. I also know exactly who you are, to him, to Hell, and to the Gods. If you need me, I choose you, my Queen. Every guard in the castle was loyal to your mate, not Ezra. Grieve as long as you need to, but he'd want you to continue. Hell still needs its savior." He bowed to me and then straightened.

Kyler had once told me that the army was not loyal to Ezra, yet they took his orders with Kyler gone.

Were they scared of him? Or were they waiting for me?

I stormed through the castle. Ezra watched, but he didn't bother getting up. I felt his anger as I walked by. He would get me back for my disobedience tonight when he came to visit, of that I was sure. I made it to my room, and the bed molded around me as I sat. This spot had been my home for so long that it became imprinted in my bed. My thoughts went back to what Orpheus said.

Hell still needs a savior.

Lucifer's reign of terror had only begun. For him to knock me down when all of Hell knew who I was proved a point I couldn't see while swallowed in grief. I needed rest and to heal, and then I would do what I needed to for Kyler.

I won't let his death be in vain.

Chapter Forty-Nine

Sapphire

After a few hours, Ezra shoved the bedroom door open. The lines on his forehead creased as he stomped into the room. His new favorite game was about to begin. He rolled up his sleeves and stood in front of the bed.

"Here. Now." He pointed to the edge of the bed, but I ignored his request. A low growl escaped his lips from my defiance. "Fine. Remember, you chose this."

Ezra walked over to where I was curled on the bed and slammed his fist into my face. Blood spilled from my nose, but still I didn't waver. Lightning formed around his fist, and he punched my stomach. He watched me waiting for a reaction, but he would get nothing from me.

He let a lightning rod continuously shoot into my body from various points. His nostrils flared at my lack of response. It didn't matter. He would never get anything from me again.

"You will give me what I want." He screamed in my face.

His fists continued to slam into me. I looked down to see a bulge in his pants. For a split second, a laugh escaped me. A pathetic sight. He got hard from punching me.

"Something funny, you vile bitch?" He showed me his fangs, and I could not help the laughter that came from me.

I continued to laugh, over and over again. Until Ezra left from frustration and my laughter turned to tears and pain. Not physical pain, but the pain from all that had conspired.

My birth parents, whom I'd never meet, my real parents, who were dead, and my friends, who I would never see again. All things I lost because of who I was, because of some destiny the Gods cursed me with. Kyler was my biggest loss. The last shred of hope inside of me slipped away.

I sat up on the bed and pulled out the picture of Apollyon and Lilith again. I decided to read my mortal mother's journal. She had a way of making me feel better as a teen, perhaps even her words on a page could take away some of the hurt I felt.

After summoning the notebook, I flipped through the pages until I reached her last passage.

My darling Sapphire,

This will be my final letter to you. I can feel the last bit of my soul slipping away. There is one more secret I kept from you. The truth of why I am dying. The only way Lilith could hide your demon was with a spell. A spell that would slowly absorb my soul over the years. Once I am gone, you will slowly take your father's soul as well. Once we are both gone, it will only be a matter of time before you awaken in your true form. Don't fret, my darling girl, we both agreed to keep you safe and to love you as our own. And we do, wholeheartedly. I would give up my life ten times over if it meant you got to fulfill your destiny. You are the savior. You, my love, are going to save the world. Please don't give up hope. All will work out in the end. Your angel will always be close by. I made him vow to be as close to you as possible despite the Gods' wishes. I may only have a day or two with you, but I am grateful for every minute. I will always be able to claim that you were a gift from the Gods, and that is something no one else will ever get to say.

Until we meet again.

~ Mom

Tears that I didn't think I had began to fall onto the paper. Blotches blurring the words. I closed the book and pulled the journal to my chest.

My mother gave her life for me. My father did too, and I hated him for drinking. Yet he knew it was his turn to die, for me. They gave up their lives because they believed in me. I closed my eyes and lay down, fighting the tears.

"Highness, Highness, wake up." Vealla shook my shoulder. I groaned, opening my eyes. I held the book close to my chest still.

What was Vealla doing in my room?

I sat up and looked at her. Behind where she stood was an oval portal. The iridescent color waved around from the magic holding it together. The scene from the oval was hard to make out, but from the dark colors of vines, I assumed it to be Dante's castle.

"Come with me, please. I have something to show you. I can only hold the portal for so long." Vealla spoke fast.

With a nod, I slid out of bed. Vealla took my hand and pulled me through the portal. An incredible burst of magic hit me as we came out the other side.

The view before me was a vision I never expected to see. I stood on the balcony of Dante's castle, and past his village were armies. To the left were his demons, the middle consisted of the witches, and right were the demon warriors. All of them must have had hundreds standing by. Blade stood with his brethren, and Esme stood in front of the witches. Alfonso, Dante, and Vealla were with me on the balcony.

"We told you we would go to war for you. None of us can take away the pain of losing a mate, but we can stand with you." Dante said, nodding his head towards the armies below.

They had gathered, ready to storm Hell for me.

"You are our chosen Queen. Kyler came to see me before we first met and told me who you were. All of us were skeptical at first; there was no way the lost Princess was here. Then we met you, and you hit Dante with your elemental power." Vealla said in her soft voice.

"Yeah, that kind of hurt." Dante snickered and rubbed the back of his neck.

Vealla rolled her eyes, "I healed his wound. The power from you lingered there, and it was strong, fierce. It was definitely you, our Queen."

"Kyler said something to us when he came to get us that night. He said, 'She will save us all, and I will go to the ends of the realms to make sure she can.' He believed in you, and that is good enough for us. I even let it slide when he threatened me for hitting on you." Alfonso teased me.

A small giggle came from my lips, and everyone turned to me. The noise surprised even me. Kyler was respected by everyone, and he wanted to help me take over Hell. The three of them stood waiting for something, for me to speak. I walked to the edge of the balcony and placed my hands on the railing. Every noise and voice turned to eerie silence. Smoke rolled around the armies standing at the ready for me. My mom's last journal entry and this army before me was the sign I needed.

It was time to use my grief as a weapon.

To get my throne and my revenge.

"We won't go to war. You all trust me enough to risk your lives; I need you to trust me enough to act like everything is the same. Ezra and Lucifer's tyranny will be dealt with in a way that no one will get hurt. You all fought for years for freedom you have yet to see. I will give it to you. That, I promise. Go home, live your life. I will take care of the rest. For my parents, for Hell, and for all of you, my subjects. *My demons.*"

Everyone bowed in unison before me.

Hell will be mine.

A plan danced in my head when I turned back to my friends. They're hopeful faces met mine.

"Thank you, Highness," Vealla said with warmth in her eyes.

"I'm doing this for Kyler. He believed in me, and I will make sure I am worthy of it. But I need you guys to do something for me." My three companions focused on me. "I need you to pretend everything is fine for a few days. Ezra's time has come."

Dante took a step towards me, "We are at your command." He bowed before me.

"Anything you need." Vealla bowed her head to me after she finished speaking.

I turned back to look at the skies beyond the balcony, "I'm the savior."

Static filled my arms as I formed balls of lightning in them. I looked up and threw bolts into the sky as a thunderous noise cracked through the air. So much power filled me. Kyler protected me with his life so I could fulfill my destiny. I'd use that knowledge and protect Hell.

"Take me home. Go take care of your kingdoms. When the time is right, I'll send word." I said, turning back to the group.

Vealla whispered the demon language until a new portal appeared. I gave them a bow of the head before stepping into it. My room in the castle was still empty as the portal dissipated. Hell and the world would see who I had become soon. My determination took over, and I opened the door to my room.

"Orpheus, bring me a soul. We need to train. Tell no one."

He looked at me with wide eyes.

"Is it time, my Queen?" He asked.

"Yes," I said simply.

He bowed and disappeared.

Chapter Fifty

Sapphire

Once Ezra left my room the next night, Orpheus and I went to the training grounds in the vampire realm. Dante and Vealla were waiting for us. I needed to train again to hone everything Kyler taught me. He fought till his death to protect me, and I'd do that for his memory and for Hell. One last training session, and then it would be time to take my rightful place.

I stood in the middle of the arena and summoned two black swords. Vealla went over to the bench by the weapon racks to stay out of the way. As I went to the middle of the sand, Blade showed up with Esme.

Blade wore Lucifer's red guard armor, and a spike of anger thralled me. Once I took over, their armor would change. A unified Hell would mean everyone would have the armor I chose. Esme bobbed over to me and bowed.

"We heard our Queen could use a hand." She grinned before darting over to Vealla's side.

Blade gave me his usual grunt, but pulled out his sword.

"Now it's a party." Dante laughed, summoning his own swords.

"One last training, and then, I do what needs to be done," I said.

Everyone bowed to me. There was one last thing I had to do before we could start. I waved my hand and summoned my black crown.

I am the Princess of Hell, and I will take what is mine.

"Let's do this," I said.

I twirled the swords in my hands, ready for a battle.

Swords began to clash above my head. I blocked as Blade went to strike with a shield he had summoned on his right arm. Dante tried to get me from the opposite side, but I ducked and slid around them. Orpheus threw a fireball that I managed to dodge. A low growl left my throat.

"I'm going to rule Hell. Stop being gentle and fight me!" I roared.

Dante swung his sword hard at me while Blade ran at me full force. I dropped a sword and pushed Blade with a burst of wind from my hand while simultaneously blocking Dante's sword. Orpheus phased in front of me and slammed his sword down on my shoulder, slicing it. My eyes darted to him and his wide eyes. I pushed the sword up and healed before pushing the blade in Orpheus' hand hard, pushing him backwards.

We battled for hours. Swords and elementals went flying in every direction. At one point, Esme had to duck from a bolt of lightning. When my body could no longer heal quicker than I got hit, I shoved everyone away with a burst of wind. I panted and kneeled on one knee, holding myself up with my sword. Vealla and Esme came over to heal everyone.

The red bow from the first time Kyler and I were here came into view. The wind blew through my hair, and I closed my eyes. I let my memories flow to remember why I was doing this. Kyler showed up at the bar, he made me smile, and his sarcasm matched mine. He and I felt created for each other. I pictured his smirk and his voice. The pain that I pushed aside rose again as a tear fell. Everyone's attention turned back to me.

"Highness, everything will be okay. If you need more time, this can wait." Blade placed a hand on my shoulder. I had never heard him speak before.

"Agreed. Kyler would understand if you needed more time, Highness." Dante said as the girls came over. Kyler's words floated in my mind then.

You never ask for more than I can give.

He was so afraid I would see him differently because of his trauma and his past. I never saw him that way, as someone less than. I took our time together for granted, and I hated myself for it.

"There's something I need to do. Orpheus, can you cover for me with Ezra?" he nodded. "Thank you all for standing by me." I waved and then let my butterflies take me away. There was one more person I needed to see.

The small home sat before me. I tapped on the door lightly. The shades of red in the sky were lighter. The way time moved in Hell made little sense to me.

Sylvie greeted me with wide eyes. When she saw me, she put up a finger and disappeared into the house. I waited for a moment, and Zariah opened the door more.

"Highness?" He asked.

"Zariah, I know Kyler is gone, but I want to get to know you. He loved you as a brother, which makes you family to me, too. I hope... I hope that's okay," Tears fell down my face as the words came out.

Zariah stared at me for a moment. His wife touched his shoulder gently.

"I would like that, Highness." His lower lip began to quiver.

"I have a few things to deal with, but I'll visit as soon as I can."

I gave them both a warm smile. I could do what I needed to. A promise to Sylvie needed to be filled. Afterward, I'd make sure Kyler had whatever kind of burial a demon should, even if he had no body. Then I'd get to know the only decent person Kyler had left in his life.

"Kill them both, make them suffer, Highness." Zariah's eyes were glowing.

"I have every intention of taking my rightful place in honor of Kyler." My voice cracked, but I tried to sound confident.

"Thank you for coming here, Highness." Sylvie bowed to me.

I gave Zariah and his wife a nod and phased away.

Standing on top of Ezra's castle, I peeked over the battlement. The village below had minimal movement. Most demons were resting now. A soft wind ruffled my hair, and another tear fell down my face.

"Kyler, I know you will never hear this, but I need to say goodbye. You gave me the strength to figure out who I am and what I

could do. You stood by me in ways no one had before. All my life, a piece of me felt lost, but never with you. Now our enemies will die. For your honor, for my destiny, and for the pain they brought us. Your brother can no longer hurt you, and soon he won't be able to hurt anyone. Until we meet again." I whispered into the wind, hoping wherever he was, he heard me.

"Ezra was angry that he could not find you last night. He would come for you now, but I lied and told him Lucifer sent for him. I don't think we have much time, Highness." Orpheus said in one breath behind me. He waved his hand and summoned a demon to take a soul from. I absorbed it and felt my power ignite within my body. I was ready.

"It will be over soon."

Ezra's demise was within my reach now.

Let's go save the world, Kyler.

Chapter Fifty-One

Sapphire

The next day, it was time to enact my plan. No one but Orpheus knew when it would happen. The others knew it could be soon, but not how soon. The fewer that were aware, the easier this would be. Ezra was going to suffer as my mate did. I went to the throne room where he had been having a meeting. It was perfect timing, and his legion would watch him die. He looked at me with anger in his eyes. I summoned my black sword, gripping the hilt.

"Ezra." I said through gritted teeth, "I think we need to talk."

"Sapphire." He stood and stared at me.

The vampires in the room darted out behind me. Anger from Ezra drifted into me. He would die a painful death.

Blood for Blood.

"It's time you learned your place, Ezra." I sang in a cool tone.

"Is that so?" He summoned his own sword and took heavy steps my way.

"I'm power. I'm the savior. You, you're nothing, have always been nothing, and will always be nothing." I lifted my sword, and the electric current of my power tingled between my fingers.

"We will see about that." Ezra let a sly grin cross his face before he charged at me.

Our swords collided, and thunder cracked through the room. Every demon who had been there scattered. I watched Ezra's feet, his every move. His anger flicked through him as I countered his every strike.

He dropped his sword and began walking around me in circles, throwing lightning my way. I used my sword to block every strike, spinning in a circle. After a short period, I used my wind power to push him away. He fell down and slid on the floor.

His black eyes met mine, a storm brewing behind his calloused smile. He shot toward me with his speed and slammed me into the wall. Ezra swung his hand to hit me, but I gripped it before impact. I let out a deep laugh.

Wrong move.

I spun him around, slamming him into the wall, reversing our positions. Ezra's eyes widened as I pinned him with my arm against his neck.

"You took everything away from me." Ezra tried to move, but my power pushed him back against the wall. "You watched as the person I love was ripped away from me, all because you wanted a weapon. Now you get to see firsthand what you created." I let out a wicked laugh.

"You do not have the gall to kill me," Ezra said, half choking from the pressure of my arms.

"Watch me."

Fire engulfed his body from my hand. I called his soul to me slowly as he burned, and his screams bounced off the castle walls. His lifeless body dropped to the ground. I looked down at his charred skin. There was nothing recognizable left.

No one would remember him years from now. I heaved and closed my eyes. His soul burned like acid inside of me for a brief moment, then my power sprang to life.

With a scream from my throat, lightning, wind, and fire circled my body as I fell to my knees. My magic surrounded me as I began to wail and cry. Ezra would no longer be a threat, but I still felt empty.

Empty and alone.

It will all be okay.

My angel's voice echoed in my mind, but I ignored him. He and the Gods abandoned me when I needed them most. I did this all on my own, without them.

I took Ezra's soul alone.

For my mate.

Footsteps echoed in my ears as demons entered the room. I turned, and the faces staring at me had smiles. Kyler's legion was mine. Ezra's soul was mine, and the new ruler of the realm was me.

Waving my hand caused Ezra's body to disappear. My powers simmered out, and I sat on his throne. The demons before me all bowed. Hell will be mine, and Lucy was next on my list to die.

"All hail our reigning Princess!" Orpheus smiled at me and took a second bow.

He was instrumental in this and I won't forget it. The demons in the room roared with cheer and yelled my name. A small sense of pride filled me despite the ache within me.

"Things are going to change around here. If anyone has a problem with the way I run things, don't be afraid to speak up. Our golden age begins." I spoke firmly, flames brewing in my black eyes. "Now leave me. Except you." I looked at Orpheus.

The room of demons disappeared as I crossed my legs. I snapped and changed the crest on the banisters to mine. Ezra's black rose no longer rests on red banners. Instead, my sword and shield rested on white banners with gold trim. That empty spot pulled at my heart as my fingers gripped the arms of the throne. I swallowed and fought back tears. Ezra was gone, a victory won, but my heart still ached. My pain still ravaged my mind. Taking a deep breath, I tried to push it aside. I would protect them all, just like Kyler protected me.

This was for him.

"I don't mean to overstep, Highness, but as the sole monarch and soon-to-be Queen of Hell, it would be helpful for you to have a second-in-command. Someone you know and trust to do your dirty work," Orpheus said, bowing his head.

"Sounds like a job for you, Orpheus. You have more than earned it." I smirked and rose from the throne. "Orpheus, with Ezra dead, any magic he used, is it gone?"

Orpheus raised his head, giving me a curious look, "Yes, Highness."

"Good to know. Keep an eye on things here, please. I have something to do, and a nap to take." Orpheus bowed fully, and my black butterflies surrounded me.

I stood in the middle of Ezra's war room as the butterflies disappeared. Anger and pain filled me. It was all for Ezra and his plan to take over Hell. My body became rife with warmth as fire surrounded my hands. I threw it at everything in the room, the walls covered in messy notes, the figurines, all of it. My eyes locked on his map, and I formed lightning in my hands. Thunder cracked as I hit the map over and over again, screaming as loud as I could.

The room was filled with smoke and ash. I sat on the floor and roared with pain. The noise of fire cracking echoed in my ears, and tears began to stream down my face. I bent my knees up and ran a hand through my ash-covered hair. The fire raged on around me, and I waited for everything to be a pile of nothing before standing back up. I waved my hand and killed the flames. The smoke that sat heavy in the room had no effect on my demon lungs. I closed my eyes momentarily and decided I needed sleep.

I phased to Kyler's room, crying tears that flowed no matter how hard I tried to stop. My love was gone, the one person who had made me feel whole. Once I entered his room, I threw my heels on the floor and plopped onto his bed. My tears continued to fall.

Nothing could take away the pain.

Even with Ezra dead, I am drowning

Chapter Fifty-Two

Sapphire

The next morning, I sat criss-cross on Kyler's bed, staring at the photos of both sets of parents and my friends. I silently cursed myself for never taking a picture with Kyler. A small smile crept on my face, thinking back to when I assumed you couldn't see vampires in mirrors.

I lifted my head at the sound of a knock on the door. Sighing, I slid the pictures into his nightstand and walked over to see who it was.

"Highness, I'm sorry to disturb you." Orpheus bowed to me.

"Orph, I want to change the legion's armor," I said before he could tell me the real reason he was here.

"To what Highness?" He tilted his head at me.

"Black armor, but the sash, I want it to be like the banners. White with gold trim and my crest. Can we do that?" I raised a brow.

"We can do whatever you'd like, My Queen. I'll be sure to get this to the legion at once. In the meantime, you have company in the throne room." He bowed the upper half of his body.

"I'll be down in a moment. Thank you."

He turned on his heels and made his way down the hall.

I looked at the bedroom and sighed. The hole in my heart that Kyler once filled rested empty again—this time, bigger, somehow. I went down to the throne room, where everyone waited.

Before my throne were the other princes and Lucifer's Officials. I took a deep breath and waited for someone to say something.

"Congratulations, it would seem you did get Ezra to Fuck off." Alfonso joked, and a small smile crossed my face. His sarcasm reminded me so much of Kyler.

"Are you okay, Highness?" Vealla walked over to the bottom of the steps, her bright smile aimed at me.

"No, but there is still one more enemy to defeat," I said, shaking my head.

I walked up the steps of the dias and sat in the throne I now claimed. The guards by the door and everyone else bowed to me. I pulled the crown off my head and stared at it.

"I need a new one. I hate the reminder this brings." I sighed and placed it down on the floor at my feet.

"We are here for whatever you might need." Esme chirped up. "What do you have in mind, Princess?"

"Gold, I want it to be gold with sapphires," I said with confidence. It was only fitting to wear a golden crown for a golden age.

"I will bring the request to Zariah," Orpheus said as he came into the room.

"Thank you," I said.

The group began to talk amongst themselves once it became clear I was done talking. It took a lot of energy to try and show face, even to them. I leaned my hand on my chin, and memories of my mortal friends and my parents flashed through my mind. I never knew my birth parents, but even their loss hits me now. I looked out at my new friends and my legion.

Snap out of it, Sapphire. Hell needs you.

A blur darted into the room. Once it stopped moving, a demon woman appeared. Her dress ran all the way to the floor, and dirt covered her face.

"Princess, I'm sorry to interrupt; there is fighting in the village." She bowed her head to me while panting.

"Where?" I asked and popped up from my throne.

"By the fountain."

"I will handle it." I darted into the village with haste.

Demons moved out of my way as I dashed along the path. A crowd formed toward the fountain, and murmurs filled the air. I spotted two vampires exchanging words with excessive voices. I hid in the back and listened.

"You stole thousands of dollars from me, you punk ass jerk." A male vampire with black hair shouted.

"It's not like you needed it, stupid prick." The blonde yelled back.

Their voices grew louder until someone threw a punch. They began to fight and throw elemental powers at each other. One fireball barely missed a child.

Okay, that's enough of that.

I phased between them and placed my hands out against their chests, pushing them apart with a brutal force of wind.

"H.... Highness." The black-haired vampire bowed. I glared at both of them as I straightened out.

"What's wrong with the two of you? It's money. You're demons, for fuck's sake," I growled at them. I didn't mean to sound so harsh, but the fighting was unnecessary.

"Forgive us, Princess. We didn't realize you were here. This is just how things get dealt with." The blonde spoke up now. The excuse for fighting made me more angry.

"That's going to change starting right now. You, what's your name?" I asked the black-haired demon.

"Blue"

"And you?" I asked the blonde.

"Kal."

"Very well, Kal, you will give him back the money you stole, or I will find you again. I promise you will not like me anymore if I do. Do I make myself clear?" I hissed at them. Both bowed before me, and I huffed. "Good." I turned on my heels and headed back to the castle.

The female demon was still there when I returned to the castle. I took my place back on the throne before speaking.

"Thank you for telling me. What's your name?" I asked her.

The others stood to the side, watching the interaction with great concentration. This was technically my first situation as a ruler.

"Phoenix, Highness." She said in a soft voice.

"Phoenix, you did me a service today. If you ever need a favor, please ask." She bowed and gave her thanks before turning away.

"Day one and she's already making moves." Dante laughed, and then everyone else did, filling the room with a lightness it had long needed.

"Orpheus, I need you to ensure some new rules get sent throughout the kingdom. My friends, thank you for coming to check on me, but it would seem my duties start now. I'll come visit all of you soon."

"You are going to make a damn fine queen. Kyler would be proud." Alfonso bowed to me.

"Thank you. I really hope he is." I said, biting my lip to hold back tears.

Everyone else bowed and left the room, leaving me and Orpheus.

He summoned a pen and paper and waited for me to tell him our new rules. I laughed internally at making a list of rules for demons in Hell, but I'd rule differently than the others. I'd make sure that if someone had a problem with a rule, demon voices would get heard. This place was not full of demons killing each other and trying to eat mortals. My subjects wanted peace after a long war and freedom to be themselves, nothing more.

"If there were grievances that needed a third party, come to me. If physical fighting happens, keep it out of the village and away from the children." I paused for a moment, allowing Orpheus to write. He gave me a nod when he was ready.

"Tell them if something is wrong, to come to me so I can fix it. Unfortunately, I never got mind-reading powers." I chuckled.

Orpheus looked up at me with a soft grin before returning to his paper.

I did not expect Hell to get fixed overnight. Lucifer still sat on his throne for now, but I could start here with my vampires. For better or worse, this had become my home. Orpheus left to make sure the realm knew.

My depression still consumed me as I sat there. Kyler's voice rang in my head. I tried to hold onto our memories. The keychain he gave me formed in my hand with a summon. A guitar: a reminder of that night we sang karaoke together. I still needed time to grieve. With sorrow heavy in my heart, I made my way back to his room.

My head lay on his pillow, and my tears began to fall once again. I did not want to leave this spot. The strength it took to leave this room for barely an hour was more than I thought I could give.

How could I kill Lucifer and rule Hell for eternity when depression ate me alive? Demons are supposed to be uncaring and soulless, yet here I was, caring too much. The conflict within myself would drive me mad. Did I save Hell and rule in honor of my mate? Or did I stay in this room and wither away forever?

The choice was obvious, no matter how hard it would be.
Save Hell for my mate.
My missing puzzle piece.
My soul.

Chapter Fifty-Three

Sapphire

"You wake her up. She chose you to be her second."

I kept my eyes closed and grumbled as voices outside my door interrupted my peace. Peeling one eye open, I could see the lighter shades of the sky peeking through the curtains.

It's too early for this.

I pulled the covers over my head and tried to drown out the noise.

"Yes, but Lucifer sent you as the errand boy," Orpheus said in his ever-calm demeanor.

What on earth was this all about? I opened my eyes and sat up, stretching my arms. At least I was learning earlier that life would always be chaotic on the throne.

"I am not waking her up! She is asleep! You never wake a sleeping bear, Orpheus. Never!"

I grumbled again and pulled the blankets off myself.

I guess I'm getting out of bed, so these two stopped fighting.

I went into the bathroom and stared at myself in the mirror. My fingers ran through my hair to brush out the mess. My mind clouded as I walked over to the full-length mirror. Bags still lay under my eyes. No matter how much rest I got, depression lingered on my face.

"You're being a baby," Orpheus' irritated voice echoed. I let out a soft laugh.

"Which one of you wants to explain what is going on?" I grumbled, pushing open the door to the room. They looked at me like a deer in headlights.

"Hi, your Highness, I, um, I... I'm here to give a message." A smaller demon tripped on his words. This was going to take forever.

"Please, shut up." I said to the kid. He instantly stopped talking.

Thank the Gods.

"Forgive Donatello, Highness. He's Lucifer's newest errand boy; he came to deliver a letter." Orpheus bowed at me, and Donatello copied him.

Donatello was short and wore glasses. He didn't wear armor but regular jeans and a T-shirt. He looked like he belonged in college, not Hell. I taped my foot on the ground.

"You're telling me Lucifer sent a *Ninja Turtle* to deliver this letter?"

They exchanged looks, and I rolled my eyes.

Does no one watch television down here?

I extended my hand, and Donatello gave me the letter. I waved a dismissive hand and turned back to the room. I imagined closing the door, and it shut behind me. I stopped in my tracks. I could move things with my mind.

When did that start happening?

I remember the book Lucifer had given me. In it, it said the alpha line could move things with their mind. Was the hold from the gods slowly weakening?

The paper crinkling in my hand drew my attention back to the letter. My eyes scanned the words.

Hello, Sapphire.

It would seem you killed Ezra. I suppose congratulations are in order. Please come back to my castle. I am sure we can come to an arrangement. There is still an empty throne here after all. I am sure one more lesson is to be learned.

-Lucy

I wanted time before seeing Lucifer again, but it would be now or never. My mind raced as I paced back and forth. He'd be expecting me to strike first. Lucifer was one of the reasons for the emptiness within my soul. He would die. One way or the other; his soul was mine.

"Orpheus!" I called out. He appeared in a blink, before bowing. "I'm going to see Lucifer. Please take care of the kingdom while I'm gone. If I don't come back, the demons are your problem permanently." I shrugged, stood up, and let out a soft chuckle. That thought gave me a bit of peace.

If Lucy killed me, would I be with Kyler?

"Highness, if I may offer a small piece of advice?" I waved my hand as a sign of agreement. "Only a select few know you heal from things that should kill you. Use it to your advantage."

"How do you know that?" I raised a brow.

"I'm just an old vampire with lots of knowledge, Princess." Orpheus shrugged.

"Thanks. See you on the flip side."

"Before you go, you might want this." Orpheus opened his hand and summoned a crown.

He passed it to me, and I took it from him, admiring Zariah's handy work. The crown was fully gold with spikes every half inch. Inside the spikes were sapphires except on the front. Two rubies perched on either side of a giant oval sapphire.

"Kyler's birthstone." Orpheus said, answering my unasked question.

"Thank you. I will be back soon."

He nodded and bowed again. I placed the crown on my head and waved goodbye as my butterflies swarmed around me.

As I entered the castle, Lucy was in the middle of something, and my butterflies disappeared. Demons gathered as he gave a speech about keeping Hell united. He talked a big game but probably cared more about the lollipop in his mouth than Hell. The demons parted ways for me as I strode to Lucifer. Their eyes followed me. If there's one thing I learned, it's not to back down. Lucifer watched my every movement.

"Sapphire, now sole Princess of the Vampires. Hmmm, an interesting turn of events, for sure." He popped a new lollipop in his mouth. "Unfortunately for you, killing a Prince is punishable by death. Do say hello to Kyler for me in the void." Lucifer smirked as he walked closer to me. The demons clapped, waiting for a killing blow. He was not ready for the show I was about to put on.

"Oh, Lucifer! Please don't kill me. I didn't know it was wrong. I just lost Kyler, and the rage of my powers took over." Tears fell as I bowed my head and collapsed to my knees. Wails of pain escaped my throat as I covered my face with my hands.

Something I didn't have to fake. Pain from my loss still sat heavy within me.

Your soul will be mine, Lucy.

He knelt and placed a hand on my shoulder.

"That is why he charred," Lucy murmured to himself. I didn't know how he knew that, but I had a plan.

"Please, My Liege, please. Have mercy." I cried out the words.

Lucifer stayed kneeling, and I could feel the heat of his glare. I continued to wail, hoping he would fall for it.

"Oh dear girl, I would like to believe you, but my spies tell me how you have been handling the vampires."

"Who else. Will. Take care. Of them?" I asked between sobs. Lucifer let out a low sigh.

"Very well. One chance." He patted my shoulder, and I looked down, hiding my mischievous grin.

Got you, motherfucker.

I popped up, smacking his chin with my head. He fell back, and fire burned in his eyes. He summoned a fireball and threw it at me. I ducked down as it hit another demon behind me. Turning my head, I watched as that demon burst into flames. A low growl sat in my throat, proof he didn't care about his united Hell.

He appeared in front of me and picked me up by my throat. I grabbed his wrist and used my weight to double-kick him in the chest. I went flying out of his hand and landed with my knee and hand on the ground.

How the Hell do I pin him?

I summoned lightning in my fingers and shot it at him. It hit him directly in the leg, and a satisfying roar left his throat.

Shooting towards me in a mad rage, Lucifer summoned a dagger, and I dodged. It wasn't a complete miss as his blade went into my side. He let out a laugh. Blood ran over my fingers as I gripped my side and fell onto my knees. Feeling myself heal, I had an idea. Pretending to faint on the ground, I left the dagger in place, so it would continue to bleed. Keeping my eyes closed, I focused on my other senses. His footsteps approached. The blood flow slowed; I hoped he didn't notice.

"Pathetic," Lucifer hissed as he kicked my stomach. Pain echoed within me, but I ignored it, keeping my body as lifeless as possible. "Let this be a lesson for everyone here. Do not kill what is not yours to kill." He kicked my body once more, and his footsteps walked away.

"Or let this be a lesson to not fuck with the most powerful demon alive." I opened my eyes and shot closer to Lucifer, shoving him against the wall with my wind power.

He went to take a step toward me, and I pushed back harder. His body jerked at the magic, and I looked into his eyes. Despite this fight, Lucy felt calm. I didn't care why. He plotted with Ezra. He stole the person I loved away. He tricked me. I was done being a puppet.

I roared, and all three of my powers surrounded us as I slammed him into the floor.

"You took what mattered most to me, and now, I'm taking the only thing that matters to you. *My* throne." I whispered in his ear.

My fingers wrapped around his neck. I couldn't tell if he wasn't fighting back because my power had a hold over him, or if he chose not to. In the end, it didn't matter as I called his soul to me. A red glow ran from his body into my arm.

"Finally. I hope the lessons I taught you will be enough. Check my desk," He whispered faintly as I called the last of his soul to me.

Was this his plan all along?

Lucifer's body went limp. The color drained from his face. His cold eyes stared at me with a haunting smile on his lips.

It's done.

My body shook, and tears rolled down my cheeks. A cascade of emotions soared through me. I grabbed at my chest, as the ache from before roared to life within me.

I would rule Hell with an empty throne beside me. I wanted to meet death so desperately. I knew Hell needed me. I knew I had to go on, but agony clung to me.

I picked myself off the ground and wiped my eyes. After straightening my crown, I went to the throne and sat down. A red aura surrounded my body before fading away. Lucifer's power tingled through every inch of my body when I focused on it.

The demons in the room bowed to me. In the distance, a bell began tolling. As it continued to ring, more and more demons appeared and bowed, including Orpheus. I realized the bells told all of Hell that Lucifer was dead.

I had taken over Hell.

My birthright, *claimed*.

The power of Lucifer felt more substantial than I could imagine. A new tightness gripped my lungs, and the air felt trapped. I scratched at my throat, trying to catch a breath. Then I realised exactly what I was feeling.

A pull.

Chapter Fifty-Four

Sapphire

I headed in the direction of the tug in my chest. Every breath felt more painful than the last. I couldn't tell why. I only knew I needed to find the source. I ignored the demons and ran out of the throne room, following the pull.

Darting to the door behind the stairs, I ripped it open. I bounced down the steps to the sentry standing before the door to the dungeons.

"Let me through, now." I growled with impatience.

The sentry said nothing; he bowed and opened the door. I darted down the hallway, checking every cell. The sound of water dripping from somewhere echoed everywhere. The smell of rotting flesh crept into my nose. In the distance, I could hear a faint, pained breathing.

Kyler.

I found him in the last cell.

Without a second thought, I ripped the cell door off and ran to his side, pulling his head into my lap. His skin looked pale, and blood covered every inch of his shirt. Burn marks and peeling skin lined the visible skin. His eyes wouldn't open as I held him in my arms. Weak whimpers escaped his lips.

What did Lucifer do to you?

There had to be a way to save him. I ripped his bloody shirt off him, and a tear fell down my face at the sight. Scars ran down his back in varying degrees of size. If Lucifer wasn't already dead, I'd have killed him all over.

"Listen here, you Gods. If you don't tell me how to save my mate right fucking now, I will spend eternity trying to find a way to kill myself. Fuck destiny if I have to do this alone." I tried to sound angry, but instead, tears filled my eyes.

Kyler took in wheezing breaths, and I ran my fingers over his face gently. Dirt covered his pale cheeks. I felt so helpless as I pulled his body closer to me.

"Take your blade and let him drink your blood. He has been tainted by bad blood."

"Don't think this makes up for abandoning me!" I shouted.

Pulling the dagger Apollyon left for me from the sheath on my thigh, I slit a cut on my wrist and pressed it to Kyler's lips.

Come on. Come on. Please wake up. Please.

I gasped as his fangs sank into my arm. The tightness in my chest disappeared, and I could breathe again. Color slowly returned to his face, and he let out a small groan.

"Fire," He said, his voice raspy as he wrapped a hand around my arm. "Don't cry, My Queen. You saved my life."

It didn't matter what he said; tears flowed out of my eyes. He sat up and wiped the blood from his mouth before pulling me into his chest. I looked at the scars on his chest that began disappearing before my eyes. His skin started to heal. We shared a look.

"A gift from the Gods, for your sacrifice." My angel said to both of us.

"Still not even." I huffed out.

"I recognize that voice, but I can't place it." Kyler murmured into my hair.

"Ezra and Lucifer are gone, Kyler. We won. We won," I cried into his chest. The pit of emptiness that consumed me for weeks disappeared. I felt whole again.

I pulled away and wiped my eyes.

"Lucifer didn't fully kill me. He put a spell on me to seem dead. I don't know what he was planning, but killing him broke the magic." Kyler watched my eyes as I nodded; tears dried on my face. "I need a new shirt."

"Majesty, I'm sorry to barge in, but many people would like to meet the new ruler of Hell." Orpheus' voice came from the hallway as he stepped over the now-broken gate.

Kyler looked at him and tilted his head.

"We'll be there in a minute, Orpheus. Thank you." I gave him a curt nod.

He smiled and gave me a quick bow before walking away. I looked back at Kyler, who had a smirk on his face.

"Are you okay? I won't do this if you're not by my side." My eyes met his. They had so much warmth, and I couldn't help the smile that crossed my face.

"I'd rather be inside of you, but I'll settle for being beside you for now."

I rolled my eyes at him. Only he could have almost died five minutes ago, and already he's trying to get between my legs. It made my heart beat faster; I felt safe again.

He was home.

We rose from the ground, and I looked at his bloody pants. He looked down and realized why I was gawking. He summoned a change of clothes. Once he was in a clean black tee and ripped jeans, he pulled me against his chest once again.

"Don't you ever fucking leave me again." I said against his body.

"I wouldn't dream of it, Fire." He kissed my forehead, and I pulled away from him.

Kyler took my hand, and I led him back out of the dungeon. He laughed briefly at the gate as we stepped over it.

I'll fix that. Eventually.

Once we returned to the throne room, I sat down, and Kyler leaned on the left side of me. I turned and looked up at him with a smile.

The Protector of Hell had a nice ring to it.

Alfonso, Dante, Blake, Esme, and Vealla all stood in a line, ready to hear what the Queen of Hell had to say. All the demons who came when the ball rang filled the room.

I did it.

I was worthy of Kyler's praise.

I cleared my throat, and the noise in the room disappeared. All eyes turned to me.

"From now on, I will personally deal with any issues here in Hell or in the mortal world. The leaders of the realms and factions will sit on my council to discuss matters that are important. Anyone who defies or plots against me will end up like ole Lucy." I stepped down two steps. "Thank you for being my friends and helping me find the strength to go on." My soft voice filled the room.

For the first time in a long time, I could breathe. My new family and I would make this realm better.

"Thank you for keeping us from going to war again." Dante bowed, and the others followed suit.

I went to speak when a black cloud of shadows formed before me. As the smoke disappeared, a tall demon replaced the space. His brown hair was slicked back, and a bit of stubble lined his face. He wore a black suit, vest, and pants. Muscles popped out from the folded suit shirt.

"I am Asmodus, a Knight of Death. It is a pleasure to meet you, my Queen." He bowed.

"I've never seen you before," I said in a firm voice. I remembered Lucifer's brief mention of who he was.

"Forgive me, My Queen. I have lived in seclusion for much longer than most of these demons have been alive. The bells ringing told me you had finally arrived. I promise to serve you and protect you with my life." Asmodus straightened, and his face stayed expressionless.

"Very well, you may all leave." I would have to figure out Asmodus later, but for now, my throne called my name. The space I fought so hard to get.

Kyler and I stepped up to the thrones and sat down. My new family bowed and left one by one.

"Fire, there's something I need to do. Will you be okay for a bit?" Kyler raised his brow at me.

"Of course. Are you ok?" I asked him.

"I will be. I'll be back soon." He stood and phased away. I wanted to ask him more, but after everything we went through, it didn't feel right.

Chapter Fifty-Five

Kyler

I stood in front of my mom's burial stone. Silence filled the air as a stern wind blew. Kneeling, I ran a hand over the rigid lines of her plaque. Time had been unkind to the column.

"Hey, Mom. I'm sorry I haven't visited in a while. I was half dead for a bit there." I ran a hand over the back of my neck. "I just wanted to say thank you for sending her to me. Somehow, I have a feeling you knew I would find her. You always said I'd find my savior, and I did. If it wasn't for all the things you taught me, I never would have been able to save her. I love you, Mom." I ignored the warmth of the tear rolling down my face and stood back up.

I promised myself I would take Fire here one day. She understood more than anyone the loss. It felt good to be home with her. I hoped she would understand needing a moment to myself.

I stayed for a few minutes, enjoying the silence. Visions of being in Lucifer's cell tried to find their way to the forefront of my mind, but I pushed them out. I didn't fight to stay alive so the old Lucifer could have some hold over me.

Phasing away, there was one more errand I had to run, and it might have been the most important one.

"Kyler! My brother, you're alive!" Zariah waltzed over to me once I entered the store.

"Zariah!" We slapped hands and gave each other a quick hug.

"How are you here?" His yellow eyes had a hint of red lines to them. He cried for me? "We watched Lucifer kill you." His voice went quiet.

"He kept me trapped in a cell and tortured me every day." I said, trying not to relive the past few weeks.

"I'm just glad you're alive, man. Sylvie will be over the moon to know you are, too. Our queen has a kind heart. She came to me and told me I was family and she wanted to get to know me." Zariah smiled at me.

Gods. She is amazing.

"She also requested a new crown. I'm sure you noticed the rubies." He gave me a sly smirk.

"That was your doing?"

"I figured she would need it, to keep going." He didn't elaborate more, but his eyes shifted towards the ground.

"I need an engagement ring."

Zariah gave me a once-over with a raised brow. "An engagement ring? Are you not going to do a ceremonial binding ritual?" He tilted his head slightly.

I shook my head, "Ezra already did a binding ceremony. I think the only reason he couldn't use it against her was that she has my essence. I can't put her through that again." I grimaced.

When she broke the bindings between them, a relief lifted off of me in a way I didn't know possible. Our matting bond felt weaker the entire time, and I hated it.

"I know that look, man, what's eating you?" Zariah leaned against the wall and crossed his arms. I rested my elbow on the counter with a sigh.

"I went to my mom's grave today. I don't know, man, it just feels like Fire was Mom's gift to me. You know what she always used to say." Sorrow filled my voice. Zariah gazed at me for a heartbeat.

"What were the words? You'll find your savior, look for the woman with fire in her eyes?" Zariah tilted his head, trying to recall the memory.

"It feels like she knew." I shook my head.

"Sapphire loves you so much, she told me, your best friend, I was family. Mates like that only come once in a blue moon. I would know." He laughed and nudged me in the ribs, "Come on, I'm sure we can find something fitting for the Queen of Hell." He led me to the front counter and pulled out a tray of rings. "What is the plan?"

"I'm going to give her a mortal proposal," I said as Zariah burst into laughter. I scowled at him.

"That is a good one, man, but really, what's the plan?"

I gave him a death glare.

"You're serious?" He put the tray of rings back into the display. "I don't know what made her fall in love with you besides the bond, but she's lucky." He laughed and tapped a finger on the counter.

"My good looks, obviously." With a smirk, I swept some invisible dust off my shoulder with one hand.

"Now we both know that's not true." Zariah mimicked my smirk.

"She saved my life probably more times than I can count. I'm the lucky one." I said, dazing off into the distance.

"Hold on, I have just the thing for you. There is only one ring fitting for the Queen of Hell, and your soul mate." Zariah held a finger up before taking off into the back.

What did he mean by that?

I looked out at the village. Fire saw this and called it a fairytale. I laughed at her, but not because of what she said. I laughed because this is Hell. I grew up here and knew the horrors of what happened here all too well. It pissed me off that she had to learn the hard way.

Relief washed over me. For the first time in my life, no one would look down on me. My brother and Lucifer were dead. I had a place beside the Queen of Hell. She didn't just save my life, she gave me a new one. She gave me a place where I belonged.

Zariah came back and placed a red velvet box down on the counter. Turning back towards him, I raised my eyes in silent question. He just pushed his hand at the box for me to open it.

My mother's wedding ring glared back at me. The silver band with 3 small diamonds on either side of the heart-shaped 14-karat diamond glistened in the light. I closed the box and looked up at Zariah, who had a giant smile. How did he have this? My mom had always said no matter how much my father changed, this ring reminded her of better days. It meant so much to her, and she told me my future wife would wear it one day. I always thought Father lost it, but it stared back at me.

"Your mother gave it to mine until you found the right woman. It's been here waiting for you." He pushed the box closer to me, and I picked it up, putting it into my jeans pocket. "Go get your queen, bother." He gave me a warm smile, and I echoed his sentiment.

"Wait a damn second, were you going to let me buy one of those other rings?" I raised a brow at him.

"You have been known to take home a woman for a night or two. Had to make sure it was real love." He gave me a shrug.

"She came to you after I died, and you're still questioning it?" My voice rose.

"Oh, please. Don't act like you're butt hurt." Zariah waved me off, and we laughed.

"I love you, brother. I don't say that enough." I said quietly.

"Oh Gods, don't get sentimental on me now, man."

I shook my head at him and laughed.

"I love you too, brother. Make sure to invite me to the wedding!"

I gave him the middle finger.

"Wait, brother."

I turned back to him.

"Are you okay?"

"No." Was my reply as I walked off into a wall of flames

Chapter Fifty-Six

Kyler

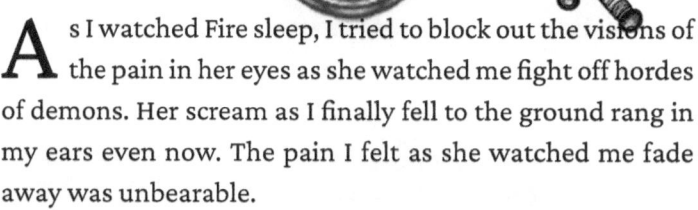

As I watched Fire sleep, I tried to block out the visions of the pain in her eyes as she watched me fight off hordes of demons. Her scream as I finally fell to the ground rang in my ears even now. The pain I felt as she watched me fade away was unbearable.

Yet somehow, here we are in bed together and safe.

It didn't matter how tightly I held her in my arms; fear still gripped me, told me that she wasn't real. She already killed Lucifer, or I'd do it myself.

Bustling outside the door drew my attention away from Fire's soft snores. I rubbed my blurry eyes. Fire looked so peaceful lying there.

Did she sleep while we were apart?

I kissed her head softly before climbing out of the sheets and stretching. With a soft grunt, I stretched my arms and summoned a clean shirt and pants, then my armor. My crest now matched hers since I was still her knight. I'd always protect her with my life; I owed her that and much more.

As I opened the door, the maids ran around. Since Fire took over, they were busy cleaning the castle and changing the crest on all the hanging banners around. Once in the throne room, I spotted Orpheus sitting by the dais, flipping through a book.

"Orpheus, I have to run an errand. Can you tell Fire if she's awake before I'm back?" I tilted my head to the side, trying to figure out what he was reading.

I spotted the other Princes standing by the wall and chatting amongst themselves. Blade looked my way and gave me a slight nod that I returned.

"She didn't sleep for weeks after we thought you died. I doubt you have to worry." He said, looking up.

"She didn't sleep for weeks?" I raised an eyebrow at him.

"No, she was so depressed and wanted to die. Ezra tortured her in ways I won't repeat. Anyway, I'll take care of things. I'm still her second-in-command until she says otherwise," Orpheus bowed his head towards me.

"What did he do?" I balled my fists at my sides.

"It's not important. Go run your errand. I'm glad you're alive, brother." Orpheus stood and patted my shoulder.

"I am, too."

What had Ezra done to my mate? I had to remind myself he was dead and could no longer hurt her. With a two-fingered salute to Orpheus, I phased to the sand oval that Fire loved so much. There were demons all over, training. I found one of the leading demons, Kaltar.

"What can I do for you?" He asked, crossing his arms. His eyes stayed locked on the vampires, failing to hold their swords properly.

"I need one of our sessions," I said. My gaze turned to the other demons fighting past us.

"Alright, but make it quick, man." Kaltar agreed.

We went to the middle of the sand and pulled out our swords, standing, ready to fight. My sword now had a sapphire gem on the hilt. I'd be sure to always carry her with me now.

We began to spar, swinging our swords hard as the other demons watched. I turned my sword for Kaltar's head, and he ducked but gave me a curious look. I had been swinging harder than usual for a simple spar. He could tell something was going on. He began to hit my sword harder as I swung back.

Kaltar was a pureblood demon and had way more power than me. I didn't care. My sword extended and tripped him onto the ground, spinning around him. I slid in the sand as he turned and pushed me with a blast of wind. Spreading my feet was the only way to slow myself down. Dashing at him, my sword swung in a circle before our weapons crashed again.

Kaltar grunted as he swung harder. I knew he was still going easy on me. Pure demons had the strength of Lucifer, and they were known for their brute force. There was no way his light swings had been even a fraction of that power. We kept going back and forth for a long time. Eventually, he swung his sword above his head, and it came down onto my shoulder, pushing me down. He was irritated now that we had fought so long. The sword cracked my armor, which was his sign that the battle was over.

"I do have actual trainees, Kyler." He stretched out a hand and helped me up. I waved a hand to fix my cracked armor. "Next time, I'm making you give a lesson instead." His lips curled in the corner. "Stay. I will be done in an hour."

"Thanks, man."

Kaltar gave a quick nod. He had been my trainer long ago, so he knew I wouldn't come here unless something were wrong.

An hour later, he found me. "Alright, start talking. You don't pick a fight with me for no reason." He crossed his arms after walking over.

"It's complicated." I shrugged.

"More complicated than being in love with the new reigning Queen of Hell?" My brow raised in question. "Lucifer made everyone watch."

I didn't respond for a minute. The realization that everyone watched Sapphire lose me brought my rage to a boiling point.

"Almost dying has brought a lot of memories to the surface." That was all that managed to come out of my mouth.

"And?"

"And, I failed Sapphire. She had to go on without me there to protect her." My eyes looked down as I kicked some sand with my foot.

"You know I'm not going to sugarcoat this. She doesn't need you and never needed you. She is the single most powerful demon of all time. She wants you, though. Can't be a failure if that's the case." Kaltar shrugged.

He was right, I needed to get over myself. Fire wanted me. I gave her the tools, but it was she who killed our enemies. I would always protect her with my life, even if she didn't need it.

"Thanks, Kaltar." I gave him a quick smile.

"No problem, kid."

I huffed at that.

"I'm almost 358, dude."

He let out a laugh and crossed his arms again.

"And I'm 537. You are a kid."

A chuckle of agreement left my throat.

"Make sure to tell her Majesty how good I am. Maybe I can get a position doing more than training newbies." Kalter gruffed.

"I'll put in a good word with our Queen." With that, I phased away.

Chapter Fifty-Seven

Kyler

I sat on the throne that Fire had kept empty and drank a bag of blood before resting my chin in my hand. She had not woken for over two weeks, and worry flooded my veins. Why was this happening to her? That's the problem with her being the only pureblooded soul eater; there was no telling what would happen. We didn't have simple answers because she was anything but.

My mind flickered back to the horrors on her face; she was so scared watching me fend off those demons. As soon as Lucifer formed a wall in front of my face, I knew it was all over. She must have known, too. I wanted to shove everything that happened from my mind, but it stayed.

Did those images flash through Fire's mind, too? Zariah said she went into a depression, but Kaltar did not mention that. Orpheus would know. I'd ask him about it later. Right now, I needed Fire to wake up. I looked over to see one of her high-command demons talking to a group of varying creatures of Hell.

"Asmodus!" I called over to him.

He laughed with the group and then walked over to me alone. He walked like every stride had a purpose.

Pretentious prick.

"It is disrespectful that you sit on her throne. We also don't answer to you until she makes you her second or consort, so I could not care less about what you want. I did not come out of seclusion after millennia for you." Asmodus spat his words at me like venom. I groaned and rubbed the furrow of my brow.

"Yes, yes, we've been over this already. I don't care. She doesn't know who you are, but I do. However, your Queen needs you to watch the throne so I can check on her."

He was an enormous prick, even more than me, and that's saying something. I didn't much care as long as he did what I needed. It pissed me off that he came out of seclusion after doing nothing, including in the war, and got such high praise. Because he was a knight of death, everyone fell at his feet.

"What is in it for me?" He crossed his arms and gave me a dirty look.

"Hmmm, let's see. How about I don't give our Queen a reason to take your soul?" I sang the words as I stood up, giving him a fake, innocent smile.

Asmodus let out a low growl in protest but gave in.

"Kyler, you know exactly what I am, so good luck with that. I will, however, still do it at the behest of my Queen." He huffed and turned on his heels.

I made my way back up to the room where she slept. She had tossed and turned in her sleep, so at least I knew she was alive. Occasionally, she let out a faint cry, and I worried about what she could be dreaming.

After she killed Lucifer, her eyes were completely red instead of all black, with a slight glow. Consuming his soul did something to her, and now she was in a coma. Who knew it was even possible?

When I opened the door to the room, Orpheus stood over her with his hand glowing white. What was he doing? That was not a vampire power.

His eyes met mine, and he sighed. From where he was, he waved a hand, closing the door behind me. She let out a painful cry in her sleep, and my heart skipped a beat. I darted to her side, ran my hand through her hair, and shushed her softly. I hated hearing those sounds.

We just got each other back, and I couldn't tell her I loved her. It was apparent then that our life would never be easy, but it didn't matter.

I will love you and protect you with my life, Fire, always.

"What were you doing, Orpheus? That is not a power a vampire can possess." I said, glaring at him.

"I can't tell you." He said, pressing his lips together in a line.

"The hell you can't. You were touching my mate with magic." I growled.

I extended my fangs and stared him down. No one would lay a fucking hand on my mate ever again.

Orpheus sighed and nodded.

"I can't tell you who I am. I can tell you that Sapphire is more than meets the eye and must be protected at all costs. That's why I'm here. The Gods sent me."

"The Gods sent you? You expect me to believe that?" I summoned my sword in my hand and laid it across my lap. I made sure it was pointed toward him. His eyes shifted, and he groaned.

"Put that away, brother. If you tell anyone the truth, I will not be able to protect her."

"You better prove it right, Gods damned now, or I will send this sword through your chest."

Orpheus took a deep breath and groaned. He backed away from Fire and, before my eyes, extended out two long white wings.

"Holy shit, you're telling me this entire time you were her angel? How did you blend in as a vampire? I've known you for 200 years!" I whisper-shouted. "It *was* you in the cell! I knew the voice was familiar!"

"I told you, I am here at the will of the Gods. Please don't ask me more, Kyler. If you love her, you will back off so I can do my job." He hid his wings again.

"One question." I put up a finger. Orpheus reluctantly nodded. "The storm is still coming, isn't it?"

"Yes, but that is all I can say. Please don't ask anything else. No one can know, not even her." He nodded his chin back toward Fire.

The tone of his voice told me to back down. I remembered the entry from Anna's journal. She said an angel came to her about Sapphire. It had to have been Orpheus. I looked back towards Fire.

"Why is she still asleep?" I asked, pulling her head into my lap.

"She's drawing too much power. She needed a reset. She will be fine, I promise." He went to walk away, but I had another question.

"What happened to her while I was away?"

His eyes scanned the room before he turned back to me.

"There was a point we feared she would kill herself. She sat on her bed and stared out the window. She didn't take in any souls or sleep. One night, I snuck off to tell Dante and Vealla, and we hatched a plan. They showed Sapphire the legions of armies who were already behind her. It was just enough to snap her out of it. She asked me for a soul, and then we trained with everyone. She trained hard, then made her move. Once Ezra was dead, though, Lucifer sent for her, and she killed him. I am unsure how that fight ended; I was with the vampires. The bell began tolling, so I knew she won." His hands were behind his back as he told me everything.

She had gone through as much as I had—our own forms of torture, together, even apart. My mind shifted to my time in the cell. The cold floor and my blood pooling at my feet. Lucifer's laughter resounded in my mind.

"How do you know all of this?" I asked, running a hand through her hair, pushing my ghost away.

"Ezra assigned me to guard her, and once he was dead, she named me her second for keeping her secrets." He shrugged.

"I still don't understand, but if you're here to protect her, then thank you."

Orpheus bowed his head.

"She will wake in a day or two." He said and left the room.

My Fire was so important that the Gods sent an angel to watch over her. Our battles were far from over. If I could guarantee one thing, I would never leave her side again.

I pulled out the box with the ring and smiled. I would give her everything within my power to give.

All of my nightmares did not matter in comparison to the strength she managed for me. We would get through whatever would come our way and whatever we needed to push through now, together.

Come heaven or Hell, we were one.

Chapter Fifty-Eight
Sapphire

I felt a warm breeze against my face, sending goosebumps down my spine. The air forced me to sit up and look over at an open window. I rubbed my eyes and flicked the corners to remove the gunk.

I guess I needed that nap.

The place beside me, where Kyler held me, was now empty. He must have gotten bored watching me sleep. Groaning, I pulled the covers off my body and put my feet on the ground. My movements felt like quicksand filled my bones.

As I went to the bathroom, I noticed my shirt felt a little tight. The dried blood must have ruined the material. Running a brush through my hair was a struggle.

How did my hair get so messy in only a few hours?

As I snapped my fingers, my outfit changed. The crown with my sapphire gem stayed on my head. The castle felt quiet, almost still, as I descended the stairs.

The throne room sat empty, leading me to wonder where everyone had gone. I made my way down a corridor towards the office. Pulling the memory of Lucy's final words, he told me to check his desk. I pushed open the doors and walked over to the mahogany desk. A letter addressed to me sat on top. I unfolded the paper and read it.

Dear Sapphire,

The crown will be yours when you read this. The burden now lies upon your head. I was never meant to hold it. Towards the end of the seventy-year war, the creator came to me and told me you'd be coming. I knew my fate that day. This was always going to play out this way. Do tell Kyler I'm sorry for the torture. Remember, you are more powerful than anyone knows. Use my soul well.

-Lucy

A knock on the door made me lift my gaze. Kyler stood leaning on the frame, his ripped jeans and leather jacket showcasing his fit body. A smile curved on my lips.

"I was starting to think you'd never wake up." He walked into the room and pulled me into his arms, causing me to drop the letter on the floor.

"It was only a nap." I laughed. He furrowed his brow and shook his head.

"My Queen, you slept for three weeks," Kyler said, looking down at me.

"What?"

"It's okay, you needed rest. The council took care of Hell while you were away. Mostly Orpheus, since he knew how you wanted the rules of the land to be." He ran his hand down my hair, and our lips met for the first time in weeks.

The static that awakened my powers surged through me, and I wrapped my arms around Kyler's neck.

"I am so glad you're home," I whispered against his lips.

"So am I, Fire. So am I. Now about this whole being inside of you thing." He pulled away from me and smirked. I laughed and covered my mouth with my hand.

"Congratulations on your victory, Sapphire." We turned our heads to see a woman with golden hair held by a crown of flowers and twigs entwined. Her white dress draped around her body, to the floor.

"Who are you?" Kyler growled.

He couldn't see what I could. Her aura was green. She radiated goodness as I had never felt before. I interlocked my fingers with Kyler's and stepped forward so he would be calmer about what I was going to say.

"She's a goddess," I said softly, as I studied her presence.

"One of many, and we need to talk." I bowed my head towards her.

Kyler grumbled inside my head.

Here we go again.

Acknowledgements

I'd like to take this opportunity to thank everyone who has helped me along the journey of reaching my dream of being an author.

To my husband, John. He sat beside me and watched me write god knows how many drafts of this story, all while cheering me on and supporting me.

To Ginger, my sister from another mister, who has also read every single version of this story that I have written. Which includes ones with no grammatical edits. She has been an enormous support and helped point me in the direction I needed to go!

To Rii, for making my beautiful cover. Thank you for lending your gift of art to me! And also for reading every draft I sent you! Your friendship kept me going when I was dragging.

To Freya for always being a voice of reason and telling me the truth about my work, even if it was hard to swallow at the time.

To Erika and Monika. For becoming friends in a way I never expected, and for giving me honest advice.

To my Ink Knights crew, I love each and every one of you. Tenny, Doc, and LC, you guys are my found family. This would have been a lonely road without you.

To Dahlia, thank you for editing my manuscript! You did me a favor, and I'm forever grateful.

And lastly, to everyone who said I'd never be good enough or didn't deserve to make it this far. This is in spite of you.

www.ingramcontent.com/pod-product-compliance
Lightning Source LLC
LaVergne TN
LVHW040131080526
838202LV00042B/2869